SAVE ME THE WALTZ

Zelda Fitzgerald was born in Montgomery, Alabama in 1900. She became a 'roarer' of the pre-1920s and met F. Scott Fitzgerald at one of the many social dances she attended. They married in 1920 and began a decade of riotous living in France and America.

Zelda wrote magazine articles and short stories, and at twenty-seven became obsessed with a career as a dancer. The couple became increasingly eccentric and erratic; Scott became an alcoholic and Zelda developed schizophrenia. In 1932 Zelda became seriously ill and wrote *Save me the Waltz* in six weeks to the envy of her husband who had been writing *Tender is the Night* for more than five years. Zelda died in a hospital fire in 1947.

ZELDA FITZGERALD

Save me the Waltz

VINTAGE BOOKS
London

Published by Vintage 2001

24

Copyright © 1932 by Charles Scribner's Sons
Copyrigh renewed 1960 by Frances Scott Fitzgerald Lanahan

First published in the United States by Scribner in 1932

First published in Great Britain in 1968 by Jonathan Cape

Vintage
Random House, 20 Vauxhall Bridge Road,
London SW1V 2SA

www.vintage-classics.info

Addresses for companies within The Random House Group Limited
can be found at: www.randomhouse.co.uk/offices.htm

The Random House Group Limited Reg. No. 954009

A CIP catalogue record for this book
is available from the British Library

ISBN 9780099286554

Penguin Random House is committed to a sustainable future for
our business, our readers and our planet. This book is made from
Forest Stewardship Council® certified paper.

MIX
Paper from
responsible sources
FSC
www.fsc.org FSC® C018179

Printed and bound in Great Britain by Clays Ltd, Elcograf S.p.A.

To Mildred Squires

SAVE ME THE WALTZ

We saw of old blue skies and summer seas
  When Thebes in the storm and rain
Reeled, like to die.
O, if thou can'st again,
  Blue sky – blue sky!

                    Oedipus, King of Thebes

I

I

'THOSE GIRLS,' people said, 'think they can do anything and get away with it.'

That was because of the sense of security they felt in their father. He was a living fortress. Most people hew the battlements of life from compromise, erecting their impregnable keeps from judicious submissions, fabricating their philosophical drawbridges from emotional retractions and scalding marauders in the boiling oil of sour grapes. Judge Beggs entrenched himself in his integrity when he was still a young man; his towers and chapels were builded of intellectual conceptions. So far as any of his intimates knew he left no sloping path near his castle open either to the friendly goatherd or the menacing baron. That inapproachability was the flaw in his brilliance which kept him from having become, perhaps, a figure in national politics. The fact that the state looked indulgently upon his superiority absolved his children from the early social efforts necessary in life to construct strongholds for themselves. One lord of the living cycle of generations to lift their experiences above calamity and disease is enough for a survival of his progeny.

One strong man may bear for many, selecting for his breed such expedient subscriptions to natural philosophy as to lend his family the semblance of a purpose. By the time the Beggs children had learned to meet the changing exigencies of their times, the devil was already upon their necks. Crippled, they clung long to the feudal donjons of their fathers, hoarding their spiritual inheritances – which might have been more had they prepared a fitting repository.

One of Millie Beggs' school friends said that she had never seen a more troublesome brood in her life than those children when they were little. If they cried for something, it was supplied by Millie within her powers or the doctor was called to subjugate the inexorabilities of a world which made, surely, but poor provision for such exceptional babies. Inadequately equipped by his own father, Austin Beggs worked night and day in his cerebral laboratory to better provide for those who were his. Millie, perforce and unreluctantly, took her children out of bed at three o'clock in the morning and shook their rattles and quietly sang to them to keep the origins of the Napoleonic code from being howled out of her husband's head. He used to say, without humor, 'I will build me some ramparts surrounded by wild beasts and barbed-wire on the top of a crag and escape this hoodlum.'

Austin loved Millie's children with that detached tenderness and introspection peculiar to important men when confronting some relic of their youth, some memory of the days before they elected to be the instruments of their experience and not its result. You will feel what is meant in hearing the kindness of Beethoven's 'Springtime' sonata. Austin might have borne a closer relation to his family had he not lost his only boy in infancy. The Judge turned savagely to worry fleeing from his disappointment. The financial worry being the only one which men and women can equally share, this was the trouble he took to Millie. Flinging the bill for the boy's funeral into her lap, he cried heartbreakingly, 'How in God's name do you expect me to pay for that?'

Millie, who had never had a very strong sense of reality, was unable to reconcile that cruelty of the man with what she knew was a just and noble character. She was never again able to form a judgment of people, shifting her actualities to conform to their inconsistencies till by a fixation of loyalty she achieved in her life a saintlike harmony.

'If my children are bad,' she answered her friend, 'I have never seen it.'

2

The sum of her excursions into the irreconcilabilities of the human temperament taught her also a trick of transference that tided her over the birth of the last child. When Austin, roused to a fury by the stagnations of civilization, scattered his disillusions and waning hope for mankind together with his money difficulties about her patient head, she switched her instinctive resentment to the fever in Joan or Dixie's twisted ankle, moving through the sorrows of life with the beatific mournfulness of a Greek chorus. Confronted with the realism of poverty, she steeped her personality in a stoic and unalterable optimism and made herself impervious to the special sorrows pursuing her to the end.

Incubated in the mystic pungence of Negro mammies, the family hatched into girls. From the personification of an extra penny, a street-car ride to whitewashed picnic grounds, a pocketful of peppermints, the Judge became, with their matured perceptions, a retributory organ, an inexorable fate, the force of law, order, and established discipline. Youth and age: a hydraulic funicular, and age, having less of the waters of conviction in its carriage, insistent on equalizing the ballast of youth. The girls, then, grew into the attributes of femininity, seeking respite in their mother from the exposition of their young-lady years as they would have haunted a shady protective grove to escape a blinding glare.

The swing creaks on Austin's porch, a luminous beetle swings ferociously over the clematis, insects swarm to the golden holocaust of the hall light. Shadows brush the Southern night like heavy, impregnated mops soaking its oblivion back to the black heat whence it evolved. Melancholic moon-vines trail dark, absorbent pads over the string trellises.

'Tell me about myself when I was little,' the youngest girl insists. She presses against her mother in an effort to realize some proper relationship.

'You were a good baby.'

The girl had been filled with no interpretation of herself, having been born so late in the life of her parents that humanity had already disassociated itself from their intimate consciousness and childhood become more of a concept than the child. She wants to be told what she is like, being too

3

young to know that she is like nothing at all and will fill out her skeleton with what she gives off, as a general might reconstruct a battle following the advances and recessions of his forces with bright-colored pins. She does not know that what effort she makes will become herself. It was much later that the child, Alabama, came to realize that the bones of her father could indicate only her limitations.

'And did I cry at night and raise Hell so you and Daddy wished I was dead?'

'What an idea! All my children were sweet children.'

'And Grandma's, too?'

'I suppose so.'

'Then why did she run Uncle Cal away when he came home from the Civil War?'

'Your Grandmother was a queer old lady.'

'Cal, too?'

'Yes. When Cal came home, Grandma sent word to Florence Feather that if she was waiting for her to die to marry Cal, she wanted the Feathers to know that the Beggs were a long-lived race.'

'Was she so rich?'

'No. It wasn't money. Florence said nobody but the Devil could live with Cal's mother.'

'So Cal didn't marry, after all?'

'No – grandmothers always have their way.'

The mother laughs – the laugh of a profiteer recounting incidents of business prowess, apologetic of its grasping security, the laugh of the family triumphant, worsting another triumphant family in the eternal business of superimposition.

'If I'd been Uncle Cal I wouldn't have stood it,' the child proclaims rebelliously. 'I'd have done what I wanted to do with Miss Feather.'

The deep balance of the father's voice subjugates the darkness to the final diminuendo of the Beggs' bedtime.

'Why do you want to rehash all that?' he says judiciously.

Closing the shutters, he boxes the special qualities of his house: an affinity with light, curtain frills penetrated by sunshine till the pleats wave like shaggy garden borders about the flowered chintz. Dusk leaves no shadows or distortions in his rooms but transfers them to vaguer, grayer worlds, intact. Winter and spring, the house is like some lovely shining place painted on a mirror. When the chairs fall to pieces and the carpets grow full of holes, it does not matter in the brightness of that presentation. The house is a vacuum for the culture of Austin Beggs' integrity. Like a shining sword it sleeps at night in the sheath of his tired nobility.

The tin roof pops with the heat; the air inside is like a breath from a long unopened trunk. There is no light in the transom above the door at the head of the upstairs hall.

'Where is Dixie?' the father asks.

'She's out with some friends.'

Sensing the mother's evasiveness, the little girl draws watchfully close, with an important sense of participation in family affairs.

'Things happen to us,' she thinks. 'What an interesting thing to be a family.'

'Millie,' her father says, 'if Dixie is out traipsing the town with Randolph McIntosh again, she can leave my house for good.'

Her father's head shakes with anger; outraged decency loosens the eyeglasses from his nose. The mother walks quietly over the warm matting of her room, and the little girl lies in the dark, swelling virtuously submissive to the way of the clan. Her father goes down in his cambric nightshirt to wait.

From the orchard across the way the smell of ripe pears floats over the child's bed. A band rehearses waltzes in the distance. White things gleam in the dark – white flowers and paving-stones. The moon on the window panes careens to the garden and ripples the succulent exhalations of the earth like a silver paddle. The world is younger than it is, and she to herself appears so old and wise, grasping her problems and wrestling with them as affairs peculiar to herself and not as racial heritages. There is a brightness and bloom over things; she inspects life proudly, as if she walked in a garden forced by herself to grow in the least hospitable of soils. She is already contemptuous of ordered planting, believing in the possibility of a wizard cultivator to bring forth sweet-smelling

5

blossoms from the hardest of rocks, and night-blooming vines from barren wastes, to plant the breath of twilight and to shop with marigolds. She wants life to be easy and full of pleasant reminiscences.

Thinking, she thinks romantically on her sister's beau. Randolph's hair is like nacre cornucopias pouring forth those globes of light that make his face. She thinks that she is like that inside, thinking in this nocturnal confusion of her emotions with her response to beauty. She thinks of Dixie with excited identity as being some adult part of herself divorced from her by transfiguring years, like a very sun-burned arm which might not appear familiar if you had been unconscious of its alterations. To herself, she appropriates her sister's love affair. Her alertness makes her drowsy. She has achieved a suspension of herself with the strain of her attenuated dreams. She falls asleep. The moon cradles her tanned face benevolently. She grows older sleeping. Some day she will awake to observe the plants of Alpine gardens to be largely fungus things, needing little sustenance, and the white discs that perfume midnight hardly flowers at all but embryonic growths; and, older, walk in bitterness the geo-metrical paths of philosophical Le Nôtres rather than those nebulous byways of the pears and marigolds of her childhood.

Alabama never could place what woke her mornings as she lay staring about, conscious of the absence of expression smothering her face like a wet bath-mat. She mobilized herself. Live eyes of a soft wild animal in a trap peered out in skeptic invitation from the taut net of her features; lemon-yellow hair melted down her back. She dressed herself for school with liberal gestures, bending forward to watch the movements of her body. The schoolbell on the still exudings of the South fell flat as the sound of a buoy on the vast mufflings of the sea. She tiptoed into Dixie's room and plastered her face with her sister's rouge.

When people said, 'Alabama, you've got rouge on your face,' she simply said, 'I've been scrubbing my face with the nail brush.'

Dixie was a very satisfactory person to her young sister; her room was full of possessions; silk things lay about. A statuette

6

of the Three Monkeys on the mantel held matches for smoking. *The Dark Flower*, *The House of Pomegranates*, *The Light that Failed*, *Cyrano de Bergerac*, and an illustrated edition of *The Rubáiyát* stretched between two plaster 'Thinkers.' Alabama knew the *Decameron* was hid in the top bureau drawer – she had read the rough passages. Over the books, a Gibson girl with a hatpin poked at a man through a magnifying glass; a pair of teddy bears luxuriated over a small white rocker. Dixie possessed a pink picture hat and an amethyst bar pin and a pair of electric curling irons. Dixie was twenty-five. Alabama would be fourteen at two o'clock in the morning on the fourteenth of July. The other Beggs sister, Joan, was twenty-three. Joan was away; she was so orderly that she made little difference in the house, anyway.

Alabama slid down the banisters expectantly. Sometimes she dreamed that she fell down the well of the staircase and was saved at the bottom by landing astride the broad railing – sliding, she rehearsed the emotions of her dream.

Already Dixie sat at table, withdrawn from the world in furtive defiance. Her chin was red and red welts stood out on her forehead from crying. Her face rose and fell in first one place and then another beneath the skin, like water boiling in a pot.

'I didn't ask to be born,' she said.

'Remember, Austin, she is a grown woman.'

'The man is a worthless cuss and an unmitigated loafer. He is not even divorced.'

'I make my own living and I'll do as I please.'

'Millie, that man is not to enter my house again.'

Alabama sat very still, anticipating some spectacular protest against her father's interruption of the course of romance. Nothing transpired but the child's stillness.

The sun on the silvery fern fronds, and the silver water pitcher, and Judge Beggs' steps on the blue and white pavings as he left for his office measured out so much of time, so much of space – nothing more. She heard the trolley stop under the catalpa trees at the corner and the Judge was gone. The light flicked the ferns with a less organized rhythm without his presence; his home hung pendant on his will.

7

Alabama watched the trumpet-vine trailing the back fence like chip coral necklaces wreathing a stick. The morning shade under the chinaberry tree held the same quality as the light – brittle and arrogant.

'Mamma, I don't want to go to school any more,' she said, reflectively.

'Why not?'

'I seem to know everything.'

Her mother stared at her in faintly hostile surprise; the child, thinking better of her intended expositions, reverted to her sister to save her face.

'What do you think Daddy will do to Dixie?'

'Oh, pshaw! Don't worry your pretty head about things like that till you have to, if that's what's bothering you.'

'If I was Dixie, I wouldn't let him stop me. I like 'Dolph.'

'It is not easy to get everything we want in this world. Run on, now – you will be late to school.'

Flushed with the heat of palpitant cheeks, the school room swung from the big square windows and anchored itself to a dismal lithograph of the signing of the Declaration of Independence. Slow days of June added themselves in a lump of sunlight on the far blackboard. White particles from the worn erasers sprayed the air. Hair and winter serge and the crust in the inkwells stifled the soft early summer burrowing white tunnels under the trees in the street and poulticing the windows with sweet sickly heat. Humming Negroid intonations circulated plaintively through the lull.

'H'ye ho' tomatoes, nice ripe tomatoes. Green, colla'd greens.'

The boys wore long black winter stockings, green in the sun.

Alabama wrote 'Randolph McIntosh' under 'A debate in the Athenian Assembly.' Drawing a ring around 'All the men were at once put to death and the women and children sold into slavery,' she painted the lips of Alcibiades and drew him a fashionable bob, closing her *Myer's Ancient History* on the transformation. Her mind rambled on irrelevantly. How did Dixie make herself so fluffy, so ready always for anything? Alabama thought that she herself would never have every

8

single thing about her just right at once – would never be able to attain a state of abstract preparedness. Dixie appeared to her sister to be the perfect instrument for life.

Dixie was the society editor of the town paper. There was telephoning from the time she came home from the office in the evening till supper. Dixie's voice droned on, cooing and affected, listening to its own vibrations.

'I can't tell you now—' Then a long slow gurgle like the water running out of a bathtub.

'Oh, I'll tell you when I see you. No, I can't tell you now.'

Judge Beggs lay on his stern iron bed sorting the sheafs of the yellowing afternoons. Calf-skin volumes of the *Annals of British Law* and *Annotated Cases* lay over his body like leaves. The telephone jarred his concentration.

The Judge knew when it was Randolph. After half an hour, he'd stormed into the hall, his voice quaking with restraint.

'Well, if you can't talk, why do you carry on this conversation?'

Judge Beggs brusquely grabbed the receiver. His voice proceeded with the cruel concision of a taxidermist's hands at work.

'I will thank you never to attempt to see or to telephone to my daughter again.'

Dixie shut herself in her room and wouldn't come out or eat for two days. Alabama revelled in her part of the commotion.

'I want Alabama to dance at the Beauty Ball with me,' Randolph had said over the wire.

Her children's tears infallibly evoked their mother.

'Why do you bother your father? You could make your arrangements outside,' she said placatingly. The wide and lawless generosity of their mother was nourished from many years of living faced with the irrefutable logic of the Judge's fine mind. An existence where feminine tolerance plays no rôle being insupportable to her motherly temperament, Millie Beggs, by the time she was forty-five, had become an emotional anarchist. It was her way of proving to herself her individual necessity of survival. Her inconsistencies seemed to assert her dominance over the scheme had she so desired.

Austin couldn't have died or got sick with three children and no money and an election next fall and his insurance and his living according to law; but Millie, by being a less closely knit thread in the pattern, felt that she could have.

Alabama mailed the letter that Dixie wrote on her mother's suggestion and they met Randolph at the 'Tip-Top' Café.

Alabama, swimming through her teens in a whirlpool of vigorous decision, innately distrusted the 'meaning' communicated between her sister and Randolph.

Randolph was a reporter for Dixie's paper. His mother kept his little girl in a paintless house down-state near the canebreaks. The curves of his face and the shape of his eyes had never been mastered by Randolph's expression, as if his corporeal existence was the most amazing experience he had ever achieved. He conducted night dancing classes for which Dixie got most of his pupils – his neckties, too, for that matter, and whatever about him that needed to be rightly chosen.

'Honey, you must put your knife on your plate when you're not using it,' Dixie said, pouring his personality into the mould of her society.

You'd never have known he had heard her, though he seemed to be always listening for something – perhaps some elfin serenade he expected, or some fantastic supernatural hint about his social position in the solar system.

'And I want a stuffed tomato and potatoes *au gratin* and corn on the cob and muffins and chocolate ice cream,' Alabama interrupted impatiently.

'My God! – So we're going to do the *Ballet of the Hours*, Alabama, and I will wear harlequin tights and you will have a tarlatan skirt and a three-cornered hat. Can you make up a dance in three weeks?'

'Sure. I know some steps from last year's carnival. It will go like this, see?' Alabama walked her fingers one over the other inextricably. Keeping one finger firmly pressed on the table to mark the place she unwound her hands and began again. '—And the next part is this way—And it ends with a br – rr – rr – oop!' she explained.

Dubiously Randolph and Dixie watched the child.

'It's very nice,' commented Dixie hesitantly, swayed by her sister's enthusiasm.

'You can make the costumes,' Alabama finished glowing with the glamour of proprietorship. Marauder of vagrant enthusiasm, she piled the loot on whatever was at hand, her sisters and their sweethearts, performances and panoplies. Everything assumed the qualities of improvisation with the constant change in the girl.

Every afternoon Alabama and Randolph rehearsed in the old auditorium till the place grew dim with dusk and the trees outside seemed bright and wet and Véronèse as if it had been raining. It was from there that the first Alabama regiment had left for the Civil War. The narrow balcony sagged on spindle iron pillars and there were holes in the floor. The sloping stairs led down through the city markets: Plymouth Rocks in cages, fish, and icy sawdust from the butcher shop, garlands of Negro shoes and a doorway full of army overcoats. Flushed with excitement, the child lived for the moment in a world of fictitious professional reserves.

'Alabama has inherited her mother's wonderful coloring,' commented the authorities, watching the gyrating figure.

'I scrubbed my cheeks with a nail brush,' she yelled back from the stage. That was Alabama's answer about her complexion; it was not always accurate or adequate, but that was what she said about her skin.

'The child has talent,' they said, 'it should be cultivated.'

'I made it up myself,' she answered, not in complete honesty.

When the curtains fell at last on the tableau at the end of the ballet she heard the applause from the stage as a mighty roar of traffic. Two bands played for the ball; the Governor led the grand march. After the dance she stood in the dark passage that led to the dressing room.

'I forgot once,' she whispered expectantly. The still fever of the show went on outside.

'You were perfect,' Randolph laughed.

The girl hung there on his words like a vestment waiting to be put on. Indulgently, Randolph caught the long arms and swept her lips with his as a sailor might search the horizons of

11

the sea for other masts. She wore this outward sign that she was growing up like a decoration for valor – it stayed on her face for days, and recurred whenever she was excited.

'You're almost grown, aren't you?' he asked.

Alabama did not concede herself the right to examine those arbitrary points of view, meeting places of the facets of herself envisaged as a woman, conjured up behind his shoulders by the kiss. To project herself therein would have been to violate her confessional of herself. She was afraid; she thought her heart was a person walking. It was. It was everybody walking at once. The show was over.

'Alabama, why won't you go out on the floor?'

'I've never danced. I'm scared.'

'I'll give you a dollar if you'll dance with a young man who's waiting.'

'All right, but s'pose I fall down or trip him up?'

Randolph introduced her. They got along quite nicely, except when the man went sideways.

'You are so cute,' her partner said. 'I thought you must be from some other place.'

She told him he could come to see her some time, and a dozen others, and promised to go to the Country Club with a red-head man who slid over the dance floor as if he were skimming milk. Alabama had never imagined what it would be like to have a date before.

She was sorry when the makeup came off of her face with washing next day. There was only Dixie's rouge pot to help her masquerading through the engagements she had made.

Sloshing his coffee with the folded *Journal*, the Judge read the account of the Beauty Ball in the morning's paper. 'The gifted Miss Dixie Beggs, oldest daughter of Judge and Mrs. Austin Beggs of this city,' the paper said, 'contributed much to the success of the occasion, acting as impresario to her talented sister, Miss Alabama Beggs, assisted by Mr. Randolph McIntosh. The dance was one of startling beauty and the execution was excellent.'

'If Dixie thinks that she can introduce the manners of a prostitute into my family, she is no daughter of mine. Identified in print with a moral scapegoat! My children have got to respect my name. It is all they will have in the world,' the Judge exploded.

It was the most Alabama had ever heard her father say about what he exacted of them. Isolated by his unique mind from the hope of any communication with his peers, the Judge lived apart, seeking only a vague and gentle amusement from his associates, asking only a fair respect for his reserve.

So Randolph came in the afternoon to say good-bye.

The swing creaked, the Dorothy Perkins browned in the dust and sun. Alabama sat on the steps watering the lawn with a hot rubber hose. The nozzle leaked lugubriously over her dress. She was sad about Randolph; she had hoped some occasion would present itself for kissing him again. Anyway, she told herself, she would try to remember that other time for years.

Her sister's eyes followed the man's hands as if she expected the path of his fingers to lead her to the ends of the earth.

'Maybe you'll come back when you've got your divorce,' Alabama heard Dixie say in a truncated voice. The shape of Randolph's eyes was heavy with finality against the roses. His distinct voice carried clear and detached to Alabama.

'Dixie,' he said, 'you taught me how to use my knife and fork and how to dance and choose my suits, and I wouldn't come back to your father's house if I'd left my Jesus. Nothing is good enough for him.'

Sure enough, he never did. Alabama had learned from the past that something unpleasant was bound to happen when-ever the Saviour made his appearance in the dialogue. The savor of her first kiss was gone with the hope of its repetition.

The bright polish on Dixie's nails turned yellow and deposits of neglect shone through the red. She gave up her job on the paper and went to work at the bank. Alabama inherited the pink hat and somebody stepped on the bar pin. When Joan got home the room was so untidy that she moved her clothes in with Alabama. Dixie hoarded her money; the only things she bought in a year were the central figures from the 'Primavera' and a German lithograph of 'September Morn.'

Dixie covered her transom with a block of pasteboard to prevent her father's knowing that she was sitting up after midnight. Girls came and went. When Laura spent the night the family was afraid of catching tuberculosis; Paula, gold and effulgent, had a father who had stood a murder trial; Marshall was beautiful and malicious with many enemies and a bad reputation; when Jessie came all the way from New York to visit she sent her stockings to the dry cleaner. There was something immoral about that to Austin Beggs.

'I don't see why,' he said, 'my daughter has to choose her companions from the scum of the earth.'

'Depending on which way you look at it,' protested Millie. 'The scum might be a valuable deposit.'

Dixie's friends read aloud to each other. Alabama sat in the little white rocker and listened, imitating their elegance and cataloguing the polite, bibelotic laughs which they collected from one another.

'She won't understand,' they reiterated, staring at the girl with liquidated Anglo-Saxon eyes.

'Understand what?' said Alabama.

The winter choked itself in a ruching of girls. Dixie cried whenever a man talked her into giving him a date. In the spring, word came about Randolph's death.

'I hate being alive,' she screamed in hysterics. 'I hate it, I hate it, I hate it! I could have married him and this wouldn't have happened.'

'Millie, will you call the doctor?'

'Nothing serious, just nervous strain, Judge Beggs. Nothing to worry about,' the doctor said.

'I cannot put up with this emotional nonsense any longer,' Austin said.

When Dixie was better she went to New York to work. She cried when she kissed them all good-bye and went off with a bunch of kiss-me-at-the-gate in her hand. She shared a room with Jessie on Madison Avenue, and looked up everybody from home who had drifted up there. Jessie got her a job with the same insurance company as herself.

'I want to go to New York, Mamma,' said Alabama as they read Dixie's letters.

'What on earth for?'

'To be my own boss.'

Millie laughed. 'Well, never mind,' she said. 'Being boss isn't a question of places. Why can't you be boss at home?'

Within three months Dixie married up there – a man from Alabama, down State. They came home on a trip and she cried a lot as if she was sorry for all the rest of the family who had to go on living at home. She changed the furniture about in the old house and bought a buffet for the dining room. She bought Alabama a Kodak and they took pictures together on the steps of the State Capitol, and under the pecan trees and holding hands on the front steps. She said she wanted Millie to make her a patchwork quilt and to have a rose garden planted around the old house, and for Alabama not to paint her face so much, that she was too young, that in New York the girls didn't.

'But I am not in New York,' said Alabama. 'When I go there, I will, anyway.'

Then Dixie and her husband went away again, out of the Southern doldrums. The day her sister left, Alabama sat on the back porch watching her mother slice the tomatoes for lunch.

'I slice the onions an hour beforehand,' Millie said, 'and then I take them out so just the right flavor stays in the salad.'

'Yes'm. Can I have those ends?'

'Don't you want a whole one?'

'No'm. I love the greenish part.'

Her mother attended her work like a chatelaine ministering to a needy peasant. There was some fine, aristocratic, personal relationship between herself and the tomatoes, dependent on Miss Millie to turn them into a salad. The lids of her mother's blue eyes rose in weary circumflex as her sweet hands moved in charity through the necessities of her circumstance. Her daughter was gone. Still there was something of Dixie in Alabama – the tempestuousness. She searched the child's face for family resemblances. And Joan would be coming home.

'Mamma, did you love Dixie very much?'

'Of course. I still do.'

'But she was troublesome.'

'No. She was always in love.'

'Did you love her better than me, for instance?'

'I love you all the same.'

'I will be troublesome, too, if I can't do as I please.'

'Well, Alabama, all people *are*, about one thing or another. We must not let it influence us.'

'Yes'm.'

Pomegranates in the leathery lacing of their foliage ripened outside the lattice to an exotic décor. The bronze balls of a mournful crape myrtle at the end of the lot split into lavender tarlatan gurgles. Japanese plums splashed heavy sacks of summer on the roof of the chicken yard.

Cluck, *cluck*, cluck, *cluck!*

'That old hen must be laying again.'

'Maybe she's caught a June bug.'

'The figs aren't ripe yet.'

A mother called her children from a house across the way. Pigeons cooed in the oak next door. The rhythmic flap of a pounding beefsteak began in a neighbor's kitchen.

'Mamma, I don't see why Dixie had to go all the way to New York to marry a man from so near home.'

'He's a very nice man.'

'But I wouldn't have married him if I was Dixie. I would have married a New Yorker.'

'Why?' said Millie curiously.

'Oh, I don't know.'

'More conquering,' Millie mocked.

'Yes'm, that's it.'

A distant trolley ground to a stop on the rusty rails.

'Isn't that the streetcar stopping? I'll bet it's your father.'

II

'And I tell you I will *not* wear it if you fix it that way,' Alabama screeched, pounding her fist on the sewing machine.

'But, dear, it's the very thing.'

'If it has to be blue serge, it *doesn't* have to be long as well.'

16

'When you're going out with boys, you can't go back to short dresses.'

'I'm not going out with boys in the day time – ever,' she said. 'I am going to play in the day and go out at night.'

Alabama tilted the mirror and inspected the long gored skirt. She began to cry with impotent rage.

'I won't have it! I really won't – how can I run or anything?'

'It's lovely, isn't it, Joan?'

'If she were my child, I'd slap her jaw,' said Joan succinctly.

'You would, would you! Well, I'd slap your own jaw.'

'When I was your age I was glad to get anything. My dresses were all made out of Dixie's old ones. You're a vixen to be so spoiled,' pursued her sister.

'Joan! Alabama just wants her dress fixed differently.'

'Mamma's little angel! It's exactly like she said she wanted it.'

'How could I tell it would look like that?'

'I know what I would do if you were mine,' Joan threatened.

Alabama stood in the special Saturday sun and straightened the sailor collar. She ran her fingers tentatively inside the breast pocket, staring pessimistically at her reflection.

'The feet look as if they were somebody's else's,' she said. 'But maybe it'll be all right.'

'I've never heard so much fuss about a dress,' said Joan. 'If I were Mamma I'd make you buy them ready-made.'

'There's none in the stores that I like. Besides, you have lace on all your things.'

'I pay for it myself.'

Austin's door slammed.

'Alabama, will you stop that dispute? I am trying to take a nap.'

'Children, your father!' said Millie in dismay.

'Yes, sir, it's Joan,' shrieked Alabama.

'My Lord! She always has to blame somebody else. If it isn't me, it's Mamma or whoever's near – never herself.'

Alabama thought resentfully of the injustice of a life which had created Joan before herself. Not only that, but had given her sister an unattainable hue of beauty, dark as a black opal.

17

Nothing Alabama ever did could turn her eyes gold and brown or hollow out those dark mysterious sockets from her cheek bones. When you saw Joan directly under a light, she seemed like a ghost of her finest points awaiting inhabitation. Transparent blue halos shone around the edge of her teeth; her hair was smooth to a colorless reflection.

People said Joey was a sweet girl – compared to the others. Being over twenty, Joan had attained her right to the family spotlight. When she heard them planning vaguely for Joan, Alabama hung on her parents' rare delvings into what she felt was the substance of herself. Hearing little bits of things about the family characteristics that she too must have in her, was like finding she had all five toes when up to the present she had been able to count only four. It was nice to have indications about yourself to go on.

'Millie,' Austin asked anxiously one night, 'is Joey going to marry that Acton boy?'

'I don't know, dear.'

'Well, I don't think she ought to have gone galavanting about the country visiting his parents if she doesn't mean business, and she is seeing too much of the Harlan man if she does.'

'I visited Acton's people from my father's house. Why did you let her go?'

'I didn't know about Harlan. There are obligations—'

'Mamma, do you remember your father well?' interrupted Alabama.

'Certainly. He was thrown from a race cart when he was eighty-three years old, in Kentucky.' That her mother's father had a graphic life of his own to dramatize was promising to Alabama. There was a show to join. Time would take care of that, and she would have a place, inevitably – somewhere to enact the story of her life.

'What about this Harlan?' pursued Austin.

'O, pshaw!' Millie said noncommittally.

'I don't know. Joey seems very fond of him. He can't make a living. Acton is well established. I will not have my daughter become a public charge.'

Harlan called every night and sang with Joan the songs she brought with her from Kentucky: 'The Time, The Place and

The Girl,' 'The Girl from the Saskatchewan,' 'The Chocolate Soldier,' songs with two-tone lithograph covers of men smoking pipes and princes on a balustrade and worlds of clouds about the moon. He had a serious voice like an organ. He stayed too much to supper. His legs were so long that the rest of him seemed merely a decorative appendage.

Alabama invented dances to show off for Harlan, tapping about the outside edges of the carpet.

'Doesn't he ever go home?' Austin fretted to Millie on each succeeding visit. 'I don't know what Acton would think. Joan must not be irresponsible.'

Harlan knew how to ingratiate himself personally; it was his status that was unsatisfactory. Marrying him would have meant, for Joan, starting over where the Judge and Millie had started, and Austin didn't have race horses to pull her background for her like Millie's father had had.

'Hello, Alabama, what a pretty bib you've got on.' Alabama blushed. She strove to sustain the pleasurable emotion. It was the first time she could remember blushing; another proof of something or other, or that all the old responses were her proper heritage – embarrassment and pride and responsibility for them.

'It's an apron. I've got on a new dress and I was helping fix supper.' She exposed the new blue serge for Harlan's admiration.

He drew the lanky child across his knee.

Alabama, unwilling to relinquish the discussion of herself, went on hurriedly, 'But I have a beautiful dress to wear to the dance, more beautiful than Joan's even.'

'You are too young to go to a dance. You look such a baby, I'd be ashamed to kiss you.' Alabama was disappointed at sensing Harlan's paternal air.

Harlan pulled the pale hair away from her face. There were many geometrical formations and shining knolls and an element of odalisque retrocession about its stillness. Her bones were stern like her father's, an integrity of muscle structure bound her still to extreme youth.

Austin came in for his paper.

'Alabama, you are too big to sprawl on young men's laps.'

19

'But he's not *my* beau, Daddy!'

'Good evening, Judge.'

The Judge spat contemplatively into the hearth, disciplining his disapproval.

'It makes no difference, you are too old.'

'Will I always be too old?'

Harlan rose to his feet spilling her to the floor. Joan stood in the door.

'Miss Joey Beggs,' he said, 'the prettiest girl in town!'

Joan giggled the way people do when, entrenched in an enviable position, they are forced to deprecate their superiority to spare others – as if she had always known she was the prettiest.

Alabama watched them enviously as Harlan held Joey's coat and took her off possessively. Speculatively she watched her sister change into a more fluctuating, more ingratiating person, as she confided herself to the man. She wished it were herself. There would be her father at the supper table. It was nearly the same; the necessity of being something that you really weren't was the same. Her father didn't know what she really was like, she thought.

Supper was fun; there was toast with a taste of charcoal and sometimes chicken, warm, like a breath of the air from beneath a quilt, and Millie and the Judge talking ceremoniously of their household and their children. Family life became a ritual passed through the sieve of Austin's strong conviction.

'I want some more strawberry jam.'

'It'll make you sick.'

'Millie, in my opinion, a respectable girl does not engage herself to one man and permit herself to be interested in another.'

'There's no harm in it. Joan's a good girl. She is not engaged to Acton.'

Her mother knew that Joan was engaged to Acton because one summer night when it poured with rain and the vines swished and dripped like ladies folding silken shirts about them, and the drains growled and choked like mournful doves and the gutters ran with foamy mud, Millie had sent Alabama with an umbrella and Alabama had found the two of them

20

clinging together like moist stamps in a pocketbook. Acton said to Millie afterwards that they were going to be married. But Harlan sent roses on Sundays. Lord knows where he got the money to buy so many flowers. He couldn't ask Joan to marry him, he was so poor.

When the town gardens began to bloom so prettily, Harlan and Joan took Alabama with them on their walks. Alabama, and the big japonicas with leaves like rusting tin, viburnum and verbena and Japanese magnolia petals lying about the lawns like scraps from party dresses, absorbed the quiet communion between them. The presence of the child held them to trivialities. By her person, they held at bay the issue.

'I want one of those bushes when I have a house,' Joan pointed out.

'Joey! I can't afford it! I'll grow a beard instead,' expostulated Harlan.

'I love little trees, arborvitae and juniper, and I'm going to have a long walk winding between like featherstitching and a terrace of Clotilde Soupert at the end.' Alabama decided that it didn't much matter whether her sister was thinking of Acton or Harlan – certainly the garden was to be very nice, for either or neither or both, she amended confusedly.

'O, Lord! Why can't I make money?' protested Harlan.

Yellow flags like anatomical sketches and pools of lotus flowers, the brown and white batik of snowball bushes, the sudden emotional gush of burning brush and the dead cream of Joey's eggshell face under her leghorn hat made up that spring. Alabama understood vaguely why Harlan rattled the keys in his pockets where there was no money and walked the streets like a dizzy man traversing a log. Other people had money; he had only enough for roses. If he did without the roses he would have nothing for ages and ages while he saved until Joan was gone or different or lost forever.

When the weather was hot they hired a buggy and drove through the dust to daisy fields like nursery rhymes where dreamy cows saddled with shade nibbled the summer off the white slopes. Alabama stood up behind and brought back the flowers. What she said in this foreign world of restraint and emotion seemed to her especially significant, as a person will

21

imagine himself wittier than usual in an unfamiliar tongue. Joan complained to Millie that Alabama talked too much for her age.

Creaking and swaying like a sail in a swelling gale, the love story breasted July. At last the letter from Acton came. Alabama saw it on the Judge's mantelpiece.

'And being able to support your daughter in comfort and I believe, in happiness, I ask your sanction to our marriage.'

Alabama asked to keep it. 'To make a family document,' she said.

'No,' said the Judge. He and Millie never kept things.

Alabama's expectations for her sister envisaged everything except that love might roll on using the bodies of its dead to fill up the craters in the path to its line of action. It took her a long time to learn to think of life unromantically as a long, continuous exposition of isolated events, to think of one emotional experience as preparation to another.

When Joey said 'Yes' Alabama felt cheated out of a drama to which she had bought her ticket with her interest. 'No show today; the leading lady has cold feet,' she thought.

She couldn't tell whether Joan was crying or not. Alabama sat polishing white slippers in the upstairs hall. She could see her sister lying on the bed, as if she had laid herself down there and gone off and forgotten to come back, but she didn't seem to be making a noise.

'Why don't you want to marry Acton?' she heard the Judge say, kindly.

'Oh – I haven't got any trunk, and it means leaving home, and my clothes are all worn out,' answered Joan evasively.

'I'll get you a trunk, Joey, and he is well able to give you clothes and a good home and all you will be needing in life.'

The Judge was gentle with Joan. She was less like him than the others; her shyness had made her appear more composed, more disposed to bear with her lot than Alabama or Dixie.

The heat pressed down about the earth inflating the shadows, expanding the door and window ledges till the summer split in a terrific clap of thunder. You could see the trees by the lightning flashes gyrating maniacally and waving their arms about like furies. Alabama knew Joan was afraid of a storm. She crept into her sister's bed and slipped her brown arm over Joan like a strong bolt over a sagging door. Alabama supposed that Joan had to do the right thing and have the right things; she could see how that might be necessary if a person was like Joan. Everything about Joan had a definite order. Alabama was like that herself sometimes on a Sunday afternoon when there was nobody in the house besides herself and the classic stillness.

She wanted to reassure her sister. She wanted to say 'And, Joey, if you ever want to know about the japonicas and the daisy fields it will be all right that you have forgotten because I will be able to tell you about how it felt to be feeling that way that you cannot quite remember – that will be for the time when something happens years from now that reminds you of now.'

'Get out of my bed,' said Joan, abruptly.

Alabama wandered sadly about, in and out through the pale acetylene flashes.

'Mamma, Joey's scared.'

'Well, do you want to lie here by me, dear?'

'*I'm* not scared; I just can't sleep. But I'll lie there, please, if I may.'

The Judge often sat reading Fielding. He closed his book over his thumb to mark the end of the evening.

'What are they doing at the Catholic Church?' the Judge said. 'Is Harlan a Catholic?'

'No, I believe not.'

'I'm glad she's going to marry Acton,' he said, inscrutably.

Alabama's father was a wise man. Alone his preference in women had created Millie and the girls. He knew everything, she said to herself. Well, maybe he did – if knowing is paring your perceptions to fit into the visible portion of life's mosaic, he did. If knowledge is having an attitude towards the things we have never experienced and preserving an agnosticism towards those we have, he did.

'I'm not glad,' Alabama said decisively. 'Harlan's hair goes up like a Spanish king. I'd rather Joey married *him*.'

'People can't live off the hair of Spanish kings,' her father answered.

Acton telegraphed that he would arrive at the end of the week and how happy he was.

Harlan and Joan rocked in the swing, jerking and creaking the chain and scraping their feet over the worn gray paint and snipping the trailers off the morning-glories.

'This porch is always the coolest, sweetest place,' said Harlan.

'That's the honeysuckle and star jasmine you smell,' said Joan.

'No,' said Millie, 'it's the cut hay across the way, and my aromatic geraniums.'

'Oh, Miss Millie, I hate to leave.'

'You'll be back.'

'No, not any more.'

'I'm very sorry, Harlan—' Millie kissed him on the cheek. 'You're just a baby,' she said, 'to care. There'll be others.'

'Mamma, that smell is the pear trees,' Joan said softly.

'It's my perfume,' said Alabama impatiently, 'and it cost six dollars an ounce.'

From Mobile, Harlan sent Joan a bucket of crabs for Acton's supper. They crawled about the kitchen and scurried under the stove and Millie dropped their live green backs into a pot of boiling water one by one.

Everybody ate them except Joan.

'They're too clumsy,' she said.

'They must have arrived in the animal kingdom just about where we have in mechanical development. They don't work any better than tanks,' said the Judge.

'They eat dead men,' said Joan.

'Joey, is that necessary at table?'

'They do, though,' Millie corroborated distastefully.

'I believe I could make one,' said Alabama, 'if I had the material.'

'Well, Mr. Acton, did you have a nice trip?'

Joan's trousseau filled the house – blue taffeta dresses and a black and white check, and a shell-pink satin, a waist of turquoise blue and black suede shoes.

Brown and yellow silk and lace and black and white and a self-important suit and sachet-pads of rose filled the new trunk.

'I don't want it that way,' she sobbed. 'My bust is too big.'

'It's very becoming and will be so useful in a city.'

'You must come to visit me,' Joan said to her friends. 'I want you all to come to see me when you come to Kentucky. Some day we'll move to New York.'

Joan held excitedly to some intangible protestation against her life's purpose like a puppy worrying a shoe string. She was irritable and exacting of Acton, as if she had expected him to furnish her store of gladness with the wedding ring.

They put them on the train at midnight. Joan didn't cry, but she seemed ashamed that she might. Walking back across the railroad tracks, Alabama felt the strength and finality in Austin more than ever. Joan was produced and nourished and disposed of; her father, in parting with his daughter, seemed to have grown the span of Joan's life older; there was only Alabama's future now standing between him and his complete possession of his past. She was the only unresolved element that remained of his youth.

Alabama thought of Joan. Being in love, she concluded, is simply a presentation of our pasts to another individual, mostly packages so unwieldy that we can no longer manage the loosened strings alone. Looking for love is like asking for a new point of departure, she thought, another chance in life. Precociously for her age, she made an addendum: that one person never seeks to share the future with another, so greedy are secret human expectations. Alabama thought a few fine and many skeptical thoughts, but they did not essentially affect her conduct. She was at seventeen a philosophical gourmand of possibilities, having sucked on the bones of frustration thrown off from her family's repasts without repletion. But there was much of her father in her that spoke for itself and judged.

From him, she wondered why that brisk important sense of being a contributory factor in static moments could not last. Everything else seemed to. With him, she enjoyed the concision and completion of her sister's transference from one family to another.

It was lonesome at home without Joan. She could almost have been reconstructed by the scraps she'd left behind.

'I always work when I'm sad,' her mother said.

'I don't see how you learned to sew so well.'

'By sewing for you children.'

'Anyway, won't you please let me have this dress without sleeves at all, and the roses up here on my shoulder?'

'All right, if you want. My hands are so rough nowadays, they stick in the silk and I don't sew so well as I did.'

'It's perfectly beautiful, though. It's better on me than it ever was on Joan.'

Alabama pulled out the full, flowing silk to see how it would blow in a breeze, how it would have looked in a museum on the 'Venus de Milo.'

'If I could just stay this way till I got to the dance,' she thought, 'it would be pretty enough. But I will all come to pieces long before then.'

'Alabama, what *are* you thinking about?'

'About fun.'

'That's good subject matter.'

'And about how wonderful she is,' teased Austin. Privy to the small vanities of his family, these things so absent in himself amused him in his children. 'She's always looking in the glass at herself.'

'Daddy! I am not!' She knew, though, that she looked more frequently than her satisfaction in her appearance justified in the hope of finding something more than she expected.

Her eyes trailed in embarrassment over the vacant lot next door that lay like a primrose dump through the windows. The vermilion hibiscus curved five brazen shields against the sun; the altheas drooped in faded purple canopies against the barn, the South phrased itself in engraved invitation – to a party without an address.

'Millie, you oughtn't to let her get so sunburned if she's going to wear that kind of clothes.'

'She's only a child yet, Austin.'

Joan's old pink was finished for the dance. Miss Millie hooked up the back. It was too hot to stay inside. One side of her hair was flattened by the sweat on her neck before she had

26

finished the other. Millie brought her a cold lemonade. The powder dried in rings around her nose. They went down to the porch. Alabama seated herself in the swing. It had become almost a musical instrument to her; by jiggling the chains she could make it play a lively tune or somnolently protest the passage of a boring date. She'd been ready so long that she wouldn't be any more by the time they got here. Why didn't they come for her, or telephone? Why didn't something happen? Ten o'clock sounded on a neighbor's clock.

'If they don't come on, it'll be too late to go,' she said carelessly, pretending she didn't care whether she missed the dance or not.

Spasmodic unobtrusive cries broke the stillness of the summer night. From far off down the street the cry of a paper boy floated nearer on the heat.

'Wuxtry! Wuxtry! Yad – y – add – vo – tize.'

The cries swelled from one direction to another, rose and fell like answering chants in a cathedral.

'What's happened, boy?'

'I don't know, Ma'am.'

'Here, boy! Gimme a paper!'

'Isn't it awful, Daddy! What does it mean?'

'It may mean a war for us.'

'But they were warned not to sail on the *Lusitania*,' Millie said.

Austin threw back his head impatiently.

'They can't do that,' he said, 'they can't warn neutral nations.'

The automobile loaded with boys drew up at the curb. A long, shrill whistle sounded from the dark; none of the boys got out of the car.

'You will not leave this house until they come inside for you,' the Judge said severely.

He seemed very fine and serious under the hall light – as serious as the war they might have. Alabama was ashamed for her friends as she compared them with her father. One of the boys got out and opened the door; she and her father could call it a compromise.

'War! There's going to be a war!' she thought.

27

Excitement stretched her heart and lifted her feet so high that she floated over the steps to the waiting automobile.

'There's gonna be a war,' she said.

'Then the dance ought to be good tonight,' her escort answered.

All night long Alabama thought about the war. Things would disintegrate to new excitements. With adolescent Nietzscheanism, she already planned to escape on the world's reversals from the sense of suffocation that seemed to her to be eclipsing her family, her sisters, and mother. She, she told herself, would move brightly along high places and stop to trespass and admire, and if the fine was a heavy one – well, there was no good in saving up beforehand to pay it. Full of these presumptuous resolves, she promised herself that if, in the future, her soul should come starving and crying for bread it should eat the stone she might have to offer without complaint or remorse. Relentlessly she convinced herself that the only thing of any significance was to take what she wanted when she could. She did her best.

III

'She's the wildest one of the Beggs, but she's a thoroughbred,' people said.

Alabama knew everything they said about her – there were so many boys who wanted to 'protect' her that she couldn't escape knowing. She leaned back in the swing visualizing herself in her present position.

'Thoroughbred!' she thought, 'meaning that I never let them down on the dramatic possibilities of a scene – I give a damned good show.'

'He's just like a very majestic dog,' she thought of the tall officer beside her, 'a hound, a noble hound! I wonder if his ears would meet over his nose.' The man vanished in metaphor.

His face was long, culminating in a point of lugubrious sentimentality at the self-conscious end of his nose. He pulled himself intermittently to pieces, showered himself in fragments above her head. He was obviously at an emotional tension.

'Little lady, do you think you could live on five thousand a year?' he asked benevolently. 'To start with,' he added, on second thought.

'I could, but I don't want to.'

'Then why did you kiss me?'

'I had never kissed a man with a moustache before.'

'That's hardly a reason—'

'No. But it's as good a reason as many people would have to offer for going into convents.'

'There's no use in my staying any longer, then,' he said sadly.

'I s'pose not. It's half-past eleven.'

'Alabama, you're positively indecent. You know what an awful reputation you've got and I offer to marry you anyway and—'

'And you're angry because I won't make you an honest man.'

The man hid dubiously beneath the impersonality of his uniform.

'You'll be sorry,' he said unpleasantly.

'I hope so,' Alabama answered. 'I like paying for things I do – it makes me feel square with the world.'

'You're a wild Comanche. Why do you try to pretend you're so bad and hard?'

'Maybe so – anyway the day that I'm sorry I'll write it in the corner of the wedding invitations.'

'I'll send you a picture, so you won't forget me.'

'All right – if you want to.'

Alabama slipped on the night latch and turned off the light. She waited in the absolute darkness until her eyes could distinguish the mass of the staircase. 'Maybe I ought to have married him, I'll soon be eighteen,' she tabulated, 'and he could have taken good care of me. You've got to have some sort of background.' She reached the head of the stairs.

'Alabama,' her mother's voice called softly, almost indistinguishable from the currents of the darkness, 'your father

29

wants to see you in the morning. You'll have to get up to breakfast.'

Judge Austin Beggs sat over the silver things about the table, finely controlled, co-ordinated, poised in his cerebral life like a wonderful athlete in the motionless moments between the launchings of his resources.

Addressing Alabama, he overpowered his child.

'I tell you that I will not have my daughter's name bandied about the street corners.'

'Austin! She's hardly out of school,' Millie protested.

'All the more reason. What do you know of these officers?'

'P – l – e – a – s – e—'

'Joe Ingham told me his daughter was brought home scandalously intoxicated and she admitted that you had given her the liquor.'

'She didn't have to drink it – it was a freshman leadout and I filled my nursing bottle with gin.'

'And you forced it on the Ingham girl?'

'I did not! When she saw people laughing, she tried to edge in on the joke, having none of her own to amuse them with,' Alabama retorted arrogantly.

'You will have to find a way of conducting yourself more circumspectly.'

'Yes, sir. Oh, Daddy! I'm so tired of just sitting on the porch and having dates and watching things rot.'

'It seems to me you have plenty to do without corrupting others.'

'Nothing to do but drink and make love,' she commented privately.

She had a strong sense of her own insignificance; of her life's slipping by while June bugs covered the moist fruit in the fig trees with the motionless activity of clustering flies upon an open sore. The bareness of the dry Bermuda grass about the pecan trees crawled imperceptibly with tawny caterpillars. The matlike vines dried in the autumn heat and hung like empty locust shells from the burned thickets about the pillars of the house. The sun sagged yellow over the grass plots and bruised itself on the clotted cotton fields. The fertile countryside that grew things in other seasons spread flat from

the roads and lay prone in ribbed fans of broken discourage-
ment. Birds sang dissonantly. Not a mule in the fields nor a
human being on the sandy roads could have borne the heat
between the concave clay banks and the mediant cypress
swamps that divided the camp from the town – privates died
of sunstroke.

The evening sun buttoned the pink folds of the sky and
followed a busload of officers into town, young lieutenants,
old lieutenants, free from camp for the evening to seek what
explanation of the world war this little Alabama town had to
offer. Alabama knew them all with varying degrees of
sentimentality.

'Is your wife in town, Captain Farreleigh?' asked a voice in
the joggling vehicle. 'You seem very high tonight.'

'She's here – but I'm on my way to see my girl. That's why
I'm happy,' the captain said shortly, whistling to himself.

'Oh.' The especially young lieutenant didn't know what to
say to the captain. It would be about like offering con-
gratulations for a stillborn child. He supposed to say to the
man, 'Isn't that splendid' or 'How nice!' He might say, 'Well,
captain, that'll be very scandalous indeed!' – if he wanted to
be court-martialed.

'Well, good luck, I'm going to see mine tomorrow,' he said
finally, and further to show that he bore no moral prejudice,
he added 'good luck.'

'Are you still panhandling in Beggs Street?' asked Farreleigh
abruptly.

'Yes,' the lieutenant laughed uncertainly.

The car deposited them in the breathless square, the centre
of the town. In the vast space enclosed by the low buildings
the vehicle seemed as minuscular as a coach in the palace yard
of an old print. The arrival of the bus made no impression on
the city's primal sleep. The old rattle-trap disgorged its cargo
of clicking masculinity and vibrant official restraint into the
lap of this invertebrate world.

Captain Farreleigh crossed to the taxi stand.

'Number five Beggs Street,' he said with loud insistence,
making sure his words reached the lieutenant, 'as fast as you
can make it.'

As the car swung off, Farreleigh listened contentedly to the officer's forced laugh stabbing the night behind him.

'Hello, Alabama!'

'Ho, there, Felix!'

'My name is not Felix.'

'It suits you, though. What is your name?'

'Captain Franklin McPherson Farreleigh.'

'The war's on my mind, I couldn't remember.'

'I've written a poem about you.'

Alabama took the paper he gave her and held it to the light falling through the slats of the shutters like a staff of music.

'It's about West Point,' she said disappointed.

'That's the same thing,' said Farreleigh. 'I feel the same way about you.'

'Then the United States Military Academy appreciates the fact that you like its gray eyes. Did you leave the last verse in the taxi or were you keeping the car in case I should shoot?'

'It's waiting because I thought we could ride. We ought not to go to the club,' he said seriously.

'Felix!' reproved Alabama, 'you know I don't mind people's jabbering about us. Nobody will notice that we are together – it takes so many soldiers to make a good war.'

She felt sorry for Felix; she was touched that he did not want to compromise her. In a wave of friendship and tenderness. 'You mustn't mind,' she said.

'This time it's my wife – she's here,' Farreleigh said crisply, 'and she might be there.'

He offered no apology.

Alabama hesitated.

'Well, come on, let's ride,' she said, at last. 'We can dance another Saturday.'

He was a tavern sort of man buckled into his uniform, strapped with the swagger of beef-eating England, buffeted by his incorruptible, insensitive, roistering gallantry. He sang 'The Ladies' over and over again as they rode along the horizons of youth and a moonlit war. A southern moon is a sodden moon, and sultry. When it swamps the fields and the rustling sandy roads and the sticky honeysuckle hedges in its sweet stagnation, your fight to hold on to reality is like a

32

protestation against a first waft of ether. He closed his arms about the dry slender body. She smelled of Cherokee roses and harbors at twilight.

'I'm going to get myself transferred,' said Felix impatiently.

'Why?'

'To avoid falling out of aeroplanes and cluttering up roadsides like your other beaux.'

'*Who* fell out of an aeroplane?'

'Your friend with the Dachshund face and the moustache, on his way to Atlanta. The mechanic was killed and they've got the lieutenant up for court-martial.'

'Fear,' said Alabama as she felt her muscles tighten with a sense of disaster, 'is nerves – maybe all emotions are. Anyway, we must hold on to ourselves and not care.

'Oh – how did it happen?' she inquired casually.

Felix shook his head.

'Well, Alabama, I *hope* it was an accident.'

'There isn't any use worrying about the dog-one,' Alabama extricated herself. 'Those people, Felix, who spread their sensibilities for the passage of events live like emotional prostitutes; they pay with a lack of responsibility on the part of others – no Walter Raleighing of the inevitable for me,' she justified.

'You didn't have the right to lead him on, you know.'

'Well, it's over now.'

'Over in a hospital ward,' commented Felix, 'for the poor mechanic.'

Her high cheek bones carved the moonlight like a scythe in a ripe wheat field. It was hard for a man in the army to censure Alabama.

'And the blond lieutenant who rode with me to town?' Farreleigh went on.

'I'm afraid I can't explain him away,' she said.

Captain Farreleigh went through the convulsive movements of a drowning man. He grabbed his nose and sank to the floor of the car.

'Heartless,' he said. 'Well, I suppose I shall survive.'

'Honor, Duty, Country, and West Point,' Alabama answered dreamily. She laughed. They both laughed. It was very sad.

'Number five Beggs Street,' Captain Farreleigh directed the taxi man, 'immediately. The house is on fire.'

The war brought men to the town like swarms of benevolent locusts eating away the blight of unmarried women that had overrun the South since its economic decline. There was the little major who stormed about like a Japanese warrior flashing his gold teeth, and an Irish captain with eyes like the Blarney stone and hair like burning peat, and aviation officers, white around their eyes from where their goggles had been with swollen noses from the wind and sun; and men who were better dressed in their uniforms than ever before in their lives communicating their consequent sense of a special occasion; men who smelled of Fitch's hair tonic from the camp barber and men from Princeton and Yale who smelled of Russian Leather and seemed very used to being alive, and trade-mark snobs naming things and men who waltzed in spurs and resented the cut-in system. Girls swung from one to another of the many men in the intimate flush of a modern Virginia reel.

Through the summer Alabama collected soldiers' insignia. By autumn she had a glove-box full. No other girl had more and even then she'd lost some. So many dances and rides and so many golden bars and silver bars and bombs and castles and flags and even a serpent to represent them all in her cushioned box. Every night she wore a new one.

Alabama quarrelled with Judge Beggs about her collection of bric-a-brac and Millie laughed and told her daughter to keep all those pins; that they were pretty.

It turned as cold as it ever gets in that country. That is to say, the holiness of creation misted the lonesome green things outside; the moon glowed and sputtered nebulous as pearls in the making; the night picked itself a white rose. In spite of the haze and the clouds in the air, Alabama waited for her date outside, pendulously tilting the old swing from the past to the future, from dreams to surmises and back again.

A blond lieutenant with one missing insignia mounted the Beggs' steps. He had not bought himself a substitute because he liked imagining the one he had lost in the battle of Alabama to be irreplaceable. There seemed to be some heavenly support beneath his shoulder blades that lifted his feet from the ground in ecstatic suspension, as if he secretly enjoyed the ability to fly but was walking as a compromise to convention. Green gold under the moon, his hair lay in Cellinian frescos and fashionable porticoes over his dented brow. Two hollows over his eyes like the ends of mysterious bolts of fantasy held those expanses of electric blue to the inspiration of his face. The pressure of masculine beauty equilibrated for twenty-two years had made his movements conscious and economized as the steps of a savage transporting a heavy load of rocks on his head. He was thinking to himself that he would never be able to say to a taxi driver 'Number five Beggs Street' again without making the ride with the ghost of Captain Farreleigh.

'You're ready already! Why outdoors?' he called. It was chilly in the mist to be swinging outside.

'Daddy has the blight and I have retired from the field of action.'

'What particular iniquity have you committed?'

'Oh, he seems to feel for one thing, that the army has a right to its epaulettes.'

'Isn't it nice that parental authority's going to pieces with everything else?'

'Perfect – I love conventional situations.'

They stood on the frosted porch in the sea of mist quite far away from each other, yet Alabama could have sworn she was touching him, so magnetic were their two pairs of eyes.

'And—?'

'Songs about summer love. I hate this cold weather.'

'And—?'

'Blond men on their way to the country club.'

The clubhouse sprouted inquisitively under the oaks like a squat clump of bulbs piercing the leaves in spring. The car drew up the gravel drive, poking its nose in a round bed of cannas. The ground around the place was as worn and used as the plot before a children's playhouse. The sagging wire about the tennis court, the peeling drag-green paint of the summer house on the first tee, the trickling hydrant, the veranda thick in dust all flavored of the pleasant atmosphere

35

of a natural growth. It is too bad that a bottle of corn liquor exploded in one of the lockers just after the war and burned the place to the ground. So much of the theoretical youth – not just transitory early years, but of the projections and escapes of inadequate people in dramatic times – had wedged itself beneath the low-hung rafters, that the fire destroying this shrine of wartime nostalgias may have been a case of combustion from emotional saturation. No officer could have visited it three times without falling in love, engaging himself to marry and to populate the countryside with little country clubs exactly like it.

Alabama and the lieutenant lingered beside the door.

'I'm going to lay a tablet to the scene of our first meeting,' he said.

Taking out his knife he carved in the door post:

'David,' the legend read, 'David, David, Knight, Knight, Knight, and Miss Alabama Nobody.'

'Egotist,' she protested.

'I love this place,' he said. 'Let's sit outside awhile.'

'Why? The dance only lasts until twelve.'

'Can't you trust me for three minutes or so?'

'I do trust you. That's why I want to go inside.' She was a little angry about the names. David had told her about how famous he was going to be many times before.

Dancing with David, he smelled like new goods. Being close to him with her face in the space between his ear and his stiff army collar was like being initiated into the subterranean reserves of a fine fabric store exuding the delicacy of cambrics and linen and luxury bound in bales. She was jealous of his pale aloofness. When she saw him leave the dance floor with other girls, the resentment she felt was not against any blending of his personality with theirs, but against his leading others than herself into those cooler detached regions which he inhabited alone.

He took her home and they sat together before the grate fire in a still suspension of externals. The flames glittered in his teeth and lit his face with transcendental qualities. His features danced before her eyes with the steady elusiveness of a celluloid target on a shooting-gallery spray. She searched her relations with her father for advice about being clever; there, she found nothing relative to human charm. Being in love, none of her personal aphorisms were of the slightest help.

Alabama had grown tall and thin in the last few years; her head was blonder for its extra distance from the earth. Her legs stretched long and thin as prehistoric drawings before her; her hands felt poignant and heavy as if David's eyes lay a weight over her wrists. She knew her face glowed in the firelight like a confectioner's brewing, an advertisement of a pretty girl drinking a strawberry sundae in June. She wondered if David knew how conceited she was.

'And so you love blond men?'

'Yes.' Alabama had a way of talking under pressure as if the words she said were some unexpected encumbrance she found in her mouth and must rid herself of before she could communicate.

He verified himself in the mirror – pale hair like eighteenth-century moonlight and eyes like grottoes, the blue grotto, the green grotto, stalactites and malachites hanging about the dark pupil – as if he had taken an inventory of himself before leaving and was pleased to find himself complete.

The back of his head was firm and mossy and the curve of his cheek a sunny spreading meadow. His hands across her shoulders fit like the warm hollows in a pillow.

'Say "dear,"' he said.

'No.'

'You love me. Why won't you?'

'I never say anything to anybody. Don't talk.'

'Why won't you talk to me?'

'It spoils things. Tell me you love me.'

'Oh – I love you. Do you love me?'

So much she loved the man, so close and closer she felt herself that he became distorted in her vision, like pressing her nose upon a mirror and gazing into her own eyes. She felt the lines of his neck and his chipped profile like segments of the wind blowing about her consciousness. She felt the essence of herself pulled finer and smaller like those streams of spun glass that pull and stretch till there remains but a glimmering

37

illusion. Neither falling nor breaking, the stream spins finer. She felt herself very small and ecstatic. Alabama was in love.

She crawled into the friendly cave of his ear. The area inside was gray and ghostly classic as she stared about the deep trenches of the cerebellum. There was not a growth nor a flowery substance to break those smooth convolutions, just the puffy rise of sleek gray matter. 'I've got to see the front lines,' Alabama said to herself. The lumpy mounds rose wet above her head and she set out following the creases. Before long she was lost. Like a mystic maze the folds and ridges rose in desolation; there was nothing to indicate one way from another. She stumbled on and finally reached the medulla oblongata. Vast tortuous indentations led her round and round. Hysterically, she began to run. David, distracted by a tickling sensation at the head of his spine, lifted his lips from hers.

'I'll see your father,' he said, 'about when we can be married.'

Judge Beggs rocked himself back and forth from his toes to his heels, sifting values.

'Um – m – m – well, I suppose so, if you think you can take care of her.'

'I'm sure of it, sir. There's a little money in the family – and my earning capacity. It will be enough.'

David thought doubtfully to himself that there wasn't much money – perhaps a hundred and fifty thousand between his mother and his grandmother, and he wanted to live in New York and be an artist. Perhaps his family wouldn't help. Well, anyway, they were engaged. He had to have Alabama, anyway, and money – well once he had dreamed of a troop of Confederate soldiers who wrapped their bleeding feet in Rebel banknotes to keep them off the snow. David, in his dream, had been there when they found that they did not feel sorry about using up the worthless money after they had lost the war.

Spring came and shattered its opalescent orioles in wreaths of daffodils. Kiss-me-at-the-gate clung to its angular branches and the old yards were covered with a child's version of flowers: snowdrops and primula veris, pussywillow and calendula. David and Alabama kicked over the oak leaves from the stumpy roots in the woods and picked white violets. They went on Sundays to the vaudeville and sat in the back of the theatre so they could hold hands unobserved. They learned to sing 'My Sweetie' and 'Baby' and sat in a box at *Hitchy-Koo* and gazed at each other soberly through the chorus of 'How Can You Tell?' The spring rains soaked the heavens till the clouds slid open and summer flooded the South with sweat and heat waves. Alabama dressed in pink and pale linen and she and David sat together under the paddles of ceiling fans whipping the summer to consequence. Outside the wide doors of the country club they pressed their bodies against the cosmos, the jibberish of jazz, the black heat from the greens in the hollow like people making an imprint for a cast of humanity. They swam in the moonlight that varnished the land like a honey-coating and David swore and cursed the collars of his uniforms and rode all night to the rifle range rather than give up his hours after supper with Alabama. They broke the beat of the universe to measures of their own conception and mesmerized themselves with its precious thumping.

The air turned opaque over the singed grass slopes, and the sand in the bunkers flew up dry as gunpowder under a niblick. Tangles of goldenrod shredded the sun; the splendid summer lay ground into powder over the hard clay roads. Moving day came and the first day of school spiced the mornings – and one summer ended with another fall.

When David left for the port of embarkation, he wrote Alabama letters about New York. Maybe, after all, she would go to New York and marry.

'City of glittering hypotheses,' wrote David ecstatically. 'Chaff from a fairy mill, suspended in penetrating blue! Humanity clings to the streets like flies upon a treacle stream. The tops of the buildings shine like crowns of gold-leaf kings in conference – and oh, my dear, you are my princess and I'd like to keep you shut forever in an ivory tower for my private delectation.'

The third time he wrote that about the princess, Alabama asked him not to mention the tower again.

She thought of David Knight at night and went to the vaudeville with the dog-faced aviation officer till the war was over. It ended one night with the flash of a message across the vaudeville curtain. There had been a war, but now there were two more acts of the show.

David was sent back to Alabama for demobilization. He told Alabama about the girl in the Hotel Astor the night he had been so drunk.

'Oh, God!' she said to herself. 'Well, I can't help it.' She thought of the dead mechanic, of Felix, of the faithful dog-lieutenant. She hadn't been too good herself.

She said to David that it didn't matter: that she believed that one person should only be faithful to another when they felt it. She said it was probably her fault for not making him care more.

As soon as David could make the arrangements, he sent for her. The Judge gave her the trip north for a wedding present; she quarrelled with her mother about her wedding clothes.

'I don't want it that way. I want it to drop off the shoulders.'

'Alabama, it's as near as I can get it. How can it stay up with nothing to hold it?'

'Aw, Mamma, you can fix it.'

Millie laughed, a pleased sad laugh, and indulgent.

'My children think I can accomplish the impossible,' she said, complacently.

Alabama left her mother a note in her bureau drawer the day she went away:

My dearest Mamma:

I have not been as you would have wanted me but I love you with all my heart and I will think of you every day. I hate leaving you alone with all your children gone. Don't forget me.

Alabama.

The Judge put her on the train.

'Good-bye, daughter.'

He seemed very handsome and abstract to Alabama. She

40

was afraid to cry; her father was so proud. Joan had been afraid, too, to cry.

'Good-bye, Daddy.'

'Good-bye, Baby.'

The train pulled Alabama out of the shadow-drenched land of her youth.

The Judge and Millie sat on the familiar porch alone. Millie picked nervously at a palmetto fan; the Judge spat occasionally through the vines.

'Don't you think we'd better get a smaller house?'

'Millie, I've lived here eighteen years and I'm not going to change my habits of life at my age.'

'There are no screens in this house and the pipes freeze every winter. It's so far from your office, Austin.'

'It suits me, and I'm going to stay.'

The old empty swing creaked faintly in the breeze that springs up from the gulf every night. Children's voices floated past from the street corner where they played some vindictive trick on time under the arc light. The Judge and Millie silently rocked the paintless porch chairs. Uncrossing his feet from the banisters, Austin rose to close the shutters for the night. It was his house at last.

'Well,' he said, 'this night next year you'll probably be a widow!'

'Pshaw!' said Millie. 'You've been saying that for thirty years.'

The sweet pastels of Millie's face faded in distress. The lines between her nose and mouth drooped like the cords of a flag at half-mast.

'Your mother was just the same,' she said, reproachfully, 'always saying she was going to die and she lived to be ninety-two.'

'Well, she did die, didn't she, at last?' the Judge chuckled.

He turned out the lights in his pleasant house and they went upstairs, two old people alone. The moon waddled about the tin roof and bounced awkwardly over Millie's window sill. The Judge lay reading Hegel for half an hour or so and fell asleep. His deeply balanced snoring through the long night reassured Millie that this was not the end of life although

Alabama's room was dark and Joan was gone and the board for Dixie's transom was long thrown away with the trash and her only boy lay in the cemetery in a little grave beside the common grave of Ethelinda and Mason Cuthbert Beggs. Millie didn't think anything much about personal things. She just lived from day to day; and Austin didn't think anything at all about them because he lived from one century to another.

It was awful, though, for the family to lose Alabama, because she was the last to go and that meant their lives would be different with her away . . .

Alabama lay thinking in room number twenty-one-o-nine of the Biltmore Hotel that her life would be different with her parents so far away. David David Knight Knight Knight, for instance, couldn't possibly make her put out her light till she got good and ready. No power on earth could make her do anything, she thought frightened, any more, except herself.

David was thinking that he didn't mind the light, that Alabama was his bride and that he had just bought her that detective story with the last actual cash they had in the world, though she didn't know it. It was a good detective story about money and Monte Carlo and love. Alabama looked very lovely herself as she lay there reading, he thought.

2

I

IT WAS the biggest bed that both of them together could imagine. It was broader than it was long, and included all the exaggerated qualities of their combined disrespect for tradition in beds. There were shining black knobs and white enamel swoops like cradle rockers, and specially made covers trailing in disarray off one side on to the floor. David rolled over on his side; Alabama slid downhill into the warm spot over the mass of the Sunday paper.

'Can't you make a little more room?'

'Jesus Chr – O Jesus,' groaned David.

'What's the matter?'

'It says in the paper we're famous,' he blinked owlishly.

Alabama straightened up.

'How nice – let's see—'

David impatiently rustled the Brooklyn real estate and Wall Street quotations.

'Nice!' he said – he was almost crying, 'nice! But it says we're in a sanitarium for wickedness. What'll our parents think when they see that, I'd like to know?'

Alabama ran her fingers through her permanent wave.

'Well,' she began tentatively. 'They've thought we ought to be there for months.'

'—But we haven't been.'

'We aren't now.' Turning in alarm she flung her arms about David. 'Are we?'

'I don't know – are we?'

They laughed.

'Look in the paper and see.'

'Aren't we silly?' they said.

'Awfully silly. Isn't it fun – well, I'm glad we're famous anyway.'

With three running steps along the bed Alabama bounced to the floor. Outside the window gray roads pulled the Connecticut horizons from before and behind to a momentous crossing. A stone minuteman kept the peace of the indolent fields. A driveway crawled from under the feathery chestnuts. Ironweed wilted in the heat; a film of purple asters matted over their stalks. Tar melted in the sun along the loping roads. The house had been there forever chuckling to itself in the goldenrod stubble.

New England summer is an Episcopal service. The land basks virtuously in a green and homespun stretch; summer hurls its thesis and bursts against our dignity explosively as the back of a Japanese kimono.

Dancing happily about, she put on her clothes, feeling very graceful and thinking of ways to spend money.

'What else does it say?'

'It says we're wonderful.'

'So you see—' she began.

'No, I don't see, but I suppose everything will be all right.'

'Neither do I – David, it must be your frescoes.'

'Naturally, it couldn't be us, megalomaniac.'

Playing about the room in the Lalique ten o'clock sun, they were like two uncombed Sealyhams.

'Oh,' wailed Alabama from the depths of the closet. 'David, just look at that suitcase, and it's the one you gave me for Easter.'

Exhibiting the gray pigskin she exposed the broad watery yellow ring disfiguring the satin lining. Alabama stared at her husband lugubriously.

'A lady in our position can't go to town with a thing like that,' she said.

'You've got to see the doctor – what happened to it?'

'I lent it to Joan the day she came to bawl me out to

44

carry the baby's diapers in.'

David laughed conservatively.

'Was she very unpleasant?'

'She said we ought to save our money.'

'Why didn't you tell her we'd spent it?'

'I did. She seemed to feel that that was wrong so I told her we were going to get some more almost immediately.'

'What'd she say to that?' asked David confidently.

'She was suspicious; she said we were against the rules.'

'Families always think the idea is for nothing to happen to people.'

'We won't call her up again – I'll see you at five, David, in the Plaza lobby – I'm gonna miss my train.'

'All right. Good-bye, darling.'

David held her seriously in his arms. 'If anybody tries to steal you on the train tell them you belong to me.'

'If you'll promise me you won't get run over—'

'Good – by – e!'

'Don't we adore each other?'

Vincent Youmans wrote the music for those twilights just after the war. They were wonderful. They hung above the city like an indigo wash, forming themselves from asphalt dust and sooty shadows under the cornices and limp gusts of air exhaled from closing windows. They lay above the streets like a white fog off a swamp. Through the gloom, the whole world went to tea. Girls in short amorphous capes and long flowing skirts and hats like straw bathtubs waited for taxis in front of the Plaza Grill; girls in long satin coats and colored shoes and hats like straw manhole covers tapped the tune of a cataract on the dance floors of the Lorraine and the St. Regis. Under the sombre ironic parrots of the Biltmore a halo of golden bobs disintegrated into black lace and shoulder bouquets between the pale hours of tea and dinner that sealed the princely windows; the clank of lank contemporaneous silhouettes drowned the clatter of teacups at the Ritz.

People waiting for other people twisted the tips of the palms into brown moustache-ends and ripped short slits about their lower leaves. It was just a lot of youngness: Lillian Lorraine would be drunk as the cosmos on top of the New

Amsterdam by midnight, and football teams breaking training would scare the waiters with drunkenness in the fall. The world was full of parents taking care of people. Debutantes said to each other 'Isn't that the Knights?' and 'I met him at a prom. My dear, please introduce me.'

'What's the use? They're c – r – a – z – y about each other,' smelted into the fashionable monotone of New York.

'Of course it's the Knights,' said a lot of girls. 'Have you seen his pictures?'

'I'd rather look at him any day,' answered other girls.

Serious people took them seriously; David made speeches about visual rhythm and the effect of nebular physics on the relation of the primary colors. Outside the windows, fervently impassive to its own significance, the city huddled in a gold-crowned conference. The top of New York twinkled like a golden canopy behind a throne. David and Alabama faced each other incompetently – you couldn't argue about having a baby.

'So what did the doctor say?' he insisted.

'I told you – he said "Hello!"'

'Don't be an ass – what else did he say? – We've got to know what he said.'

'So then we'll have the baby,' announced Alabama, proprietarily.

David fumbled about his pockets. 'I'm sorry – I must have left them at home.' He was thinking that then they'd be three.

'What?'

'The bromides.'

'I said "Baby."'

'Oh.'

'We should ask somebody.'

'Who'll we ask?'

Almost everybody had theories: that the Longacre Pharmacies carried the best gin in town; that anchovies sobered you up; that you could tell wood alcohol by the smell. Everybody knew where to find the blank verse in Cabell and how to get seats for the Yale game, that Mr. Fish inhabited the aquarium, and that there were others besides the sergeant ensconced in the Central Park Police Station – but nobody knew how to have a baby.

'I think you'd better ask your mother,' said David.

'Oh, David – don't! She'd think I wouldn't know how.'

'Well,' he said tentatively, 'I could ask my dealer – he knows where the subways go.'

The city fluctuated in muffled roars like the dim applause rising to an actor on the stage of a vast theatre. *Two Little Girls in Blue* and *Sally* from the New Amsterdam pumped in their eardrums and unwieldy quickened rhythms invited them to be Negroes and saxophone players, to come back to Maryland and Louisiana, addressed them as mammies and millionaires. The shopgirls were looking like Marilyn Miller. College boys said Marilyn Miller where they had said Rosie Quinn. Moving picture actresses were famous. Paul Whiteman played the significance of amusement on his violin. They were having the bread line at the Ritz that year. Everybody was there. People met people they knew in hotel lobbies smelling of orchids and plush and detective stories, and asked each other where they'd been since last time. Charlie Chaplin wore a yellow polo coat. People were tired of the proletariat – everybody was famous. All the other people who weren't well known had been killed in the war; there wasn't much interest in private lives.

'There they are, the Knights, dancing together,' they said, 'isn't it nice? There they go.'

'Listen, Alabama, you're not keeping time,' David was saying.

'David, for God's sake will you try to keep off of my feet?'

'I never could waltz anyway.'

There were a hundred thousand things to be blue about exposed in all the choruses.

'I'll have to do lots of work,' said David. 'Won't it seem queer to be the centre of the world for somebody else?'

'Very. I'm very glad my parents are coming before I begin to get sick.'

'How do you know you'll get sick?'

'I should.'

'That's no reason.'

'No.'

'Let's go some place else.'

Paul Whiteman played 'Two Little Girls in Blue' at the Palais Royal; it was a big expensive number. Girls with piquant profiles were mistaken for Gloria Swanson. New York was more full of reflections than of itself – the only concrete things in town were the abstractions. Everybody wanted to pay the cabaret checks.

'We're having some people,' everybody said to everybody else, 'and we want you to join us,' and they said, 'We'll telephone.'

All over New York people telephoned. They telephoned from one hotel to another to people on other parties that they couldn't get there – that they were engaged. It was always tea-time or late at night.

David and Alabama invited their friends to throw oranges into the drum at the Plantation and themselves into the fountain at Union Square. Up they went, humming the New Testament and Our Country's Constitution, riding the tide like triumphant islanders on a surf board. Nobody knew the words to 'The Star-Spangled Banner.'

In the city, old women with faces as soft and ill-lit as the side-streets of Central Europe offered their pansies; hats floated off the Fifth Avenue bus; the clouds sent out a prospectus over Central Park. The streets of New York smelled acrid and sweet like drippings from the mechanics of a metallic night-blooming garden. The intermittent odors, the people and the excitement, suctioned spasmodically up the side-streets from the thoroughfares, rose in gusts on the beat of their personal tempo.

Possessing a rapacious engulfing ego their particular genius swallowed their world in its swift undertow and washed its cadavers out to sea. New York is a good place to be on the up-grade.

The clerk in the Manhattan thought they weren't married but he gave them the room anyway.

'What's the matter?' David said from the twin-bed under the cathedral print. 'Can't you make it?'

'Sure. What time is the train?'

'Now. I've got just two dollars to meet your family,' said

David searching his clothes.

'I wanted to buy them some flowers.'

'Alabama,' said David sententiously, 'that's impractical. You've become nothing but an aesthetic theory – a chemistry formula for the decorative.

'There's nothing we can do with two dollars anyway,' she protested in a logical tone.

'I s'pose not—'

Attenuated odors from the hotel florist tapped the shell of the velvet vacuum like silver hammers.

'Of course, if we have to pay the taxi—'

'Daddy'll have some money.'

Puffs of white smoke aspired against the station skylight. Lights like unripe citrus fruits hung in the gray day from the steel rafters. Swarms and swarms of people passed each other coming up the stairway. The train clicked up with the noise of many keys turning in many rusty locks.

'If I'd only known it would be like that at Atlantic City,' they said – or, 'Could you believe it, we're half hour late?' – or, 'The town hasn't changed much without us,' they said, rustling their packages and realizing their hats were all wrong for wear in the city.

'There's Mamma!' cried Alabama.

'Well, how do ye do—'

'Isn't it a great city, Judge?'

'I haven't been here since eighteen-eighty-two. There's been considerable change since then,' said the Judge.

'Did you have a nice trip?'

'Where is your sister, Alabama?'

'She couldn't come down.'

'She couldn't come down,' corroborated David lamely.

'You see,' went on Alabama at her mother's look of surprise, 'the last time Joan came she borrowed my best suitcase to carry away wet diapers and since then we've – well, we haven't seen her so much.'

'Why shouldn't she?' the Judge demanded sternly.

'It was my best suitcase,' explained Alabama patiently.

'But the poor little baby,' sighed Miss Millie. 'I suppose we can telephone them.'

'You will feel differently about things like that after you have children of your own,' said the Judge.

Alabama wondered suspiciously if her figure showed.

'But I can see how she felt about the suitcase,' continued Millie magnanimously. 'Even as a baby, Alabama was particular like that about her own things – never wanted to share them, even then.'

The taxi steamed up the vaporous chute of the station runway.

Alabama didn't know how to go about asking the Judge to pay the taxi – she hadn't been absolutely sure of how to go about anything since her marriage had precluded the Judge's resented direction. She didn't know what to say when girls postured in front of David hoping to have him sketch them on his shirt front, or what to do when David raved and ranted and swore that it ruined his talent to have his buttons torn off in the laundry.

'If you children will get these suitcases into the train, I'll pay the taxi,' said the Judge.

The green hills of Connecticut preached a sedative sermon after the rocking of the gritty train. The gaunt, disciplined smells of New England lawn, the scent of invisible truck gardens bound the air in tight bouquets. Apologetic trees swept the porch, insects creaked in the baking meadows widowed of their crops. There didn't seem room in the cultivated landscape for the unexpected. If you wanted to hang anybody, reflected Alabama, you'd have to do it in your own back yard. Butterflies opened and shut along the roads like the flash of white in a camera lens. 'You couldn't be a butterfly,' they said. They were silly butterflies, flying about that way and arguing with people about their potentialities.

'We meant to get the grass cut,' began Alabama – 'but—'

'It's much better this way,' finished David. 'It's more picturesque.'

'Well, I like the weeds,' the Judge said amiably.

'They make it smell so sweet in the country,' Miss Millie added. 'But aren't you lonely out here at night?'

'Oh, David's friends from college come out occasionally and sometimes we go into town.'

Alabama didn't add how often they went in to New York to waste the extra afternoons sloshing orange juice through bachelor sanctuaries, droning the words to summer behind insoluble locks. They went there ahead, awaiting the passage of that progressive celebration that a few years later followed the boom about New York like the Salvation Army follows Christmas, to absolve themselves in the waters of each other's unrest.

'Mister,' Tanka greeted them from the steps, 'and Missy.'

Tanka was the Japanese butler. They couldn't have afforded him without borrowing from David's dealer. He cost money; that was because he constructed botanical gardens out of cucumbers and floral displays with the butter and made up the money for his flute lessons from the grocery bills. They had tried to do without him till Alabama cut her hand on a can of baked beans and David sprained his painting wrist on the lawn mower.

The Oriental swept the floor in an inclusive rotation of his body, indicating himself as the axis of the earth. Bursting suddenly into a roar of disquieting laughter, he turned to Alabama.

'Missy, kin see you jessy minute – jessy minute, this way, please.'

'He's going to ask for change,' thought Alabama uneasily following him to the side porch.

'Look!' said Tanka. With a gesture of negation, he indicated the hammock swung between the columns of the house where two young men lay uproariously asleep with a bottle of gin by their sides.

'Well,' she said hesitantly, 'you'd better tell Mister – but not in front of the family, Tanka.'

'Velly careful,' nodded the Jap, making a shushing sound and barring his lips with his fingers.

'Listen, Mamma, I think you'd better come upstairs and rest before dinner,' suggested Alabama. 'You must be tired after your trip.'

From the sense that she had nothing whatever to do with herself which radiated from the girl as she descended from her parents' room David knew that something was wrong.

'What's the matter?'

'Matter! There are drunks in the hammock. If Daddy sees *that* there'll be hell to pay!'

'Send them away.'

'They can't move.'

'My God! Tanka'll just have to see that they stay outside until after dinner.'

'Do you think the Judge would understand?'

'I'm afraid so—'

Alabama stared about disconsolately.

'Well – I suppose there comes a moment when people must chose between their contemporaries and their families.'

'Are they in very bad shape?'

'Pretty hopeless. If we send for the ambulance, it would just make a scene,' she said tentatively.

The moiré sheen of the afternoon polished the sterility of the rooms' colonial picturesqueness and scratched itself on the yellow flowers that trailed the mantel like featherstitching. It was a priestly light curving in the dips and hollows of a melancholic waltz.

'I don't see what we can do about it,' they agreed.

Alabama and David stood there anxiously in the quiet till the clang of a spoon on a tin waiter summoned them to dinner.

'I'm glad to see,' said Austin over the beets like roses, 'that you have succeeded in taming Alabama a little. She seems to have become a very good housekeeper since her marriage.' The Judge was impressed with the beets.

David thought of his buttons upstairs. They were all off.

'Yes,' he said vaguely.

'David has been working very well out here,' Alabama broke in nervously.

She was about to paint a picture of their domestic perfections when a loud groan from the hammock warned her. Staggering through the dining room door with a visionary air, the young man eyed the gathering. On the whole he was all there; just a little awry – his shirt tail was out.

'Good evening,' he said formally.

'I think your friend had better have some dinner,' suggested the baffled Austin.

The friend exploded in foolish laughter.

Miss Millie confusedly inspected Tanka's flowery architecture. Of course, she *wanted* Alabama to have friends. She had always brought up her children with that in mind, but circumstances were, at times, dubious.

A second dishevelled phantom groped through the door; the silence was broken only by squeaky grunts of suppressed hysteria.

'He does that way because he's been operated on,' said David hastily. The Judge bristled.

'They took out his larynx,' David added in alarm. His eyes wildly sought the protoplasmic face. Luckily, the fellows seemed to be listening to what he was saying.

'One's mute,' Alabama explained with inspiration.

'Well, I'm glad of that,' answered the Judge enigmatically. His tone was not without hostility. He seemed chiefly relieved that any further conversation was precluded.

'I can't speak a word,' burst from the ghost unexpectedly. 'I'm mute.'

'Well,' thought Alabama, 'this is the end. *Now* what can we say?'

Miss Millie was saying that salt air spoiled the table silver. The Judge faced his daughter implacable and reproving. The necessity for saying anything was dispelled by a weird and self-explanatory carmagnole about the table. It was not exactly a dance; it was an interpretive protest against the vertebrate state punctuated by glorious ecstatic paeans of rhythmic back-slappings and loud invitations to the Knights to join the party. The Judge and Miss Millie were generously included in the invitation.

'It's like a frieze, a Greek frieze,' commented Miss Millie distractedly.

'It's not very edifying,' supplemented the Judge.

Exhausted, the two men wobbled unsteadily to the floor.

'If David could lend us twenty dollars,' gasped the mass, 'we were just going on to the roadhouse. Of course, if he can't we'll stay a little longer, maybe.'

'Oh,' said David, spellbound.

'Mamma,' said Alabama, 'can't you let us have twenty dollars till we can get to the bank tomorrow?'

'Certainly, my dear – upstairs in my bureau drawer. It's a pity your friends have to leave; they seem to be having such a good time,' she continued vaguely.

The house settled. The cool chirp of the crickets like the crunching of fresh lettuce purged the living room of dissonance. Frogs wheezed in the meadow where the goldenrod would bloom. The family group yielded itself to the straining of the night lullaby through the boughs of the oak.

'Escaped,' sighed Alabama as they snuggled together in the exotic bed.

'Yes,' said David, 'it's all right.'

There were people in automobiles all along the Boston Post Road thinking everything was going to be all right while they got drunk and ran into fireplugs and trucks and old stone walls. Policemen were too busy thinking everything was going to be all right to arrest them.

It was three o'clock in the morning when the Knights were awakened by a stentorian whispering on the lawn.

An hour passed after David dressed and went down. The noise rose in increasingly uproarious muffles.

'Well, then, I'll take a drink with you if you'll try to make a little less noise,' Alabama heard David say as she meticulously put on her clothes. Something was sure to happen; it was better to be looking your best when the authorities arrived. They must be in the kitchen. She stuck her head truculently through the swinging door.

'Now, Alabama,' David greeted her, 'I would advise you to keep your nose out of this.' In a husky melodramatic aside he continued confidentially, 'This is the most expedient way I could think of—'

Alabama stared infuriated over the carnage of the kitchen.

'Oh, shut up!' she yelled.

'Now listen, Alabama,' began David.

'It was you who said all the time that we should be so respectable and now look at you!' she accused.

'He's all right. David's perfectly all right,' the prostrate men

54

muttered feebly.

'And what if my father comes down now? What'll *he* have to say about this being all right?' Alabama indicated the wreckage. 'What are all those old cans?' she demanded contemptuously.

'Tomato juice. It sobers you up. I've just been giving some to the guests,' explained David. 'First I give them tomato juice and then I give them gin.'

Alabama snatched at the bottle in David's hand. 'Give me that bottle.' As he fended her off, she slid against the door. To save the noise of a crash in the hall, she precipitated her body heavily into the jamb. The swinging door caught her full in the face. Her nose bled jubilantly as a newly discovered oil well down the front of her dress.

'I'll see if there's a beefsteak in the icebox,' proffered David. 'Stick it under the sink, Alabama. How long can you hold your breath?'

By the time the kitchen was in some kind of order, the Connecticut dawn drenched the countryside like a firehose. The two men staggered off to sleep at the inn. Alabama and David surveyed her black eyes disconsolately.

'They'll think I did it,' he said.

'Of course – it won't make any difference what I say.'

'When they see us together you'd think they'd believe.'

'People always believe the best story.'

The Judge and Miss Millie were down early to breakfast. They waited amidst the soggy mountains of damp bloated cigarette butts while Tanka burnt the bacon in his expectation of trouble. There was hardly a place to sit without sticking to dried rings of gin and orange juice.

Alabama's head felt as if somebody had been making popcorn in her cranium. She tried to conceal her bruised eyes with heavy coatings of face powder. Her face felt peeled under the mask.

'Good morning,' she said brightly.

The Judge blinked ferociously.

'Alabama,' he said, 'about that telephone call to Joan – your mother and I felt that we'd better make it today. She will be needing help with the baby.'

'Yes, sir.'

Alabama had known this would be their attitude but she couldn't prevent a cataclysmic chute of her insides. She had known that no individual can force other people forever to sustain their own versions of that individual's character – that sooner or later they will stumble across the person's own conception of themselves.

'Well!' she said defiantly to herself, 'families have no right to hold you accountable for what they inculcate before you attain the age of protestation!'

'And since,' the Judge continued, 'you and your sister do not seem to be on the best of terms, we thought we would join her alone tomorrow morning.'

Alabama sat silently inspecting the débris of the night.

'I suppose Joan will stuff them with moralities and tales about how hard it is to get along,' she said to herself bitterly, 'and neatly polish us off in contrast to herself. We're sure to come out of this picture black demons, any way you look at it.'

'Understand,' the Judge was saying, 'that I am not passing a moral judgment on your personal conduct. You are a grown woman and that is your own affair.'

'I understand,' she said. 'You just disapprove, so you're not going to stand it. If I don't accept your way of thinking, you'll leave me to myself. Well, I suppose I have no right to ask you to stay.'

'People who do not subscribe,' answered the Judge, 'have no rights.'

The train that carried the Judge and Miss Millie to the city was lumbered with milk cans and the pleasant paraphernalia of summer in transit. Their attitude was one of reluctant disavowal as they said good-bye. They were going south in a few days. They couldn't come back to the country again. David would be away seeing to his frescoes, and they thought Alabama would be better off at home during his absence. They were glad of David's success and popularity.

'Don't be so desolate,' said David. 'We'll see them again.'

'But it will never be the same,' wailed Alabama. 'Our rôle will always be discounting the character they think we are from now on.'

'Hasn't it always been?'

'Yes – but David, it's very difficult to be two simple people at once, one who wants to have a law to itself and the other who wants to keep all the nice old things and be loved and safe and protected.'

'So,' he said, 'I believe many people have found out before. I suppose all we can really share with people is a taste for the same kinds of weather.'

Vincent Youmans wrote a new tune. The old tunes floated through the hospital windows from the hurdy-gurdies while the baby was being born and the new tunes went the luxurious rounds of lobbies and grills, palm-gardens and roofs.

Miss Millie sent Alabama a box of baby things and a list of what must be done for bathing infants to pin on the bathroom door. When her mother got the telegram about Bonnie's birth, she wired Alabama, 'My blue-eyed baby has grown up. We are so proud.' It came through Western Union 'glue-eyed.' Her mother's letters asked her simply to behave; they implied that Alabama and David were wanton to a certain extent. As Alabama read them over she could hear the slow springs creaking in on the rusty croaking of the frogs in the cypress swamps at home.

The New York rivers dangled lights along the banks like lanterns on a wire; the Long Island marshes stretched the twilight to a blue Campagna. Glimmering buildings hazed the sky in a luminous patchwork quilt. Bits of philosophy, odds and ends of acumen, the ragged ends of vision suicided in the sentimental dusk. The marshes lay black and flat and red and full of crime about their borders. Yes, Vincent Youmans wrote the music. Through the labyrinthine sentimentalities of jazz, they shook their heads from side to side and nodded across town at each other, streamlined bodies riding the prow of the country like metal figures on a fast-moving radiator cap.

Alabama and David were proud of themselves and the baby, consciously affecting a vague *bouffant* casualness about the fifty thousand dollars they spent on two years' worth of polish for life's baroque façade. In reality, there is no materialist like the artist, asking back from life the double and the wastage and the cost on what he puts out in emotional usury.

People were banking in gods those years.

'Good morning,' the bank clerks said in the marble foyers, 'did you want to draw on your Pallas Athene?' and 'Shall I credit the Diana to your wife's account?'

It costs more to ride on the tops of taxis than on the inside; Joseph Urban skies are expensive when they're real. Sunshine comes high to darn the thoroughfares with silver needles – a thread of glamor, a Rolls-Royce thread, a thread of O. Henry. Tired moons ask higher wages. Lustily splashing their dreams in the dark pool of gratification, their fifty thousand dollars bought a cardboard baby-nurse for Bonnie, a second-hand Marmon, a Picasso etching, a white satin dress to house a beaded parrot, a yellow chiffon dress to snare a field of ragged-robins, a dress as green as fresh wet paint, two white knickerbocker suits exactly alike, a broker's suit, an English suit like the burnt fields of August, and two first class tickets for Europe.

In the packing case a collection of plush teddy bears, David's army overcoat, their wedding silver and four bulging scrapbooks full of all the things people envied them for were ready to be left behind.

'Good-bye,' they had said on steel station stairways. 'Some day you must try our home brew,' or 'The same band will play at Baden-Baden for the summer, perhaps we'll see you there,' they said, or 'Don't forget what I told you and you'll find the key in the same old place.'

'Oh,' groaned David from the depths of the bed's sagacious enamel billows, 'I'm glad we're leaving.'

Alabama inspected herself in the hand-mirror.

'One more party,' she answered, 'and I'd have to see Viollet-le-Duc about my face.'

David inspected her minutely.

'What's the matter with your face?'

'Nothing, only I've been picking at it so much I can't go to the tea.'

'Well,' said David blankly, 'we've got to go to the tea – it's because of your face that they're having it.'

58

'If there'd been anything else to do, I wouldn't have done the damage.'

'Anyway, you're coming, Alabama. How would it look for people to say, "And how is your charming wife, Mr. Knight?" "My wife, oh, she's at home picking at her face." How do you think I'd feel about that?'

'I could say it was the gin or the climate or something.'

Alabama stared woefully at her reflection. The Knights hadn't changed much externally – the girl still looked all day long as if she'd just got up; the man's face was still as full of unexpected lilts and jolts as riding the amusements on the Million-Dollar Pier.

'I want to go,' said David, 'look at this weather! I can't possibly paint.'

The rain spun and twisted the light of their third wedding anniversary to thin prismatic streams; alto rain, soprano rain, rain for Englishmen and farmers, rubber rain, metal rain, crystal rain. The distant philippics of spring thunder hurtled the fields in thick convolutions like heavy smoke.

'There'll be people,' she demurred.

'There'll always be people,' agreed David. 'Don't you want to say good-bye to your beaux?' he teased.

'David! I'm much too much on their side to be very romantic to men. They've always just floated through my life in taxis full of cold smoke and metaphysics.'

'We won't discuss it,' said David peremptorily.

'Discuss what?' Alabama asked idly.

'The somewhat violent compromises of certain American women with convention.'

'Horrors! Please let's not. Do you mean to say that you're jealous of me?' she asked incredulously.

'Of course. Aren't you?'

'Terribly. But I thought we weren't supposed to be.'

'Then we're even.'

They looked at each other compassionately. It was funny, compassion under their untidy heads.

The muddy afternoon sky disgorged a white moon for teatime. It lay wedged in a split in the clouds like the wheel of a gun-carriage in a rutted, deserted field of battle, slender, and tender and new after the storm. The brownstone apartment was swarming with people; the odor of cinnamon toast embalmed the entry.

'The master,' the valet pronounced as they rang, 'left word, sir, to the guests that he was escaping, that they were to make themselves at home.'

'He did!' commented David. 'People are always running all over the place to escape each other, having been sure to make a date for cocktails in the first bar outside the limits of convenience.'

'Why did he leave so suddenly?' asked Alabama disappointed.

The valet considered gravely, Alabama and David were old clients.

'The master,' he decided to trust them, 'has taken one hundred and thirty hand-woven handkerchiefs, the *Encyclopaedia Britannica*, two dozen tubes of Frances Fox ointment and sailed. Don't you find, sir, the luggage a bit extraordinary?'

'He might have said good-bye,' pursued Alabama petulantly. 'Since he knew we were going and he wouldn't see us for ages.'

'Oh, but he did leave word, Madam. "Good-bye," he said.'

Everybody said that they wished they could get away themselves. They all said they would be perfectly happy if they didn't have to live the way they lived. Philosophers and expelled college boys, movie-directors and prophets predicting the end said people were restless because the war was over.

The tea party told them that nobody stayed on the Riviera in summer – that the baby would take cholera if they carried her into the heat. Their friends expected they'd be bitten to death by French mosquitoes and find nothing to eat but goat. They told them they'd find no sewage on the Mediterranean in summer and remembered the impossibility of ice in the highballs; there was some suggestion of packing a trunk with canned goods.

The moon slid mercurially along the bright mathematical lines of the ultra-modern furniture. Alabama sat in a twilit corner, reassuring herself of the things that made up her life. She had forgotten to give the Castoria to a neighbor. And Tanka could just as well have had the half-bottle of gin. If the nurse was letting Bonnie sleep at this hour at the hotel, she wouldn't sleep on the boat – first class passengers, midnight sailing, C deck, 35 and 37; she could have telephoned her mother to say good-bye but it would only have frightened her from so far away. It was too bad about her mother.

Her eyes strayed over the rose-beige living room full of people. Alabama said to herself they were happy – she had inherited that from her mother. 'We are very happy,' she said to herself, as her mother would have said, 'but we don't seem to care very much whether we are or not. I suppose we expected something more dramatic.'

The spring moonlight chipped the pavement like an ice pick; its shy luminosity iced the corners of the buildings with glittering crescents.

It would be fun on the boat; there'd be a ball and the orchestra would play that thing that goes 'um – ah – um' – you know – the one Vincent Youmans wrote with the chorus explaining why we were blue.

The air was sticky and stuffy in the ship's bar. Alabama and David sat in their evening clothes, sleek as two borzois on the high stools. The steward read the ship's news.

'There's Lady Sylvia Priestly-Parsnips. Shall I ask her to have a drink?'

Alabama stared dubiously about. There was nobody else in the bar. 'All right – but they say she sleeps with her husband.'

'But not in the bar. How do you do, Madam?'

Lady Sylvia flapped across the room like an opaque protoplasm propelling itself over a sand bank.

'I have been chasing you two over the entire boat,' she said, 'we have word that the ship is about to sink, so they are giving the ball tonight. I want you for my dinner party.'

'You do not owe us a party, Lady Parsnips, and we are not the sort of people who pay steerage rates and ride in the honeymoon suite. So what is it?'

'I am quite altruistic,' she expostulated. 'I've got to have *somebody* for the party, though I hear you two are quite mad about each other. Here's my husband.'

Her husband thought of himself as an intellectual; his real talent was piano playing.

'I've been wanting to meet you. Sylvia here – that's my wife – tells me you are an old-fashioned couple.'

'A Typhoid Mary of time-worn ideals,' supplied Alabama, 'but I consider it only fair to tell you we are not paying any wine checks.'

'Oh, we didn't expect you to. None of my friends pay for us any more – I can't trust them at all since the war.'

'It seems there's going to be a storm,' said David.

Lady Sylvia belched. 'The trouble with emergencies is,' she said, 'that I always put on my finest underwear and then nothing happens.'

'I find the easiest way to provoke the unexpected is by deciding to sleep in pore-cream,' Alabama crossed her legs to above the table-top in a triangular check mark.

'My place in the sun of incalculability could be had with five Octagon soap wrappers,' said David emphatically.

'There are my friends,' interrupted Lady Sylvia. 'These Englishmen were sent to New York to save them from decadence and the American gentleman is seeking refinements in England.'

'So we pool our resources and think we'll be able to live out the trip.' They were a handsome quartet intent on portraying the romantic ends they anticipated.

'And Mrs. Gayle's joining us, aren't you, dear?'

Mrs. Gayle blinked her round eyes with conviction.

'I'd just love to, but parties nauseate my husband, Lady Sylvia. He really can't stand them.'

'That's all right, my dear, so do they me,' said Lady Sylvia. 'No more than the rest of us.'

'But more actively,' her ladyship insisted. 'I've given parties in one room after another of my house till finally I had to leave because of the broken fixtures, there being no place left to read.'

'Why didn't you have them mended?'

'I needed the money for more parties. Of course, *I* didn't

want to read – that was my husband. I spoil him so.'

'Boxing with the guests broke Sylvia's lights,' added milord, 'and she was very unpleasant about it, bringing me to America and back this way.'

'You loved the rusticity once you became accustomed to it,' said his wife decisively.

The dinner was one of those ship's meals with everything tasting of salty mops.

'We must all have an air of living up to something,' Lady Sylvia directed, 'to please the waiters.'

'But I do,' sang Mrs. Gayle. 'I really have to. There's been so much suspicion of us about, that I've been afraid to have children for fear they'd be born with almond-shaped eyeballs or blue fingernails.'

'It's one's friends,' said Lady Sylvia's husband. 'They rope you into dull dinners, cut you on the Riveria, devour you in Biarritz, and spread devastating rumors about your upper bicuspids over the whole of Europe.'

'When I marry a woman she will have to avoid social criticism by dispensing with all natural functions,' said the American.

'You must be sure you dislike her to escape her condemnation,' David said.

'It's approval you need to avoid,' said Alabama emphatically.

'Yes,' commented Lady Sylvia, 'tolerance has reached such a point that there's no such thing as privacy in relations any more.'

'By privacy,' said her husband, 'Sylvia means something disreputable.'

'Oh, it's all the same, my dear.'

'Yes, I suppose it actually is.'

'One is so sure to be outside the law these days.'

'There's such a crowd behind the barn,' Lady Sylvia sighed, 'one can't find a place to show off one's defense mechanism.'

'I suppose marriage is the only concept we can never fully work out of our system,' said David.

'But there are reports about that you two have made a success of your marriage.'

'We are going to present it to the Louvre,' Alabama corroborated. 'It's been accepted already by the French Government.'

'I thought for a long time that Lady Sylvia and I were the only ones who'd stuck together – of course, it's more difficult when you're not in the arts.'

'Most people feel nowadays that marriage and life do not go together,' said the American gentleman.

'But nothing does go with life,' echoed the Englishman.

'If you feel,' interrupted Lady Parsnips, 'that we are now well enough established in the eyes of our public, we might have some more champagne.'

'Oh, yes, it's better to be well started on our dissolution before the storm begins.'

'I've never seen a storm at sea. I suppose it will be a fiasco after all they've led us to expect.'

'The theory is not to drown, I believe.'

'But, my dear, my husband says you're safer on a boat than anywhere at all if you're at sea when there's a storm.'

'Oh, much better off.'

'Decidedly.'

It began very suddenly. A billiard table crashed a pillar in the salon. The sound of splintering subdued the ship like a presage of death. A quiet, desperate organization pervaded the boat. Stewards sped through the corridors, hastily lashing the trunks to the wash basins. By midnight the ropes were broken and fixtures loosened from the walls. Water flooded the ventilators and sogged the passage and word went round that the ship had lost her radio.

The stewards and stewardesses stood in formation at the foot of the stairway. The strained faces and roving, self-conscious eyes of people whose routed confidence would lead you to believe that they are contemptuous of the forces which dissipate their superficial disciplinary strength to a more direct egotism, surprised Alabama. She'd never thought of training as being superimposed on temperaments, but as temperaments being fit to carry the burden of selfless routines.

'Everybody can share the worst things,' she thought as she dashed along the soggy corridors to her cabin, 'but there's almost nobody at the top. I s'pose that's why my father was always so alone.' A heave threw her across from one berth to another. Her back felt as if it must be broken. 'Oh, God, can't it stop rocking for a minute, before it goes down?'

Bonnie peered at her mother dubiously. 'Don't be 'fraid,' said the child.

Alabama was scared half to death.

'I'm not frightened, dear,' she said. 'Bonnie, if you move from the berth you will be killed, so lie there and hold on to the sides while I look for Daddy.'

Rocking and whipping with the ship, she clung to the rails. The faces of the personnel stared at her blankly as she passed, as if she had lost her mind.

'Why don't they signal for the lifeboats?' Alabama shrieked hysterically in the calm face of the radio officer.

'Go back to your cabin,' he said. 'No boat could be launched in a sea like this.'

She found David in the bar with Lord Priestly-Parsnips. The tables were massed one on top of the other; heavy chairs were bolted to the floor and bound with ropes. They were drinking champagne, sloshing it over the place like tilted slop pails.

'It's the worst I've seen since I came back from Algiers. Then I literally walked on my cabin walls,' milord was saying placidly, 'and then, too, the transport during the war was pretty bad. I thought we should certainly lose her for ages.'

Alabama crawled across the bar, lunging from one post to another. 'David, you've got to come down to the cabin.'

'But, dearest,' he protested – he was fairly sober, more so than the Englishman, anyway – 'what on earth can *I* do?'

'I thought we'd better all go down together—'

'Rot!'

Launching herself along the room, she heard the Britisher's voice trailing after her. 'Isn't it funny how danger makes people passionate? During the war—'

Frightened, she felt very second rate. The cabin seemed to grow smaller and smaller as if the reiterant shocks were mashing in the sides. After awhile she grew accustomed to the suffocation and the intestinal ripping. Bonnie slept quietly by her side.

There was nothing but water outside the port hole, no sky at all. The motion made her whole body itch. She thought all night that they would be dead by morning.

By morning Alabama was too sick and nervous to bear the stateroom any longer. David helped her along the rail to the bar. Lord Parsnips slept in a corner. A low conversation issued from the backs of two deep leather chairs. She ordered a baked potato and listened, wishing something would prevent the two men from talking. 'I'm very antisocial,' she tabulated. David said all women were. 'I guess so,' she thought resignedly.

One of the voices resounded with the conviction of learning. It had the tone with which doctors of mediocre intelligence expound the medical theories of more brilliant colleagues to their patients. The other spoke with the querulous ponderousness of a voice which is dominant only in the subconscious.

'It's the first time I ever started thinking about things like that – about the people in Africa and all over the world. It made me think that men don't know as much as they think they do.'

'What do you mean?'

'Well, hundreds of years ago those fellows knew nearly as much about saving life as we do. Nature certainly looks after itself. You can't kill anything that's going to live.'

'Yes, you can't exterminate anything that's got a will to live. You can't kill 'em!'

The voice grew alarmingly accusative. The other voice changed the subject defensively.

'Did you go to many shows in New York?'

'Three or four, and of all the trivial indecent things! You never get a thing to take away with you. There's nothing to it,' the second voice welled in accusation.

'They've got to give the public what it wants.'

'I was talking to a newspaper man the other day and he said just that, and I told him just look at the Cincinnati *Enquirer*. They never carry a word of all this scandal and stuff, and it's one of the biggest papers in the country.'

'It's not the public – they have to take what they get.'

'Of course, I just go myself to see what's doing.'

'I don't go much myself – not more than three or four times a month.'

Alabama staggered to her feet. 'I can't stand it!' she said. The bar smelled of olive brine and dead ashes. 'Tell the man I want the potato outdoors.'

Clinging to the rail, she reached the back sun parlor. A gigantic swish and suction burst over the deck. She heard the chairs go overboard. The waves closed like marble tombstones over her vision and opened again and no water showed. The boat floated precariously in the sky.

'Everything in America is like its storms,' drawled the Englishman, 'or would you say we were in Europe?'

'Englishmen are never frightened,' she remarked.

'Don't worry about Bonnie, Alabama,' said David. 'She's, after all, a child. She doesn't feel things very much, yet.'

'Then it would be more horrible if anything should happen to her!'

'No. If I had to choose between the saving of you two theoretically, I'd take the proven material.'

'I wouldn't. I'd save her first. She may be some wonderful person.'

'Maybe, but none of us are, and we know *we're* not absolutely terrible.'

'Seriously, David, do you think we'll get through?'

'The purser says it's a Florida tidal wave with a ninety-mile wind – seventy's a hurricane. The ship's listing thirty-seven degrees. It won't go over till we hit forty. They think the wind may drop. Anyway, we can't do anything about it.'

'No. What do you think about?'

'Nothing. I'm ashamed to confess, I've been having too many *fines*. It's made me sort of sick.'

'I don't think, either. The elements are splendid – I don't really care if we sink. I've grown very savage.'

'Yes, when we find we have to dispense with so much of ourselves to function, we do – to save the rest.'

'Anyway, there's nobody in this boat or in any other gathering I have examined at first hand that it would matter a damn if they were lost.'

'You mean geniuses?'

'No. Links in that intangible thread of evolution which we call first science, then civilization – instruments of purpose.'

'As denominators to sense the past?'

'More to imagine the future.'

'Like your father?'

'In a way. He's done his job.'

'So have the others.'

'But they don't know it. Consciousness is the goal, I feel.'

'Then the direction of education should be to teach us to dramatize ourselves, to realize to the fullest extent the human equipment?'

'That's what I think.'

'Well, it's hooey!'

After three days the salon opened its doors again. Bonnie clamored to see the ship's movie.

'Do you think she ought to? I believe it's full of sex-appeal,' Alabama said.

'Most certainly,' replied Lady Sylvia. 'If I had a daughter, I'd send her to every performance so she should learn something useful for when she grew up. After all, it's the parents who pay.'

'I don't know what I think about things.'

'Nor I – but sex-appeal is in a class by itself, my dear.'

'Which would you rather have, Bonnie, sex-appeal, or a walk in the sun on the deck?'

Bonnie was two, priestess of obscure wisdoms and reverenced of her parents as if she were two hundred. The Knight household having exhausted the baby interest during the long months of weaning, her standing was that of a voting member.

'Bonnie walks *afterwards*,' the child responded promptly.

The air felt already very un-American. The sky was less energetic. The luxuriance of Europe had blown up with the storm.

Clamp – clamp – clamp – clamp, their feet fell on the resounding deck. She and Bonnie stopped against the rail.

'A ship must be very pretty passing in the night,' said Alabama.

'See the dipper?' pointed Bonnie.

'I see Time and Space wedded in painted static. I have seen it in a little glass case in a planetarium, the way it was years ago.'

'Did it change?'

'No, people just saw it differently. It was something different from what they were thinking all along.'

The air was salty, such beautiful air, from the ship's rail.

'It's the quantity that makes it so beautiful,' thought Alabama. 'Immensity is the most beautiful of all things.'

A shooting star, ectoplasmic arrow, sped through the nebular hypothesis like a wanton hummingbird. From Venus to Mars to Neptune it trailed the ghost of comprehension, illuminating far horizons over the pale battlefields of reality.

'It's pretty,' said Bonnie.

'This will be in a case for your grandchildren's grand-children's grandchildren.'

'Child'en's child'en in a case,' commented Bonnie profoundly.

'No dear, the stars! Perhaps they will use the same case – externals seem to be all that survive.'

Clamp – clamp! Clamp – clamp! round the deck they went. The night air felt so good.

'You must go to bed, my baby.'

'There won't be any stars when I wake up.'

'There will be others.'

David and Alabama climbed together to the prow of the boat. Phosphorescent, their faces gleamed in the moonlight. They sat on a coil of rope and looked back on the netted silhouette.

'Your picture of a boat was wrong; those funnels are ladies doing a very courteous minuet,' she commented.

'Maybe. The moon makes things different. I don't like it.'

'Why not?'

'It spoils the darkness.'

'Oh, but it's so unhallowed!' Alabama rose to her feet. Contracting her neck, she pulled herself high on her toes.

'David, I'll fly for you, if you'll love me!'

'Fly, then.'

'I can't fly, but love me anyway.'

'Poor wingless child!'

'Is it so hard to love me?'

'Do you think you are easy, my illusive possession?'

'I did so want to be paid, somehow, for my soul.'

'Collect from the moon – you'll find the address under Brooklyn and Queens.'

'David! I love you even when you are attractive.'

'Which isn't very often.'

'Yes, often and most impersonal.'

Alabama lay in his arms feeling him older than herself. She did not move. The boat's engine chugged out a deep lullaby.

'It's been a long time since we've had a passage like this.'

'Ages. Let's have one every night.'

'I've composed a poem for you.'

'Go on.'

> *Why am I this way, why am I that?*
> *Why do myself and I constantly spat?*
> *Which is the reasonable, logical me?*
> *Which is the one who must will it to be?*

David laughed. 'Am I expected to answer that?'

'No.'

'We've reached the age of caution when everything, even our most personal reactions, must pass the test of our intellects.'

'It's very fatiguing.'

'Bernard Shaw says all people over forty are scoundrels.'

'And if we do not achieve that desirable state by then?'

'Arrested development.'

'We're spoiling our evening.'

'Let's go in.'

'Let's stay – maybe the magic will come back.'

'It will. Another time.'

On the way down they passed Lady Sylvia rapturously kissing a shadow behind a lifeboat.

'Was that her husband? It must have been true – that about their being in love.'

'A sailor – sometimes I'd like to go to a Marseille dance hall,' said Alabama vaguely.

'What for?'

'I don't know – like eating rump steak, I suppose.'

'I would be furious.'

'You would be kissing Lady Sylvia behind the lifeboat.'

'Never.'

The orchestra blared out the flower duet from *Madame Butterfly* in the ship's salon.

> *There's David for Mignonette*
> *And somebody else for the violette,*

hummed Alabama.

'Are you artistic?' asked the Englishman.

'No.'

'But you were singing.'

'Because I am happy to find that I am a very self-sufficient person.'

'Oh, but are you? How narcissistic!'

'Very. I am very pleased with the way I walk and talk and do almost everything. Shall I show you how nicely I can?'

'Please.'

'Then treat me to a drink.'

'Come along to the bar.'

Alabama swung off in imitation of some walk she had once admired. 'But I warn you,' she said, 'I am only really myself when I'm somebody else whom I have endowed with these wonderful qualities from my imagination.'

'But I shan't mind that,' said the Englishman, feeling vaguely that he should be expectant. Anything incomprehensible has a sexual significance to many people under thirty-five.

'And I warn you that I am a monogamist at heart if not in theory,' said Alabama, sensing his difficulty.

'Why?'

'A theory that the only emotion which cannot be repeated is the thrill of variety.'

'Are you wise-cracking?'

71

'Of course. None of my theories work.'

'You're as good as a book.'

'I am a book. Pure fiction.'

'Then who invented you?'

'The teller of the First National Bank, to pay for some mistakes he made in mathematics. You see, they would have fired him if he hadn't got the money *some* way,' she invented.

'Poor man.'

'If it hadn't been for him I should have had to go on being myself forever. And then I shouldn't have had all these powers to please you.'

'You would have pleased me anyway.'

'What makes you think so?'

'You are a solid person at heart,' he said seriously.

Afraid of having compromised himself, he added hastily, 'I thought your husband promised to join us.'

'My husband is up enjoying the stars behind the third lifeboat on the left-hand side.'

'You're kidding! You couldn't know; how could you?'

'Occult gifts.'

'You're an outrageous faker.'

'Obviously. And I'm very fed up with myself. Let's talk about you.'

'I meant to make money in America.'

'Everybody intends to.'

'I had letters.'

'You can put them in your book when you write it.'

'I am not a writer.'

'All people who have liked America write books. You will get neurosis when you have recovered from your trip, then you will have something that had so much better be left unsaid that you will try to get it published.'

'I should like to write about my travels. I liked New York.'

'Yes, New York is like a Bible illustration, isn't it?'

'Do you read the Bible?'

'The book of Genesis. I love the part about God's being so pleased with everything. I like to think that God is happy.'

'I don't see how he could be.'

'I don't either, but I suppose *somebody* has to feel every

72

possible way about everything that happens. Nobody else claiming that particular attribute, we have accredited it to God – at least, Genesis has.'

The coast of Europe defied the Atlantic expanse; the tender slid into the friendliness of Cherbourg amidst the green and far-away bells and the clump of wooden shoes over the cobbles.

New York lay behind them. The forces that produced them lay behind them. That Alabama and David would never sense the beat of any other pulse half so exactly, since we can only recognize in other environments what we have grown familiar with in our own, played no part in their expectations.

'I could cry!' said David, 'I want to get the band to play on the deck. It's the most thrilling God-damned thing in the world – all the experiences of man lie there to choose from!'

'Selection,' said Alabama, 'is the privilege for which we suffer in life.'

'It's so magnificent! It's glorious! We can have wine with our lunch!'

'Oh, Continent!' she apostrophized, 'send me a dream!'

'You have one now,' said David.

'But where? It will only be the place where we were younger in the end.'

'That's all any place is.'

'Crab!'

'Soap-box orator! I could bowl a comb through the Bois de Boulogne!'

Passing Lady Sylvia at the douane, she called to them from a heap of fine underwear, a blue hot-water bag, a complicated electrical appliance and twenty-four pairs of American shoes.

'You will come out with me tonight? I will show you the beautiful city of Paris to portray in your pictures.'

'No,' said David.

'Bonnie,' counselled Alabama, 'if you walk into the trucks, they'll almost certainly mash your feet, which would be neither "chic" nor "élégante" – France, I am told, is full of such fine distinctions.'

The train bore them down through the pink carnival of Normandy, past the delicate tracery of Paris and the high

73

terraces of Lyon, the belfries of Dijon and the white romance of Avignon into the scent of lemon, the rustle of black foilage, clouds of moths whipping the heliotrope dusk – into Provence, where people do not need to see unless they are looking for the nightingale.

The deep Greek of the Mediterranean licked its chops over the edges of our febrile civilization. Keeps crumbled on the gray hillsides and sowed the dust of their battlements beneath the olives and the cactus. Ancient moats slept bound in tangled honeysuckle; fragile poppies bled the causeways; vineyards caught on the jagged rocks like bits of worn carpet. The baritone of tired mediæval bells proclaimed disinterestedly a holiday from time. Lavender bloomed silently over the rocks. It was hard to see in the vibrancy of the sun.

'Isn't it wonderful?' said David. 'It's so utterly blue, except when you examine it. Then it's gray and mauve and if you look closely, it's harsh and nearly black. Of course, on close inspection, it's literally an amethyst with opal qualities. What *is* it, Alabama?'

'I can't see for the view. Wait a minute.' Alabama pressed her nose against the mossy cracks of the castle wall. 'It's really Chanel, Five,' she said positively, 'and it feels like the back of your neck.'

'Not Chanel!' David protested. 'I think it's more robe de style. Get over there, I want to take your picture.'

'Bonnie, too?'

'Yes. I guess we'll have to let her in.'

'Look at Daddy, privileged infant.'

The child wooed its mother with wide incredulous eyes.

'Alabama, can't you tilt her a little bit? Her cheeks are wider than her forehead and if you could lean her a little bit forward, she wouldn't look so much like the entrance to the Acropolis.'

'Boo, Bonnie,' Alabama essayed.

They both toppled over in a clump of heliotrope.

'My God! I've scratched its face. You haven't got any Mercurochrome with you, have you?'

She inspected the sooty whirlpools that formed the baby's knuckles.

'It doesn't seem to be serious, but we ought to go home and disinfect, I suppose.'

'Baby home,' Bonnie pronounced ponderously, pushing the words between her teeth like a cook straining a purée.

'Home, home, home,' she chanted tolerantly, bobbing down the hill on David's arm.

'There it is, my dear. "The Grand Hotel of Petronius and the Golden Isles." See?'

'I think, David, that maybe we should have gone to the Palace and the Universe. They have more palms in their garden.'

'And pass up a name like ours? Your lack of a historical sense is the biggest flaw in your intelligence, Alabama.'

'I don't see why I should have to have a chronological mind to appreciate these white-powdered roads. We remind me of a troupe of troubadours, your carrying the baby like that.'

'Exactly. Please don't pull Daddy's ear. Have you ever seen such heat?'

'And the flies! I don't know how people stand it.'

'Maybe we'd better move further up the coast.'

'These cobbles make you feel as if you had a peg leg. I'm going to get some sandals.'

They followed the pavings of the French Republic past the bamboo curtains of Hyères, past strings of felt slippers and booths of women's underwear, past gutters flush with the lush wastage of the south, past the antics of exotic dummies inspiring brown Provençal faces to dream of the freedom of the Foreign Legion, past scurvy-eaten beggars and bloated clots of bougainvillea, dust and palms, a row of horse-cabs, the tooth-paste display of the village coiffeur exuding the smell of Chypre, and past the caserne which drew the town together like a family portrait will a vast disordered living room.

'There.'

David deposited Bonnie in the damp cool of the hotel lobby on a pile of last year's *Illustrated London News*.

'Where's Nanny?'

Alabama poked her head into the bilious plush of the lace parlor.

'Madam Tussaud's is deserted. I s'pose she's out gathering material for her British comparison table so when she gets back to Paris she can say "Yes, but the clouds in Hyères were a touch more battleship gray when I was there with the David Knights."'

'She'll give Bonnie a sense of tradition. I like her.'

'So do I.'

'Where's Nanny?' Bonnie rolled her eyes in alarm.

'Darling! She'll be back. She's out collecting you some nice opinions.'

Bonnie looked incredulous.

'Buttons,' she said, pointing to her dress. 'I want some orange jluice.'

'Oh, all right – but you'll find opinions will be much more useful when you grow up.'

David rang the bell.

'Can we have a glass of orange juice?'

'Ah, Monsieur, we are completely desolated. There aren't any oranges in summer. It's the heat; we had thought of closing the hotel since one can have no oranges because of the weather. Wait a minute, I'll see.'

The proprietor looked like a Rembrandt physician. He rang the bell. A valet de chambre, who also looked like a Rembrandt physician, responded.

'Are there any oranges?' the proprietor asked.

'Not even one,' the man responded with gloomy emphasis.

'You see, Monsieur,' the proprietor announced in a tone of relief, 'there is not even one orange.'

He rubbed his hands contentedly – the presence of oranges in his hotel would certainly have caused him much trouble.

'Orange jluice, orange jluice,' bawled the baby.

'Where in the hell is that woman?' shrieked David.

'Mademoiselle?' the proprietor asked. 'But she is in the garden, under an olive tree that is over one hundred years old. What a splendid tree! I must show you.'

He followed them out of the door.

'Such a pretty little boy,' he said. 'He will speak French. I have spoke very good English before.'

Bonnie's femininity was the most insistent thing about her.

'I'm sure you have,' said David.

Nanny had constructed a boudoir out of the springy iron chairs. Sewing was scattered about, a book, several pairs of glasses, Bonnie's toys. A spirit lamp burned on the table. The garden was completely inhabited. On the whole, it might have been an English nursery.

'I looked on the menu, Madam, and there was goat again, so I just stopped in at the butcher's. I'm making Bonnie a little stew. This is the filthiest place, if you'll pardon me, Madam. I don't believe we shall be able to stand it.'

'We think it *is* too hot,' Alabama said apologetically. 'Mr. Knight's going to look for a villa further up the coast if we don't find a house this afternoon.'

'I'm sure we could be better pleased. I have spent some time in Cannes with the Horterer-Collins, and we found it very comfortable. Of course, in summer, *they* go to Deauville.'

Alabama felt, somehow, that they, perhaps, should have gone to Deauville – some obligation on their parts to Nanny.

'I might try Cannes,' David said impressed.

The deserted dining room buzzed with the turbulent glare of midday in the tropics. A decrepit English couple teetered over the rubbery cheese and soggy fruit. The old woman leaned across and distantly rubbed one finger over Bonnie's flushed cheeks.

'So like my little granddaughter,' she said patronizingly.

Nanny bristled. 'Madam, you will please not to stroke the baby.'

'I wasn't stroking the baby. I was only touching her.'

'This heat has upset her stomach,' concluded Nanny, peremptorily.

'No dinner. I won't have my dinner,' Bonnie broke the long silence of the English encounter.

'I don't want mine either. It smells of starch. Let's get the real-estate man now, David.'

Alabama and David stumbled through the seething sun to

the main square. An enchantment of lethargy overwhelmed the enclosure. The cabbies slept under whatever shade they could find, the shops were closed, no shadows broke the tenacious, vindictive glare. They found a sprawling carriage and managed to wake the driver by jumping on the step.

'Two o'clock,' the man said irritably. 'I am closed till two o'clock!'

'Well, go to this address anyway,' David insisted. 'We'll wait.'

The cabby shrugged his shoulders reluctantly.

'To wait is ten francs an hour,' he argued disgruntled.

'All right. We are American millionaires.'

'Let's sit on the robe,' said Alabama, 'the cab looks full of fleas.'

They folded the brown army-issue blanket under their soaking thighs.

'Tiens! there is the Monsieur!' The cabby pointed indolently at a handsome meridional with a patch over one eye who was engrossed in removing the handle from his shop door directly across the way.

'We want to see a villa, the "Blue Lotus," which I understand is for rent,' David began politely.

'Impossible. For nothing in the world is it barely possible. I have not had my lunch.'

'Of course, Monsieur will allow me to pay for his free time—'

'That is different,' the agent beamed expansively. 'Monsieur understands that since the war things are different and one must eat.'

'Of course.'

The rickety cab rolled along past fields of artichoke blue as spots of the hour's intensity, through long stretches of vegetation shimmering in the heat like submarine growths. A parasol pine rose here and there in the flat landscape, the road wound hot and blinding ahead to the sea. The water, chipped by the sun, spread like a floor of luminous shavings in a workshop of light.

'There she is!' the man cackled proudly.

The 'Blue Lotus' parched in a treeless expanse of red clay.

They opened the door and stepped into the coolness of the shuttered hall.

'This is the master's bedroom.'

On the huge bed lay a pair of batik pajamas and a chartreuse pleated nightgown.

'The casualness of life in this country amazes me,' Alabama said. 'They obviously just spent the night and went off.'

'I wish we could live like that, without premeditation.'

'Let's see the plumbing.'

'But, Madame, the plumbing is a perfection. You see?'

A massive carved door swung open on a Copenhagen toilet-bowl with blue chrysanthemums climbing over the edge in a wild Chinese delirium. The walls were tiled with many-colored fishing scenes of Normandy. Alabama tentatively tested the brass rod designed to operate these pictorial fantasies.

'It doesn't work,' she said.

The man raised his eyebrows Buddhistically.

'But! It must be because we have had no rain! Sometimes when it doesn't rain, there is no water.'

'What do you do if it doesn't rain again all summer?' David asked, fascinated.

'But then, Monsieur, it is sure to rain,' the agent smiled cheerfully.

'And in the meantime?'

'Monsieur is unnatural.'

'Well, we've got to have something more civilized than this.'

'We ought to go to Cannes,' Alabama said.

'I'll take the first train when we get back.'

David telephoned her from St-Raphaël.

'Just the place,' he said, 'for sixty dollars a month – garden, water works, kitchen stove, wonderful composition from the cupola – metal roofing of an aviation field, I understand – I'll be over for you tomorrow morning. We can move right in.'

The day enveloped them in an armor of sunshine. They hired a limousine stuffy with reminiscences of state occasions. Paper nasturtiums fading in the cubism of a cut glass triangle obscured the view along the coast.

'Drive, drive, why can't I drive?' Bonnie screamed.

'Because the golf sticks have to go there, and, David, you can get your easel back here.'

'Um – um – um,' the baby droned, content with the motion. 'Nice, nice, nice.'

The summer ate its way into their hearts and crooned along the shaggy road. Tabulating the past, Alabama could find no real upheavals in spite of the fact that its tempo created the illusion that she lived in madcap abandon. Feeling so wonderful, she wondered why they had ever left home.

Three o'clock in July, and Nanny gently thinking of England from hilltops and rented motor cars and under all unusual circumstances, white roads and pines – life quietly humming a lullaby. Anyway, it was fun being alive.

'Les Rossignols' was back from the sea. The smell of tobacco flowers permeated the faded blue satin of the Louis XV parlor; a wooden cuckoo protested the gloom of the oak dining room; pine needles carpeted the blue and white tiles of the balcony; petunias fawned on the balustrade. The gravel drive wound round the trunk of a giant palm sprouting geraniums in its crevices and lost itself in the perspective of a red-rose arbor. The cream calcimined walls of the villa with its painted windows stretched and yawned in the golden shower of late sun.

'There's a summer house,' said David proprietorily, 'built of bamboo. It looks as if Gauguin had put his hand to landscape gardening.'

'It's heavenly. Do you suppose there really is a rossignol?'

'Undoubtedly – every night on toast for supper.'

'Comme ça, Monsieur, comme ça,' Bonnie sang exultantly.

'Look! She can speak French already.'

'It's a marvellous, marvellous place, this France. Isn't it, Nanny?'

'I've lived here for twenty years, Mr. Knight, and I've never got to understand these people. Of course, I haven't had much opportunity to learn French, being always with the better class of family.'

'Quite,' said David emphatically. Whatever Nanny said sounded like an elaborate recipe for making fudge.

'The ones in the kitchen,' said Alabama, 'are a present from the house agent, I suppose.'

'They are – three magnificent sisters. Perhaps the Three Fates, who knows?'

Bonnie's babbling rose to an exultant yell through the dense foliage.

'Swim! Now swim!' she cried.

'She's thrown her doll in the goldfish pool,' observed Nanny excitedly. 'Bad Bonnie! To treat little Goldilocks that way.'

'Her name's "Comme ça,"' Bonnie expostulated. 'Did you see her swimming?'

The doll was just visible at the bottom of the sleek green water.

'Oh, we are going to be so happy away from all the things that almost got us but couldn't quite because we were too smart for them!' David grabbed his wife about the waist and shoved her through the wide windows on to the tile floors of their new home. Alabama inspected the painted ceiling. Pastel cupids frolicked amidst the morning-glories and roses in garlands swelled like goiters or some malignant disease.

'Do you think it will be as nice as it seems?' she said skeptically.

'We are now in Paradise – as nearly as we'll ever get – there's the pictorial evidence of the fact,' he said, following her eyes.

'You know, I can never think of a rossignol without thinking of the *Decameron*. Dixie used to hide it in her top drawer. It's funny how associations envelop our lives.'

'Isn't it? People can't really jump from one thing to another, I don't suppose – there's always something carried over.'

'I hope it's not our restlessness, this time.'

'We'll have to have a car to get to the beach.'

'Sure. But tomorrow we'll go in a taxi.'

Tomorrow was already bright and hot. The sound of a Provençal gardener carrying on his passive resistance to effort woke them. The rake trailed lazily over the gravel; the maid put their breakfast on the balcony.

'Order us a cab, will you, daughter of this flowery republic?'

David was jubilant. It was unnecessary to be anything so dynamic before breakfast, commented Alabama privately with matinal cynicism.

'And so, Alabama, we have never known in our times the touch of so strong and sure a genius as we have before us in the last canvases of one David Knight! He begins work after a swim every day, and he continues until another swim at four o'clock refreshes his self-satisfaction.'

'And I luxuriate in this voluptuous air and grow fat on bananas and Chablis while David Knight grows clever.'

'Sure. A woman's place is with the wine,' David approved emphatically. 'There is art to be undone in the world.'

'But you're not going to work all the time, are you?'

'I hope so.'

'It's a man's world,' Alabama sighed, measuring herself on a sunbeam. 'This air has the most lascivious feel—'

The machinery of the Knights' existence, tended by the three women in the kitchen, moved without protest through the balmy world while the summer puffed itself slowly to pompous exposition. Flowers bloomed sticky and sweet under the salon; the stars at night caught in the net of the pine tops. The garden trees said, 'Whip – poor – will,' the warm black shadows said 'Whoo – oo.' From the windows of 'Les Rossignols' the Roman arena at Fréjus swam in the light from the moon bulging low over the land like a full wineskin.

David worked on his frescoes; Alabama was much alone.

'What'll we *do*, David,' she asked, 'with ourselves?'

David said she couldn't always be a child and have things provided for her to do.

A broken-down carry-all transported them every day to the beach. The maid referred to the thing as 'la voiture' and announced its arrival in the mornings with much ceremony during their brioche and honey. There was always a family argument about how soon it was safe to swim after a meal.

The sun played lazily behind the Byzantine silhouette of the town. Bath houses and a dancing pavilion bleached in the white breeze. The beach stretched for miles along the blue. Nanny habitually established a British Protectorate over a generous portion of the sands.

'It's bauxite makes the hills so red,' Nanny said. 'And, Madam, Bonnie will need another bathing costume.'

'We can get it at the Galeries des Objectives Perdues,' Alabama suggested.

'Or the Occasion des Perspectives Oubliés,' said David.

'Sure. Or off a passing porpoise, or out of that man's beard.'

Alabama indicated a lean burned figure in duck trousers with shiny ribs like an ivory Christ and faunlike eyes beckoning in obscene fantasy.

'Good morning,' the figure said formidably. 'I have often seen you here.'

His voice was deep and metallic and swelled with the confidence of a gentleman.

'I am the proprietor of my little place. We have eating and there is dancing in the evenings. I am glad to welcome you to St-Raphaël. There are not many people in the summer, as you see, but we make ourselves very happy. My establishment would be honored if you would accept an American cocktail after your bath.'

David was surprised. He hadn't expected a welcoming committee. It was as if they had passed a club election.

'With pleasure,' he said hastily. 'Do we just come inside?'

'Yes, inside. Then I am Monsieur Jean to my friends! But you must surely meet the people, so charming people,' he smiled contemplatively and vanished in splinters on the sparkle of the morning.

'There aren't any people,' Alabama said, staring about.

'Maybe he keeps them in bottles inside. He certainly looks enough like a genie to be capable of it. We'll soon know.'

Nanny's voice, ferocious in its disapproval of gin and genies, called Bonnie from over the sands.

'I said no! I said no! I said no!' The child raced to the water's edge.

'I'll get her, nurse.'

The David Knights precipitated themselves into the blue dye after the child.

'You ought to come out a sailor, somehow,' Alabama suggested.

'But I'm being Agamemnon,' protested David.

'I'm a little teeny fish,' Bonnie contributed. 'A lovely fish, I am!'

'All right. You can play if you want to. Oh, my! Isn't it wonderful to feel that nothing could disturb us now and life can go on as it should?'

'Perfectly, radiantly, gorgeously wonderful! But I want to be Agamemnon.'

'Please be a fish with me,' Bonnie inveigled. 'Fishes are nicer.'

'Very well. I'll be an Agamemnon fish. I can only swim with my legs, see?'

'But how can you be two things at once?'

'Because, my daughter, I am so outrageously clever that I believe I could be a whole world to myself if I didn't like living in Daddy's better.'

'The salt water's pickled your brain, Alabama.'

'Ha! Then I shall have to be a pickled Agamemnon fish, and that's much harder. It has to be done without the legs as well,' Alabama gloated.

'Much easier, I should think, after a cocktail. Let's go in.'

The room was cool and dark after the glare of the beach. A pleasantly masculine smell of dried salt water lurked in the draperies. The rising waves of heat outside gave the bar a sense of motion as if the stillness of the interior were a temporary resting place for very active breezes.

'Combs, yes we have no combs today,' Alabama sang, inspecting herself in the mildewed mirror behind the bar. She felt so fresh and slick and salty! She decided the part was better on the other side of her head. In the dim obliteration of the ancient mirror she caught the outline of a broad back in the stiff white uniform of the French Aviation. Gesticulating Latin gallantries, indicating first her, then David, the glass blurred the pantomime. The head of the gold of a Christmas coin nodded urgently, broad bronze hands clutched the air in the vain hope that its tropical richness held appropriate English words to convey so Latin a meaning. The convex shoulders were slim and strong and rigid and slightly hunched in the man's effort to communicate. He produced a small red comb from his pocket and nodded pleasantly to Alabama. As her eyes met those of the officer, Alabama experienced the emotion of a burglar unexpectedly presented with the combination of a difficult safe by the master of the house. She felt as if she had been caught red-handed at some outrageous act.

'Permettez?' said the man.

She stared.

'Permettez,' he insisted, 'that means, in English, "permettez" you see?'

The officer lapsed into voluble incomprehensible French.

'No understand,' said Alabama.

'Oui understand,' he repeated superiorily. 'Permettez?' He bowed and kissed her hand. A smile of tragic seriousness lit the golden face, an apologetic smile – his face had the charm of an adolescent forced to enact unexpectedly in public some situation long rehearsed in private. Their gestures were exaggerated as if they were performing a rôle for two other people in the distance, dim spectres of themselves.

'I am not a "germe,"' he said astonishingly.

'Oui can see – I mean, it's obvious,' she said.

'Regardez!' The man ran the comb effectively through his hair to demonstrate its functions.

'I'd love using it,' Alabama looked dubiously at David.

'This, Madame,' boomed Monsieur Jean, 'is the Lieutenant Jacques Chevre-Feuille of the French Aviation. He is quite harmless and these are his friends, the Lieutenant Paulette et Madame, Lieutenant Bellandeau, Lieutenant Montague, who is a Corse, as you will see – and those over there are René and Bobbie of St-Raphaël, who are very nice boys.'

The grilled red lamps, the Algerian rugs precluding the daylight, the smell of brine and incense gave Jean's Plage the sense of a secret place – an opium den or a pirate's cave. Scimitars lined the walls; bright brass trays set on African drumheads glowed in the dark corners; small tables encrusted with mother-of-pearl accumulated the artificial twilight like coatings of dust.

Jacques moved his sparse body with the tempestuous spontaneity of a leader. Back of his flamboyant brilliance stretched his cohort; the fat and greasy Bellandeau who

85

shared Jacques' apartment and had matured in the brawls of Montenegro; the Corse, a gloomy romantic, intent on his own desperation, who flew his plane so low along the beach in the hope of killing himself that the bathers could have touched the wings; the tall, immaculate Paulette followed continually by the eyes of a wife out of Marie Laurencin. René and Bobbie protruded insistently from their white beach clothes and talked in undertones of Arthur Rimbaud. Bobbie pulled his eyebrows and his feet were flat and silent butler's feet. He was older and had been in the war and his eyes were as gray and desolate as the churned spaces about Verdun – during that summer, René painted their rainwashed shine in all the lights of that varied sea. René was the artistic son of a Provençal avocat. His eyes were brown and consumed by the cold fire of a Tintoretto boy. The wife of an Alsatian chocolate manufacturer furtively brooded over the cheap phonograph and pandered loudly to her daughter Raphaël, burned black to the bone of her unforgotten, southern, sentimental origin. The white tight curls of two half-Americans in the early twenties, torn between Latin curiosity and Anglo-Saxon caution, hovered through the gloom like a cherub detail from a dark corner of a Renaissance frieze.

David's pictorial sense rose in wild stimulation on the barbaric juxtapositions of the Mediterranean morning.

'So now I will buy the drinks, but they will have to be a Porto because I have no money, you see.' Despite Jacques' grandiloquent attempts at English he made known his desires with whatever dramatic possibilities he found at hand for expansive gesture.

'Do you think he actually *is* a god?' Alabama whispered to David. 'He looks like you – except that he is full of the sun, whereas you are a moon person.'

The Lieutenant stood by her side experimentally handling things that she had touched, making tentative emotional connections between their persons like an electrician installing a complicated fuse. He gesticulated volubly to David and pretended a vast impassivity to Alabama's presence, to hide the quickness of his interest.

'And so I will come to your home in my aeroplane,' he

said generously, 'and I will be here each afternoon to swim.'

'Then you must drink with us this afternoon,' said David amused, 'because now we've got to get back to lunch and there isn't time for another.'

The rickety taxi poured them through the splendid funnels of Provençal shade and scrambled them over the parched stretches between the vineyards. It was as if the sun had absorbed the coloring of the countryside to brew its sunset mixtures, boiling and bubbling the tones blindingly in the skies while the land lay white and devitalized awaiting the lavish mixture that would be spread to cool through the vines and stones in the late afternoon.

'Look, Madam, at the baby's arms. We shall want a sunshade certainly.'

'Oh, Nanny, do let her tan! I love these beautiful brown people. They seem so free of secrets.'

'But not too much, Madam. They say it spoils the skin for afterwards, you know. We must always think of the future, Madam.'

'Well, I personally,' said David, 'am going to grill myself to a high-mulatto. Alabama, do you think it would be effeminate if I shaved my legs? They'd burn quicker.'

'Can I have a boat?' Bonnie's eyes roved the horizon.

'The *Aquitania*, if you like, when I've finished my next picture.'

'It's too démodé,' Alabama joined in, 'I want a nice beautiful Italian liner with gallons of the Bay of Naples in the hold.'

'Reversion to type,' David said, 'you've gone Southern again – but if I catch you making eyes at that young Dionysus, I'll wring his neck, I warn you.'

'No danger. I can't even speak intelligibly to him.'

A lone fly beat its brains against the light over the unsteady lunch table; it was a convertible billiard table. The holes in the felt top stuck up in bumps through the cloth. The Graves Monopole Sec was green and tepid and unappetizing colored by blue wineglasses. There were pigeons cooked with olives for lunch. They smelled of a barnyard in the heat.

'Maybe it would be nicer to eat in the garden,' suggested David.

'We should be devoured by insects,' said Nanny.

'It does seem silly to be uncomfortable in this lovely country,' agreed Alabama. 'Things were so nice when we first came.'

'Well, they get worse and more expensive all the time. Did you ever find out how much a kilo is?'

'It's two pounds, I believe.'

'Then,' stormed David, 'we can't have eaten fourteen kilos of butter in a week.'

'Maybe it's *half-a-pound*,' said Alabama apologetically. 'I hope you're not going to spoil things over a kilo—'

'You have to be very careful, Madam, in dealing with the French.'

'I don't see why,' expostulated David, 'when you complain of having nothing to do, you can't run this house satisfactorily.'

'What do you expect me to do? Every time I try to talk to the cook she scuttles down the cellar stairs and adds a hundred francs to the bill.'

'Well – if there's pigeon again tomorrow I'm not coming to lunch,' David threatened. 'Something has got to be done.'

'Madam,' said Nanny, 'have you seen the new bicycles the help have bought since we arrived here?'

'Miss Meadow,' David interrupted abruptly, 'would you mind helping Mrs. Knight with the accounts?'

Alabama wished David wouldn't drag Nanny in. She wanted to think about how brown her legs were going to be and how the wine would have tasted if it had been cold.

'It's the Socialists, Mr. Knight. They're ruining the country. We shall have another war if they aren't careful. Mr. Horterer-Collins used to say—'

Nanny's clear voice went on and on. It was impossible to miss a word of the clear enunciation.

'That's sentimental tommyrot,' David retorted irritably. 'The Socialists are powerful because the country is in a mess already. Cause and effect.'

'I beg your pardon, sir, the Socialists caused the war, really, and now—' The crisp syllables expounded Nanny's unlimited political opinions.

In the cool of the bedroom where they were supposed to be resting, Alabama protested.

'We can't have that every day,' she said. 'Do you think she's gonna talk like that through every meal?'

'We can have them eat upstairs at night. I suppose she's lonely. She's been just sitting by herself on the beach every morning.'

'But it's awful, David!'

'I know – but *you* needn't complain. Suppose you had to be thinking of composition while it was going on. She'll find somebody to unload herself on. Then it will be better. We mustn't let externals ruin our summer.'

Alabama wandered in idleness from one room to another of the house; usually only the distant noise of a functioning ménage interrupted the solitude. This last noise was the worst of all – a fright. The villa must be falling to pieces.

She rushed to the balcony; David's head appeared in the window.

The beating, drumming whirr of an aeroplane sounded above the villa. The plane was so low that they could see the gold of Jacques' hair shining through the brown net about his head. The plane swooped malevolently as a bird of prey and soared off in a tense curve, high into the blue. Banking swiftly back, the wings glittering in the sun, it dropped in a breathless spiral, almost touching the tile roof. As the plane straightened itself, they saw Jacques wave with one hand and drop a small package in the garden.

'That damn fool will kill himself! It gives me heart failure,' protested David.

'He must be terribly brave,' said Alabama dreamily.

'*Vain*, you mean,' he expostulated.

'Voilà! Madame, Voilà! Voilà! Voilà!'

The excited maid presented the brown despatch box to Alabama. There was no thought in the French fastnesses of her mind that it might have been for the masculine element of the family that a machine would fly so dangerously low to leave a message.

Alabama opened the box. On a leaf of squared notebook paper was written diagonally in blue pencil 'Toutes mes amitiés du haut de mon avion. Jacques Chevre-Feuille.'

'What do you suppose it means?' Alabama asked.

'Just greetings,' David said. 'Why don't you get a French dictionary?'

Alabama stopped that afternoon at the librairie on the way to the beach. From rows of yellow-paper volumes she chose a dictionary and *Le Bal du Comte d'Orgel* in French to teach herself the language.

Beginning at four by prearrangement, the breeze blew a blue path through sea-drenched shadows at Jean's. A three-piece version of a jazz band protested the swoop of the rising tide with the melancholia of American popular music. A triumphant rendering of 'Yes, We Have No Bananas' brought several couples to their feet. Bellendeau danced in mock coquetry with the lugubrious Corsican; Paulette and Madame hurtled wildly through the intricacies of what they believed to be an American fox trot.

'Their feet look like a tightrope walker's gymnastics,' commented David.

'It looks fun. I'm going to learn to do it.'

'You'll have to give up cigarettes and coffee.'

'I suppose. Will you teach me to do that, Monsieur Jacques?'

'I am a bad dancer. I have only danced with men in Marseilles. It is not for real men, dancing well.'

Alabama didn't understand his French. It didn't make any difference. The man's valvating golden eyes drew her back and forth, back and forth obliviously through the great Republic's lack of bananas.

'You like France?'

'I love France.'

'You cannot love France,' he said pretentiously, 'to love France you must love a Frenchman.'

Jacques' English was more adequate about love than about anything else. He pronounced the word 'lahve' and emphasized it roundly as if he were afraid of its escaping him.

'I have bought a dictionary,' he said. 'I will learn English.'

Alabama laughed.

'I'm learning French,' she said, 'so I can love France more articulately.'

'You must see Arles. My mother was an Arlésienne,' he confided. 'The Arlésienne women are very beautiful.'

The sad romanticism in his voice reduced the world to ineffable inconsequence. Together they skimmed the boom of the blue sea and gazed out over the tip of the blue horizon.

'I'm sure,' she murmured – what about, she had forgotten.

'And your mother?' he asked.

'My mother is old. She is very gentle. She spoiled me and gave me everything I wanted. Crying for things I couldn't have grew to be quite characteristic of me.'

'Tell me about when you were a little girl,' he said tenderly.

The music stopped. He drew her body against him till she felt the blades of his bones carving her own. He was bronze and smelled of the sand and sun; she felt him naked underneath the starched linen. She didn't think of David. She hoped he hadn't seen; she didn't care. She felt as if she would like to be kissing Jacques Chevre-Feuille on the top of the Arc de Triomphe. Kissing the white-linen stranger was like embracing a lost religious rite.

Nights after dinner David and Alabama drove into St-Raphaël. They bought a little Renault. Only the façade of the town was illuminated like a shallow stage-set to cover a change of scene. The moon excavated fragile caverns under the massive plane trees back from the water. The village band played 'Faust' and merry-go-round waltzes in a round pavilion by the sea. An itinerant street fair pitched its panoplies and the young Americans and the young officers swung into the southern heavens on the cable swings of chevaux de bois.

'A breeding place for whooping cough, that square, Madam,' Nanny admonished.

She and Bonnie waited in the car to avoid the germs or took slow walks in the swept place before the station. Bonnie became intractable and howled so lustily for the night life of the fair that finally they had to leave the nurse and child at home in the evenings.

Every night they met Jacques and his friends at the Café de la Flotte. The young men were uproarious and drank many beers and Portos and even champagne when David was paying, addressing the waiters boisterously as 'Amiraux.' René drove his yellow Citroën up the steps of the Hotel Continental. The fliers were Royalists. Some were painters and some tried to write when they weren't flying their aeroplanes and all were amateurs of garrison life. For flying at night they got extra pay. The red and green lights of Jacques and Paulette swept over the sea front in aerial fête very often. Jacques hated David to pay for his drinks and Paulette needed the money – he and Madame had a baby in Algiers with his parents.

The Riviera is a seductive place. The blare of the beaten blue and those white palaces shimmering under the heat accentuates things. That was before the days when High Potentates of the Train Bleu, First Muck-a-mucks of the Biarritz-Backs and Dictators-in-Chief to interior decorators employed its blue horizons for binding their artistic enterprises. A small horde of people wasted their time being happy and wasted their happiness being time beside the baked palms and vines brittlely clawing the clay banks.

Alabama read Henry James in the long afternoons. She read Robert Hugh Benson and Edith Wharton and Dickens while David worked. The Riviera afternoons are long and still and full of a consciousness of night long before evening falls. Boatloads of bright backs and the rhythmic chugging of motor launches tow the summer over the water.

'What can I do with myself,' she thought restlessly. She tried to make a dress; it was a failure.

Desultorily, she asserted herself on Nanny. 'I think Bonnie is getting too much starch in her food,' she said authoritatively.

'*I* do not think so, Madam,' Nanny answered curtly. 'No child of mine in twenty years has ever got too much starch.'

Nanny took the matter of the starch to David.

'Can't you at least not interfere, Alabama?' he said. 'Peace is absolutely essential to my work at present.'

When she was a child and the days slipped lazily past in the

same indolent fashion, she had not thought of life as furnish-
ing up the slow uneventful sequence, but of the Judge as
meting it out that way, curtailing the excitement she
considered was her due. She began to blame David for the
monotony.

'Well, why don't you give a party?' he suggested.

'Who'll we ask?'

'I don't know – the real-estate lady and the Alsatian.'

'They're horrible—'

'They're all right if you think of them as Matisse.'

The women were too bourgeoise to accept. The rest of the
party met in the Knights' garden and drank Cinzano.
Madame Paulette plucked the lilt of 'Pas Sur la Bouche' from
the tinny teakwood piano. The French talked volubly and
incomprehensively to David and Alabama about the works of
Fernand Léger and René Crevel. They bent from the waist as
they spoke and were strained and formal in acknowledgment
of the oddity of their presence there – all but Jacques. He
dramatized his unhappy attraction to David's wife.

'Aren't you afraid when you do stunts?' Alabama asked.

'I am afraid whenever I go in my aeroplane. That is why I
like it,' he answered defiantly.

If the sisters of the kitchen were wanting on week-days they
rose like July fireworks to special occasions. Venomous
lobsters writhed in traps of celery, salads fresh as an Easter
card sprouted in mayonnaise fields. The table was insistently
wreathed in smilax; there was even ice, Alabama confirmed,
on the cement floor of the basement.

Madame Paulette and Alabama were the only women.
Paulette held himself aloof and watchful of his wife. He
seemed to feel that dining with Americans was as risqué a
thing to do as attending the Quatre-Arts ball.

'Ah, oui,' smiled Madame, 'mais oui, certainement oui, et
puis o – u – i.' It was like the chorus of a Mistinguett song.

'But in Monte-Negro – you know Monte-Negro, of
course?' said the Corse – '*all* the men wear corsets.'

Somebody poked Bellandeau about the ribs.

Jacques kept his eyes fastened disconsolately on Alabama.

'In the French Navy,' he declaimed, 'the Commandant is

glad, proud to sink with his ship. – *I am an officer of the French Marine!*'

The party soared on the babble of French phrases senseless to Alabama; her mind drifted inconsequently.

'Do let me offer you a taste of the Doge's dress,' she said, dipping into the currant jelly, 'or a nice spoonful of Rembrandt?'

They sat in the breeze on the balcony and talked of America and Indo-Chine and France and listened to the screech and moan of night-birds out of the darkness. The unjubilant moon was tarnished with much summer use in the salt air and the shadows black and communicative. A cat clambered over the balcony. It was very hot.

René and Bobbie went for ammonia to keep off the mosquitoes; Bellandeau went to sleep; Paulette went home with his wife, careful of his French proprieties. The ice melted on the pantry floor; they cooked eggs in the blackened iron pans of the kitchen. Alabama and David and Jacques drove in the copper dawn to Agay against the face of the cool golden morning into the patterns of the creamy sun on the pines and the white odors of closing flowers of the night.

'Those are the caves of Neathandral man,' David said, pointing to the purple hollows in the hills.

'No,' said Jacques, 'it was at Grenoble that they found the remains.'

Jacques drove the Renault. He drove it like an aeroplane, with much speed and grinding and protesting tensions scattering echoes of the dawn like swarms of migrating birds.

'If this car were my own I'd drive into the ocean,' he said. They sped down the dim obliteration of Provence to the beach, following the languorously stretching road where it crinkled the hills like rumpled bed clothes.

It was going to cost five hundred francs at least to get the car repaired, thought David, as he deposited Jacques and Alabama at the pavilion to swim.

David went home to work till the light changed – he insisted he couldn't paint anything but exteriors in the noon light of the Midi. He walked to the beach to join Alabama for a quick plunge before lunch. He found her and Jacques sitting in the sand like a couple of – well a couple of something, he said to himself distastefully. They were as wet and smooth as two cats who had been licking themselves. David was hot from the walk. The sun in the perspiration of his neck stung like a nettled collar.

'Will you go in with me again?' He felt he had to say something.

'Oh, David – it's awfully chilly this morning. There's going to be a wind.' Alabama employed an expletive tone as if she were brooking a child's unwelcome interruption.

David swam self-consciously alone, looking back at the two figures glittering in the sun side-by-side.

'They are the two most presumptuous people I have ever seen,' he said to himself angrily.

The water was already cold from the wind. The slanting rays of the sun cut the Mediterranean to many silver slithers and served it up on the deserted beach. As David left them to dress he saw Jacques lean over and whisper to Alabama through the first gusts of a mistral. He could not hear what they were saying.

'You'll come?' Jacques whispered.

'Yes – I don't know. Yes,' she said.

When David came out of the cabin the blowing sand stung his eyes. Tears were pouring over Alabama's cheeks, strained till the deep tan glowed yellow on her cheek bones. She tried to blame it on the wind.

'You're sick, Alabama, insane. If you see that man any more, I'll leave you here and go back to America alone.'

'You can't do that.'

'You'll see if I can't!' he said threateningly.

She lay in the sand in the smarting wind, miserable.

'I'm going – he can take you home in his aeroplane.' David strode off. She heard the Renault leave. The water shone like a metal reflector under the cold white clouds.

Jacques came; he brought a Porto.

'I have been to get you a taxi,' he said. 'If you like, I will not come here again.'

'If I do not come to your apartment day after tomorrow when he goes to Nice, you must not come again.'

95

'Yes—' He waited to serve her. 'What will you say to your husband?'

'I'll have to tell him.'

'It would be unwise,' said Jacques in alarm. 'We must hang on to our benefits—'

The afternoon was harsh and blue. The wind swept cold clots of dust about the house. You could hardly hear yourself speaking out of doors.

'We don't need to go to the beach after lunch, Nanny. It's too cold to swim.'

'But, Madam, Bonnie gets so restless with this wind. I think we should go, Madam, if you don't mind. We needn't bathe – it makes a change, you know. Mr. Knight was willing to take us.'

There was nobody at all on the plage. The crystalline air parched her lips. Alabama lay sunning herself, but the wind blew the sun away before it warmed her body. It was unfriendly.

René and Bobbie strolled out of the bar.

'Hello,' said David shortly.

They sat down as if they shared some secret that might concern the Knight family.

'Have you noticed the flag?' said René.

Alabama turned in the direction of the aviation field.

The flag blew rigidly out at half-mast over the metallic cubistic roofs, brilliant in the thin light.

'Somebody is killed,' René went on. 'A soldier say it is Jacques – flying in this mistral.'

Alabama's world grew very silent as if it had stopped, as if an awful collision of astral bodies were imminent.

She rose vaguely. 'I've got to go,' she said quietly. She felt cold and sick at her stomach. David followed her to the car.

He slammed the Renault angrily into gear. It wouldn't go any faster.

'Can we go in?' he said to the sentry.

'Non, Monsieur.'

'There has been an accident – Could you tell me who it is?'

'It is against the rules.'

In the glare of a white sandy stretch before the walls, an

avenue of oleanders bent behind the man in the mistral.

'We are interested to know if it was the Lieutenant Chevre-Feuille.'

The man scrutinized Alabama's miserable face.

'That, Monsieur – I will see,' he said at last.

They waited interminably in the malevolent gusts of the wind.

The sentry returned. Courageous and proprietary, Jacques swung along behind him to the car, part of the sun and part of the French aviation and part of the blue and the white collar of the beach, part of Provence and the brown people living by the rigid discipline of necessity, part of the pressure of life itself.

'Bonjour,' he said. He took her hand firmly as if he were dressing a wound.

Alabama was crying to herself.

'We had to know,' said David tensely as he started the car – 'but my wife's tears are for me.'

Suddenly David lost his temper.

'God damn it!' he shouted. 'Will you fight this out?'

Jacques spoke steadily into Alabama's face.

'I cannot fight,' he said gently. 'I am much stronger than he.'

His hands gripping the side of the Renault were like iron mitts.

Alabama tried to see him. The tears in her eyes smeared his image. His golden face and the white linen standing off from him exhaling the gold glow of his body ran together in a golden blur.

'You couldn't either,' she cried out savagely. 'You couldn't either beat him!'

Weeping, she flung herself on David's shoulder.

The Renault shot furiously off into the wind. David drew the car short with a crash before Jean's picket fence. Alabama reached for the emergency brake.

'Idiot!' David pushed her angrily away, 'keep your hands off those brakes!'

'I'm sorry I didn't let him beat you to a pulp,' she yelled infuriated.

'I could have killed him if I had wanted,' said David contemptuously.

'Was it anything serious, Madam?'

'Just somebody killed, that's all. I don't see how they stand their lives!'

David went straight to the room at 'Les Rossignols' that he had arranged as a studio. The soft Latin voices of two children gathering figs from the tree at the end of the garden drifted up on the air in a low hum lulled louder and softer by the rise and fall of the twilit wind.

After a long time, Alabama heard him shout out the window: 'Will you get the hell out of that tree! Damn this whole race of Wops!'

They hardly spoke to each other at dinner.

'These winds are useful, though,' Nanny was saying. 'They blow the mosquitoes inland and the atmosphere is so much clearer when they fall, don't you find, Madam? But my, how they used to upset Mr. Horterer-Collins! He was like a raging lion from the moment the mistral commenced. You don't feel it *very* much, do you, Madam?'

Hardened to a quiet determination to settle the row, David insisted on driving downtown after dinner.

René and Bobbie were alone at the café drinking verveine. The chairs were piled on the tables out of the mistral. David ordered champagne.

'Champagne is not good when there is the wind,' René advised – but he drank it.

'Have you seen Chevre-Feuille?'

'Yes, he tells me he goes to Indo-Chine.'

Alabama was afraid from his tone that David was going to fight if he found Jacques.

'When is he leaving?'

'A week – ten days. When he can get transferred.'

The lush promenade under the trees so rich and full of life and summer seemed swept of all its content. Jacques had passed over that much of their lives like a vacuum cleaner. There was nothing but a cheap café and the leaves in the gutter, a dog prowling about, and a Negro named 'Sans-Bas' with a sabre-cut over one cheek who tried to sell them a paper. That was all there was left of July and August.

David didn't say what he wanted with Jacques.

'Perhaps he is inside,' René suggested.

David crossed the street.

'Listen, René,' Alabama said quickly, 'you *must* see Jacques and tell him I cannot come – just that. You will do this for me?'

Compassion lit his dreamy, passionate face. René took her hand and kissed it.

'I am very sorry for you. Jacques is a good boy.'

'You are a good boy, too, René.'

Jacques was not on the beach next morning.

'Well, Madame,' Monsieur Jean greeted them. 'You have had a nice summer?'

'It's been lovely,' Nanny answered, 'but I think Madam and Monsieur will soon have had enough of it here.'

'Well, the season will soon be over,' Monsieur Jean commented philosophically.

There were pigeons for lunch and the rubbery cheese. The maid fluttered about with the account book; Nanny talked too much.

'It has been very pleasant, I must say, here this summer,' she commented.

'I hate it. If you can have our things packed by tomorrow we're going to Paris,' said David fiercely.

'But there's a law in France that you must give the servants ten days' notice, Mr. Knight. It's an absolute law,' expostulated Nanny.

'I'll give them money. For two francs, you could buy the President, the lousy Kikes!'

Nanny laughed, flustered by David's violence. 'They are certainly very pecuniary.'

'I'll pack tonight. I'm going walking,' Alabama said.

'You won't go into town without me, Alabama?'

Their resistance met and clung with the taut suspense of two people seeking mutual support in a fast dance turn.

'No, I promise you, David. I'll take Nanny with me.'

She roamed through the pine forests and over the high roads back of the villa. The other villas were boarded up for the summer. The plane trees covered the driveways with leaves. The jade porcelain gods in front of the heathen cemetery seemed very indoor gods and out of place on the bauxite terrace. The roads were smooth and new up there to make walking easier for the British in winter. They followed a sandy path between the vineyards. It was just a wagon track. The sun bled to death in a red and purple hemorrhage – dark arterial blood dyeing the grape leaves. The clouds were black and twisted horizontally and the land spread biblical in the prophetic light.

'No Frenchman ever kisses his wife on the mouth,' said Nanny confidentially. 'He has too much respect for her.'

They walked so far that Alabama carried Bonnie astride her back to rest the short legs.

'Git up, horsey, Mummy, why won't you run?' the baby whined.

'Sh – sh – sh. I'm an old tired horse with hoof-and-mouth disease, darling.'

A peasant in the hot fields gestured lasciviously and beckoned to the women. Nanny was frightened.

'Can you imagine that, Madam, and we with a little child? I shall certainly speak to Mr. Knight. The world is not safe since the war.'

At sundown the tom-toms beat in the Senegalese camp – rites they performed for the dead in their monster-guarded burial ground.

A lone shepherd, brown and handsome, herded a thick drove of sheep along the stubbly tracks leading to the villa. They swept around Alabama and the nurse and child, whirling up the dust with their pattering feet.

'J'ai peur,' she called to the man.

'Oui,' he said gently, 'vous avez peur! Gi – o.' He clucked the sheep on down the road.

They couldn't get away from St-Raphaël until the end of the week. Alabama stayed at the villa and walked with Bonnie and Nanny.

Madame Paulette telephoned. Would Alabama come to see her in the afternoon? David said she could go to say good-bye.

Madame Paulette gave her a picture from Jacques and a

long letter.

'I am very sorry for you,' Madame said. 'We had not thought that it was so serious an affair – we had thought it was just an affair.'

Alabama could not read the letter. It was in French. She tore it in a hundred little pieces and scattered it over the black water of the harbor beneath the masts of many fishing boats from Shanghai and Madrid, Colombia and Portugal. Though it broke her heart, she tore the picture too. It was the most beautiful thing she'd ever owned in her life, that photograph. What was the use of keeping it? Jacques Chevre-Feuille had gone to China. There wasn't a way to hold on to the summer, no French phrase to preserve its rising broken harmonies, no hopes to be salvaged from a cheap French photograph. Whatever it was that she wanted from Jacques, Jacques took it with him to squander on the Chinese. You took what you wanted from life, if you could get it, and you did without the rest.

The sand on the beach was as white as in June, the Mediterranean as blue as ever from the windows of the train that extracted the Knights from the land of lemon trees and sun. They were on their way to Paris. They hadn't much faith in travel nor a great belief in a change of scene as a panacea for spiritual ills; they were simply glad to be going. And Bonnie was glad. Children are always glad of something new, not realizing that there is everything in anything if the thing is complete in itself. Summer and love and beauty are much the same in Cannes or Connecticut. David was older than Alabama; he hadn't really felt glad since his first success.

III

Nobody knew whose party it was. It had been going on for weeks. When you felt you couldn't survive another night, you went home and slept and when you got back, a new set of people had consecrated themselves to keeping it alive. It must have started with the first boatloads of unrest that emptied themselves into France in nineteen twenty-seven. Alabama and David joined in May, after a terrible winter in a Paris flat that smelled of a church chancery because it was impossible to ventilate. That apartment, where they had fastened themselves up from the winter rain, was a perfect breeding place for the germs of bitterness they brought with them from the Riviera. From out their windows the gray roofs before shaved the gray roofs behind like lightly grazing fencing foils. The gray sky came down between the chimneys in inverted ethereal Gothic dividing the horizon into spires and points which hung over their unrest like the tubes of a vast incubator. The etching of the balconies of the Champs-Elysées and the rain on the pavements about the Arc de Triomphe was all they could see from their red and gilt salon. David had a studio on the Left Bank in that quarter of the city beyond the Pont de l'Alma, where rococo apartment buildings and long avenues of trees give on colorless openings with no perspective.

There he lost himself in the retrospect of autumn disembodied from its months, from heat and cold and holidays, and produced his lullabies of recapitulation that drew vast crowds of the advance guard to the Salon des Independents. The frescoes were finished: this was a new, more personal, David on exhibit. You heard his name in bank lobbies and in the Ritz Bar, which was proof that people were saying it in other places. The steely concision of his work was making itself felt even in the lines of interior decoration. *Des Arts Décoratifs* carried a dining room after one of his interiors painted because of a gray anemone; the *Ballet Russe* accepted a décor – fantasmagoria of the light on the plage at St-Raphaël to represent the beginning of the world in a ballet called *Evolution*.

The rising vogue of the David Knights brought Dickie Axton flying symbolically across their horizons, scribbling over the walls of their prosperity a message from Babylon which they did not bother to read, being at that time engrossed in the odor of twilit lilacs along the Boulevard St-Germain and the veiling of the Place de la Concorde in the expensive mysticism of the Blue Hour.

The telephone rang and rang and rustled their dreams to

pale Valhallas, Ermenonville, and the celestial twilight passages of padded hotels. As they slept in their lyric bed dreaming the will of the world to be probate, the bell rained on their consciousness like the roll of distant hoops; David grabbed the receiver.

'Hello. Yes, this is both the Knights.'

Dickie's voice slid down the telephone wire from high-handed confidence to a low wheedle.

'I hope you're coming to my dinner.' The voice descended by its teeth like an acrobat from the top of a circus tent. The limits of Dickie's activities stopped only at the borders of moral, social and romantic independence, so you can well imagine that her scope was not a small one. Dickie had at her beck and call a catalogue of humanity, an emotional casting agency. Her existence was not surprising in this age of Mussolinis and sermons from the mount by every passing Alpinist. For the sum of three hundred dollars she scraped the centuries' historic deposits from under the nails of Italian noblemen and passed it off as caviar to Kansas débutantes; for a few hundreds more she opened the doors of Bloomsbury and Parnassus, the gates of Chantilly or the pages of Debrett's to America's post-war prosperity. Her intangible commerce served up the slithered frontiers of Europe in a céleri-rave – Spaniards, Cubans, South Americans, even an occasional black floating through the social mayonnaise like bits of truffle. The Knights had risen to so exalted a point in the hierarchy of the 'known' that they had become material for Dickie.

'You needn't be so high-hat,' Alabama protested to David's lack of enthusiasm. 'All the people will be white – or were once.'

'We'll come, then,' said David into the receiver.

Alabama twisted her body experimentally. The patrician sun of late afternoon spread itself aloofly over the bed where she and David untidily collected themselves.

'It's very flattering,' she said, propelling herself to the bathroom, 'to be sought after, but more provident, I suppose, to seek.'

David lay listening to the violent flow of the water and the quake of the glasses in their stands.

'Another jag!' he yelled. 'I find I can get along very well without my basic principles, but I cannot sacrifice my weaknesses – one being an insatiability about jags.'

'What did you say about the Prince of Wales being sick?' called Alabama.

'I don't see why you can't listen when I'm talking to you,' David answered crossly.

'I hate people who begin to talk the minute you pick up a toothbrush,' she snapped.

'I said the sheets of this bed are actually scorching my feet.'

'But there isn't any potash in the liquor over here,' said Alabama incredulously. 'It must be a neurosis – have you a new symptom?' she demanded jealously.

'I haven't slept in so long I would be having hallucinations if I could distinguish them from reality.'

'Poor David – what will we do?'

'I don't know. Seriously, Alabama' – David lit a cigarette contemplatively – 'my work's getting stale. I need new emotional stimulus.'

Alabama looked at him coldly.

'I see.' She realized that she had sacrificed forever her right to be hurt on the glory of a Provençal summer. 'You might follow the progress of Mr. Berry Wall through the columns of the *Paris Herald*,' she suggested.

'Or choke myself on a chiaroscuro.'

'If you *are* serious, David, I believe it has always been understood between us that we would not interfere with each other.'

'Sometimes,' commented David irrelevantly, 'your face looks like a soul lost in the mist on a Scotch moor.'

'Of course, no allowance has been made in our calculations for jealousy,' she pursued.

'Listen, Alabama,' interrupted David, 'I feel terrible; do you think we can make the grade?'

'I want to show off my new dress,' she said decisively.

'And I've got an old suit I'd like to wear out. You know we shouldn't go. We should think of our obligations to humanity.' Obligations were to Alabama a plan and a trap laid by civilization to ensnare and cripple her happiness and hobble the feet of time.

'Are you moralizing?'

'No. I want to see what her parties are like. The last of Dickie's soirées netted no profits to charity though hundreds were turned away at the gates. The Duchess of Dacne cost Dickie three months in America by well-placed hints.'

'They're like all the others. You just sit down and wait for the inevitable, which is the only thing that never happens.'

The post-war extravagance which had sent David and Alabama and some sixty thousand other Americans wandering over the face of Europe in a game of hare without hounds achieved its apex. The sword of Damocles, forged from the high hope of getting something for nothing and the demoralizing expectation of getting nothing for something, was almost hung by the third of May.

There were Americans at night, and day Americans, and we all had Americans in the bank to buy things with. The marble lobbies were full of them.

Lespiaut couldn't make enough flowers for the trade. They made nasturtiums of leather and rubber and wax gardenias and ragged robins out of threads and wires. They manufactured hardy perennials to grow on the meagre soil of shoulder straps and bouquets with long stems for piercing the loamy shadows under the belt. Modistes pieced hats together from the toy-boat sails in the Tuileries; audacious dressmakers sold the summer in bunches. The ladies went to the foundries and had themselves some hair cast and had themselves half-soled with the deep chrome fantasies of Helena Rubenstein and Dorothy Gray. They read off the descriptive adjectives on the menu-cards to the waiters and said, 'Wouldn't you like' and 'Wouldn't you really' to each other till they drove the men out to lose themselves in the comparative quiet of the Paris streets which hummed like the tuning of an invisible orchestra. Americans from other years bought themselves dressy house with collars and cuffs in Neuilly and Passy, stuffed themselves in the cracks of the rue du Bac like the Dutch boy saving the dikes. Irresponsible Americans suspended themselves on costly eccentricities like Saturday's servants on a broken Ferris wheel and made so many readjustments that a constant addenda went on about them like the clang of a Potin cash register. Esoteric pelletiers robbed a secret clientele in the rue des Petits-Champs; people spent fortunes in taxis in search of the remote.

'I'm sorry I can't stay, I just dropped in to say "hello,"' they said to each other and refused the table d'hôte. They ordered Veronese pastry on lawns like lace curtains at Versailles and chicken and hazelnuts at Fontainebleau where the woods wore powdered wigs. Discs of umbrellas poured over suburban terraces with the smooth round ebullience of a Chopin waltz. They sat in the distance under the lugubrious dripping elms, elms like maps of Europe, elms frayed at the end like bits of chartreuse wool, elms heavy and bunchy as sour grapes. They ordered the weather with a continental appetite, and listened to the centaur complain about the price of hoofs. There were bourgeois blossoms on the bill-of-fare and tall architectural blossoms on the horse-chestnut and crystallized rose-buds to go with the Porto. The Americans gave indications of themselves but always only the beginning like some eternal exposition, a clef before a bar of music to be played on the minors of the imagination. They thought all French school boys were orphans because of the black dresses they wore, and those of them who didn't know the meaning of the word 'insensible' thought the French thought that they were crazy. All of them drank. Americans with red ribbons in their buttonholes read papers called the *Éclaireur* and drank on the sidewalks, Americans with tips on the races drank down a flight of stairs, Americans with a million dollars and a standing engagement with the hotel masseuses drank in suites at the Meurice and the Crillon. Other Americans drank in Montmartre, 'pour le soif' and 'contre la chaleur' and 'pour la digestion' and 'pour se guérir.' They were glad the French thought they were crazy.

Over fifty thousand francs' worth of flowers had wilted to success on the altars of Notre-Dames-des-Victoires during the year.

'Maybe something will happen,' said David.

Alabama wished nothing ever would again but it was her turn to agree – they had evolved a tacit arrangement about waiting on each other's emotions, almost mathematical like the trick combination of a safe, which worked by the mutual assumption that it would.

'I mean,' he pursued, 'if somebody would come along to remind us about how we felt about things when we felt the way they remind us of, maybe it would refresh us.'

'I see what you mean. Life has begun to appear as tortuous as the sentimental writings of a rhythmic dance.'

'Exactly. I want to make some protestations since I'm largely too busy to work very well.'

'Mama said "Yes" and Papa said "Yes"' to the gramophone owners of France. 'Ariel' passed from the title of a book to three wires on the house-top. What did it matter? It had already gone from a god to a myth to Shakespeare – nobody seemed to mind. People still recognized the word: 'Ariel!' it was. David and Alabama hardly noticed the change.

In a Marne taxicab they clipped all the corners of Paris precipitous enough to claim their attention and descended at the door of the Hôtel George-V. An atmosphere of convivial menace hung over the bar. Delirious imitations of Picabia, the black lines and blobs of a commercial attempt at insanity squeezed the shiplike enclosure till it communicated the sense of being corseted in a small space. The bartender inspected the party patronizingly. Miss Axton was an old customer, always bringing somebody new; Miss Dickie Axton, he knew. She'd been drinking in his bar the night she shot her lover in the Gare de l'Est. Alabama and David were the only ones he'd never seen before.

'And has Mademoiselle Axton completely recovered from so stupid a contretemps?'

Miss Axton affirmed in a magnetic, incisive voice that she had, and that she wanted a gin highball damn quick. Miss Axton's hair grew on her head like the absent-minded pencil strokes a person makes while telephoning. Her long legs struck forcefully forward as if she pressed her toes watchfully on the accelerator of the universe. People said she had slept with a Negro. The bartender didn't believe it. He didn't see where Miss Axton would have found the time between white gentlemen – pugilists, too, sometimes.

Miss Douglas, now, was a different proposition. She was

English. You couldn't tell whom she had slept with. She had even stayed out of the papers. Of course she had money, which makes sleeping considerably more discreet.

'We will drink the same as usual, Mademoiselle?' He smiled ingratiatingly.

Miss Douglas opened her translucent eyes; she was so much the essence of black chic that she was nothing but a dark aroma. Pale and transparent, she anchored herself to the earth solely by the tenets of her dreamy self-control.

'No, my friend, this time it's Scotch and soda. I'm getting too much of a stomach for sherry flips.'

'There's a scheme,' said Miss Axton, 'you put six encyclopædias on your stomach and recite the multiplication table. After a few weeks your stomach is so flat that it comes out at the back, and you begin life again hind part before.'

'Of course,' contributed Miss Douglas, punching herself where a shade of flesh rose above her girdle like fresh rolls from a pan, 'the only sure thing is' – leaning across she sputtered something in Miss Axton's ear. The two women roared.

'Excuse me,' finished Dickie hilariously, 'and in England they take it in a highball.'

'I never exercise,' pronounced Mr. Hastings with unenthusiastic embarrassment. 'Ever since I got my ulcers I've eaten nothing but spinach so I manage to avoid looking well that way.'

'A glum sectarian dish,' concluded Dickie sepulchrally.

'I have it with eggs and then with croutons and sometimes with—'

'Now, dear,' interrupted Dickie, 'you mustn't excite yourself.' Blandly explaining, she elaborated. 'I have to mother Mr. Hastings; he's just come out of an asylum, and when he gets nervous he can't dress or shave himself without playing his phonograph. The neighbors have him locked up whenever it happens, so I have to keep him quiet.'

'It must be very inconvenient,' muttered David.

'Frightfully so – travelling all the way to Switzerland with all those discs, and ordering spinach in thirty-seven different languages.'

108

'I'm sure Mr. Knight could tell us some way of staying young,' suggested Miss Douglas, 'he looks about five years old.'

'He's an authority,' said Dickie, 'a positive authority.'

'What about?' inquired Hastings skeptically.

'Authorities are all about women this year,' said Dickie.

'Do you care for Russians, Mr. Knight?'

'Oh, very much. We love them,' said Alabama. She had a sense that she hadn't said anything for hours and that something was expected of her.

'We don't,' said David. 'We don't know anything about music.'

'Jimmie,' Dickie seized the conversation rapaciously, 'was going to be a celebrated composer, but he had to take a drink every sixteen measures of counterpoint to keep the impetus of the thing from falling and his bladder gave out.'

'I couldn't sacrifice myself for success the way some people do,' protested Hastings querulously implying that David had sold himself, somehow, to something.

'Naturally. Everybody knows you anyway – as the man without any bladder.'

Alabama felt excluded by her lack of accomplishment. Comparing herself with Miss Axton's elegance, she hated the reticent solidity, the savage sparse competence of her body – her arms reminded her of a Siberian branch railroad. Compared with Miss Douglas' elimination, her Patou dress felt too big along the seams. Miss Douglas made her feel that there was a cold cream deposit at the neckline. Slipping her fingers into the tray of salted nuts, she addressed the barman dismally, 'I should think people in your profession would drink themselves to death.'

'Non, Madame. I did use to like a good sidecar but that was before I became so well-known.'

The party poured out into the Paris night like dice shaken from a cylinder. The pink flare from the street lights tinted the canopy scalloping of the trees to liquid bronze: those lights are one of the reasons why the hearts of Americans bump spasmodically at the mention of France; they are identical with the circus flares of our youth.

The taxi careened down the boulevard along the Seine. Careening and swerving, they passed the brittle mass of Notre-Dame, the bridges cradling the river, the pungence of the baking parks, the Norman towers of the Department of State, the pungence of the baking parks, the bridges cradling the river, the brittle mass of Notre-Dame, sliding back and forth like a repeated newsreel.

The Ile St-Louis is boxed by many musty courtyards. The entry-ways are paved with the black-and-white diamonds of the Sinister Kings and grilles dissect the windows. East Indians and Georgians serve the deep apartments opening on the river.

It was late when they arrived at Dickie's.

'So, as a painter,' Dickie said as she opened the door, 'I wanted your husband to meet Gabrielle Gibbs. You must, sometime; if you're knowing people.'

'Gabrielle Gibbs,' echoed Alabama, 'of course, I've heard of her.'

'Gabrielle's a half-wit,' continued Dickie calmly, 'but she's very attractive if you don't feel like talking.'

'She has the most beautiful body,' contributed Hastings, 'like white marble.'

The apartment was deserted; a plate of scrambled eggs hardened on the centre table; a coral evening cape decorated a chair.

'Qu'est-ce tu fais ici?' said Miss Gibbs feebly from the bathroom floor as Alabama and Dickie penetrated the sanctuary.

'I can't speak French,' Alabama answered.

The girl's long blonde hair streamed in chiselled segments about her face, a platinum wisp floated in the bowl of the toilet. The face was as innocent as if she had just been delivered from the taxidermist's.

'Quelle dommage,' she said laconically. Twenty diamond bracelets clinked against the toilet seat.

'Oh, dear,' said Dickie philosophically, 'Gabrielle can't speak English when she's drunk. Liquor makes her highbrow.'

Alabama appraised the girl; she seemed to have bought herself in sets.

'Christ,' the inebriate remarked to herself morosely, 'etait né en quatre cent Anno Domini. C'etait vraiment *très* dommage.' She gathered herself together with the careless precision of a scene-shifter, staring skeptically into Alabama's face from eyes as impenetrable as the background of an allegorical painting.

'I've got to get sober,' the face quickened to momentary startled animation.

'You certainly do,' Dickie ordered. 'There's a man outside such as you have never met before especially lured here by the prospect of meeting you.'

'Anything can be arranged in the toilet,' Alabama thought to herself. 'It's the woman's equivalent for the downtown club since the war.' She'd say that at table, she thought.

'If you'll leave me I'll just take a bath,' Miss Gibbs proposed majestically.

Dickie swept Alabama out into the room like a maid gathering dust off the parlor floor.

'We think,' Hastings was saying in a tone of finality, 'that there's no use working over human relations.'

He turned accusingly to Alabama. 'Just who is this hypothetical we?'

Alabama had no explanation to offer. She was wondering if this was the time to use the remark about the toilet when Miss Gibbs appeared in the doorway.

'Angels,' cried the girl, peering about the room.

She was as dainty and rounded as a porcelain figure; she sat up and begged; she played dead-dog, burlesquing her own ostentation attentively as if each gesture were a configuration in some comic dance she composed as she went along and meant to perfect late. It was obvious that she was a dancer – clothes never become part of their sleek bodies. A person could have stripped Miss Gibbs by pulling a central string.

'Miss Gibbs!' said Dickie quickly. 'Do you remember the man who wrote you all those mash notes back in nineteen-twenty?'

The fluttering eyes ruminated over the scene uncritically. 'So,' she said, 'it is you whom I am to meet. But I've heard you were in love with your wife.'

111

David laughed. 'Slander. Do you disapprove?'

Miss Gibbs withdrew behind the fumes of Elizabeth Arden and the ripples of a pruned international giggle. 'It seems rather cannibalistic in these days.' The tone changed to one of exaggerated seriousness; her personality was alive like a restless pile of pink chiffon in a breeze.

'I dance at eleven, and we must dine if you ever had that intention. Paris!' she sighed – 'I've been in a taxi since last week at half-past four.'

From the long trestle table a hundred silver knives and forks signalled the existence of as many million dollars in curt cubistic semaphore. The grotesquerie of fashionable tousled heads and the women's scarlet mouths opening and gobbling the candle-light like ventriloquists' dummies brought the quality of a banquet of a mad, mediæval monarch to the dinner. American voices whipped themselves to a frenzy with occasional lashings of a foreign tongue.

David hung over Gabrielle. 'You know,' Alabama heard the girl say, 'I think the soup needs a little more eau de Cologne.'

She was going to have to overhear Miss Gibbs' line all during dinner, which fact considerably hampered her own.

'Well,' she began bravely – 'the toilet for women—'

'It's an outrage – a conspiracy to cheat us,' said the voice of Miss Gibbs, 'I wish they'd use more aphrodisiac.'

'Gabrielle,' yelled Dickie, 'you've no idea how expensive such things are since the war.'

The table achieved a shuttlecock balance which gave the illusion of looking out on the world from a fast-flying train window. Immense trays of ornamental foods passed under their skeptical distraught eyes.

'The food,' said Hastings crabbily, 'is like something Dickie found in a geologist's excavation.'

Alabama decided to count on his being cross at the right point; he was always a little bit cross. She had almost thought of something to say when David's voice floated up like driftwood on a tidal wave.

'A man told me,' he was saying to Gabrielle, 'that you have the most beautiful blue veins all over your body.'

'I was thinking, Mr. Hastings,' said Alabama tenaciously,

'that I would like somebody to lock me up in a spiritual chastity belt.'

Having been brought up in England, Hastings was intent on his food.

'Blue ice cream!' he snorted contemptuously. 'Probably frozen New England blood extracted from the world by the pressure of modern civilization on inherited concepts and acquired traditions.'

Alabama went back to her original premise that Hastings was hopelessly calculating.

'I wish,' said Dickie unpleasantly, 'that people would not flagellate themselves with the food when they're dining with me.'

'I have no historical sense! I am an unbeliever!' shouted Hastings. 'I don't know what you're talking about!'

'When Father was in Africa,' interrupted Miss Douglas, 'they climbed inside the elephant and ate the entrails with their hands – at least, the Pygmies did; Father took pictures.'

'And,' said David's voice excitedly, 'he said that your breasts were like marble dessert – a sort of blancmange, I presume.'

'It would be quite an experience,' yawned Miss Axton idly, 'to seek stimulation in the church and asceticism in sex.'

The party lost body with the end of dinner – the people, intent on themselves in the big living room, moved about like officials under masks in an operating room. A visceral femininity suffused the umber glow.

Night lights through the windows glittered miniature and precise as carvings of stars in a sapphire bottle. Quiet sound from the street rose above the party's quiescence. David passed from one group to another, weaving the room into a lacy pattern, draping its substance over Gabrielle's shoulders.

Alabama couldn't keep her eyes off them. Gabrielle was the centre of something; there was about her that suspension of direction which could only exist in a centre. She lifted her eyes and blinked at David like a complacent white Persian cat.

'I imagine you wear something startling and boyish underneath your clothes,' David's voice droned on, 'BVD's or something.'

Resentment flared in Alabama. He'd stolen the idea from her. She'd worn silk BVD's herself all last summer.

'Your husband's too handsome,' said Miss Axton, 'to be so well known. It's an unfair advantage.'

Alabama felt sick at her stomach – controllably, but too sick to answer – champagne is a filthy drink.

David opened and closed his personality over Miss Gibbs like the tentacles of a carnivorous maritime plant. Dickie and Miss Douglas leaning against the mantel suggested the weird Artic loneliness of totem poles. Hastings played the piano too loud. The noise isolated them all from each other.

The doorbell rang and rang.

'It must be the taxis come to take us to the ballet,' Dickie sighed with relief.

'Stravinsky is conducting,' supplied Hastings. 'He's a plagiarist,' he added lugubriously.

'Dickie,' said Miss Gibbs peremptorily, 'could you just leave me the key? Mr. Knight will see me to the Acacias – that is, if you don't mind.' She beamed on Alabama.

'Mind? Why should I?' Alabama answered disagreeably. She wouldn't have minded if Gabrielle had been unattractive.

'I don't know. I'm in love with your husband. I thought I'd try to make him if you didn't mind – of course, I'd try anyway – he's such an angel.' She giggled. It was a sympathetic giggle covering any unexpected failure in its advance apology.

Hastings helped Alabama with her coat. She was angry about Gabrielle – Gabrielle made her feel clumsy. The party burrowed into their wraps.

The lamps swung and swayed soft as the ribbons of a Maypole along the river; the spring sniggered quietly to itself on the street corners.

'But what a "lahvely" night!' Hastings proffered facetiously.

'Weather is for children.'

Somebody mentioned the moon.

'Moons?' said Alabama contemptuously. 'They're two for five at the Five and Ten, full or crescent.'

'But this is an especially nice one, Madam. It has an especially fashionable way of looking at things!'

In her deepest moods of discontent, Alabama, on looking

back, found the overlying tempo of that period as broken and strident as trying to hum a bit of *La Chatte*. Afterwards, the only thing she could place emotionally was her sense of their all being minor characters and her dismay at David's reiterance that many women were flowers – flowers and desserts, love and excitement, and passion and fame! Since St-Raphaël she had had no uncontested pivot from which to swing her equivocal universe. She shifted her abstractions like a mechanical engineer might surveying the growing necessities of a construction.

The party was late at the Châtelet. Dickie hustled them up the converging marble stairs as if she directed a processional to Moloch.

The décor swarmed in Saturnian rings. Spare, immaculate legs and a consciousness of rib, the vibrant suspension of lean bodies precipitated on the jolt of reiterant rhythmic shock, the violins' hysteria, evolved themselves to a tortured abstraction of sex. Alabama's excitement rose with the appeal to the poignancy of a human body subject to its physical will to the point of evangelism. Her hands were wet and shaking with its tremulo. Her heart beat like the fluttering wings of an angry bird.

The theatre settled in a slow nocturne of plush culture. The last strain of the orchestra seemed to lift her off the earth in inverse exhilaration – like David's laugh, it was, when he was happy.

Down the stairs many girls looked back at important men with silver-fox hair from the marble balustrade and influential men looked from side to side jingling things in their pockets – private lives and keys.

'There is the Princess,' said Dickie. 'Shall we take her along? She used to be very famous.'

A woman with a shaved head and the big ears of a gargoyle paraded a Mexican hairless through the lobby.

'Madame used to be in the ballet until her husband exhausted her knees so she couldn't dance,' went on Dickie introducing the lady.

'It is many years since my knees have grown quite ossified,' the woman said plaintively.

'How did you manage?' said Alabama breathlessly. 'How did you get in the ballet? And get to be important?'

The woman regarded her with velvety bootblack's eyes, begging the world not to forget her, that she herself might exist oblivious.

'But I was born in the ballet.' Alabama accepted the remark as if it were an explanation of life.

There were many dissensions about where to go. As a compliment to the Princess the party chose a Russian boîte. The voice of a fallen aristocracy tethered its wails to the flexible notes of Tzigane guitars; the low clang of bottles against champagne buckets jangled the tone of the dungeon of pleasure like the lashing of spectral chains. Cold-storage necks and throats like vipers' fangs pierced the ectoplasmic light; eddying hair whirled about the shallows of the night.

'Please, Madame,' Alabama persisted intently, 'would you give me a letter to whoever trains the ballet? I would do anything in the world to learn to do that.'

The shaved head scanned Alabama enigmatically.

'Whatever for?' she said. 'It is a hard life. One suffers. Your husband could surely arrange—'

'But why should any one want to do *that*?' Hastings interrupted. 'I'll give you the address of a Black-Bottom teacher – of course, he's colored, but nobody cares any more.'

'I do,' said Miss Douglas. 'The last time I went out with Negroes I had to borrow from the headwaiter to pay the check. Since then I've drawn the color line at the Chinese.'

'Do you think, Madame, that I am too old?' Alabama persisted.

'Yes,' said the Princess briefly.

'They live on cocaine anyway,' said Miss Douglas.

'And pray to Russian devils,' added Hastings.

'But some of them do lead actual lives, I believe,' said Dickie.

'Sex is such a poor substitute,' sighed Miss Douglas.

'For what?'

'For sex, idiot.'

'I think,' said Dickie surprisingly, 'that it would be the very thing for Alabama. I've always heard she was a little peculiar

116

– I don't mean actually batty – but a little difficult. An art would explain. I really think you ought, you know,' she said decisively. 'It would be almost as exotic as being married to a painter.'

'What do you mean "exotic"?'

'Running around caring about things – of course, I hardly know you, but I do think dancing would be an asset if you're going to care *anyhow*. If the party got dull you could do a few whirly-gigs,' Dickie illustrated her words by gouging a hole in the tablecloth with her fork, 'like that!' she finished enthusiastically. 'I can see you now!'

Alabama visualized herself suavely swaying to the end of a violin bow, spinning on its silver bobbin, the certain disillusions of the past into uncertain expectancies of the future. She pictured herself as an amorphous cloud in a dressing-room mirror which would be framed with cards and papers, telegrams and pictures. She followed herself along a stone corridor full of electric switches and signs about smoking, past a water cooler and a pile of Lily Cups and a man in a tilted chair to a gray door with a stencilled star.

Dickie was a born promoter. 'I'm sure you can do it – you certainly have the body!'

Alabama went secretly over her body. It was rigid, like a lighthouse. 'It might do,' she mumbled, the words rising through her elation like a swimmer coming up from a deep dive.

'Might?' echoed Dickie with conviction, 'you could sell it to Cartier's for a gold mesh sweat shirt!'

'Who can give me a letter to the necessary people?'

'I will, my dear – I have all the unobtainable entrées in Paris. But it's only fair to warn you that the gold streets of heaven are hard on the feet. You'd better take along a pair of crepe soles when you're planning the trip.'

'Yes,' Alabama agreed unhesitantly. 'Brown, I suppose, because of the gutters – I've always heard star-dust shows up on the white.'

'It's a tomfool arrangement,' said Hastings abruptly. 'Her husband says she can't even carry a tune!'

Something must have happened to make the man so

grouchy – or maybe it was that nothing had. They were all grouchy, nearly as much so as herself. It must be nerves and having nothing to do but write home for money. There wasn't even a decent Turkish bath in Paris.

'What have you been doing with – *your*self?' she said.

'Using up my war medals for pistol-practice targets,' he answered acidly.

Hastings was as sleek and brown as pulled molasses candy. He was an intangible reprobate, discouraging people and living like a moral pirate. Many generations of beautiful mothers had endowed him with an inexhaustible petulance. He wasn't half as good company as David.

'I see,' said Alabama. 'The arena is closed today, since the matador had to stay home and write his memoirs. The three thousand people can go to the movies instead.'

Hastings was annoyed at the tartness in her tone.

'Don't blame me,' he said, 'about Gabrielle's borrowing David.' Seeing the earnestness in her face he continued helpfully, 'I don't suppose you'd want me to make love to you?'

'Oh, no, it's quite all right – I like martyrdom.'

The small room smothered in smoke. A powerful drum beleaguered the drowsy dawn; bouncers from other cabarets drifted in for their morning supper.

Alabama sat quietly humming, 'Horses, Horses, Horses,' in a voice like the whistle of boats putting out to sea in a fog.

'This is my party,' she insisted as the check appeared. 'I've been giving it for years.'

'Why didn't you invite your husband?' said Hastings maliciously.

'Damn it,' said Alabama hotly. 'I did – so long ago that he forgot to come.'

'You need somebody to take care of you,' he said seriously. 'You're a man's woman and need to be bossed. No, I mean it,' he insisted when Alabama began to laugh.

Nourishing his roots on the disingenuous expectations of ladies whose exploits permitted them a remembrance of the fairy tales, Alabama concluded that he was nevertheless not a prince.

'I was just going to begin doing it myself,' she chuckled. 'I made a date with the Princess and Dickie to arrange for a future. In the meantime, it is exceedingly difficult to direct a life which has no direction.'

'You've a child, haven't you?' he suggested.

'Yes,' she said, 'there's the baby – life goes on.'

'This party,' said Dickie, 'has been going on forever. They're saving the signatures on the earliest checks for the war museum.'

'What we need is new blood in the party.'

'What we all need,' said Alabama impatiently, 'is a good—'

The dawn swung over the Palace Vendôme with the slow silver grace of a moored dirigible. Alabama and Hastings spilled into the Knights' gray apartment on the morning like a shower of last night's confetti shaken from the folds of a cloak.

'I thought David would be at home,' she said, searching the bedroom.

'I didn't,' Hastings mocked. 'For I, thy God, am a Jewish God, Baptist God, Catholic God—'

She had wanted to cry for a long time, she realized suddenly. In the weary stuffiness of the salon she collapsed. Sobbing and shaking, she did not lift her face when David finally stumbled into the dry, hot room. She lay sprawled like a damp wrung towel over the window sill, like the transparent shed carcass of a brilliant insect.

'I suppose you're awfully angry,' he said.

Alabama didn't speak.

'I've been out all night,' explained David cheerfully, 'on a party.'

She wished she could help David to seem more legitimate. She wished she could do something to keep everything from being so undignified. Life seemed so uselessly extravagant.

'Oh, David,' she sobbed. 'I'm much too proud to care – pride keeps me from feeling half the things I ought to feel.'

'Care about what? Haven't you had a good time?' mumbled David placatively.

'Perhaps Alabama's angry about my not getting sentimental about her,' said Hastings, hastily extricating himself.

'Anyway I'll just run along if you don't mind. It must be quite late.'

The morning sun shone brightly through the windows.

For a long time she lay sobbing. David took her on his shoulder. Under his arms smelled warm and clean like the smoke of a quiet fire burning in a peasant's mountain cottage.

'There's no use explaining,' he said.

'Not the slightest.'

She tried to see him through the early dusk.

'Darling!' she said, 'I wish I could live in your pocket.'

'Darling,' answered David sleepily, 'there'd be a hole you'd forgotten to darn and you'd slip through and be brought home by the village barber. At least, that's been my experience with carrying girls about in my pockets.'

Alabama thought she'd better put a pillow under David's head to keep him from snoring. She thought he looked like a little boy who had just been washed and brushed by a nurse a few minutes before. Men, she thought, never seem to become the things they do, like women, but belong to their own philosophic interpretations of their actions.

'I don't care,' she repeated convincingly to herself: as neat an incision into the tissue of life as the most dextrous surgeon could hope to produce over a poisoned appendix. Filing away her impressions like a person making a will, she bequeathed each passing sensation to that momentary accumulation of her self, the present, that filled and emptied with the overflow.

It's too late in the morning for peccadilloes; the sun bathes itself with the night's cadavers in the typhus-laden waters of the Seine; the market carts have long since rumbled back to Fontainebleau and St-Cloud; the early operations are done in the hospitals; the inhabitants of the Ile de la Cité have had their bowl of café-au-lait and the night chauffeurs 'un verre.' The Paris cooks have brought down the refuse and brought up the coal, and many people with tuberculosis wait in the damp bowels of the earth for the Metro. Children play in the grassplots about the Tour Eiffel and the white floating veils of English nannies and the blue veils of the French nounous flap out the news that all is well along the Champs-Elysées. Fashionable women powder their noses in their Porto glasses under the trees of the Pavillon Dauphine, just now opening its doors to the creak of Russian leather riding boots. The Knights' femme de chambre has orders to wake her masters in time for lunch in the Bois de Boulogne.

When Alabama tried to get up she felt nervous, she felt monstrous, she felt bilious.

'I can't stand this any longer,' she screamed at the dozing David. 'I don't want to sleep with the men or imitate the women, and I can't stand it!'

'Look out, Alabama, I've got a headache,' David protested.

'I won't look out! I won't go to lunch! I'm going to sleep till time to go to the studio.'

Her eyes glowed with the precarious light of a fanatic determination. There were white triangles under her jaw bone and blue rings around her neck. Her skin smelled of dry dirty powder from the night before.

'Well, you can't sleep sitting up,' he said.

'I can do exactly as I please,' she said; 'anything! I can sleep when I'm awake if I want to!'

David's delight in simplicity was something very complex that a simple person would never have understood. It kept him out of many arguments.

'All right,' he said, 'I'll help you.'

The macabre who lived through the war have a story they love to tell about the soldiers of the Foreign Legion giving a ball in the expanses around Verdun and dancing with the corpses. Alabama's continued brewing of the poisoned filter for a semiconscious banquet table, her insistence on the magic and glamor of life when she was already feeling its pulse like the throbbing of an amputated leg, had something of the same sinister quality.

Women sometimes seem to share a quiet, unalterable dogma of persecution that endows even the most sophisticated of them with the inarticulate poignancy of the peasant. Compared to Alabama's, David's material wisdom was so profound that it gleamed strong and harmonious through the confusion of these times.

'Poor girl,' he said, 'I understand. It must be awful just waiting around eternally.'

'Aw, shut up!' she answered ungratefully. She lay silent for a long time. 'David,' she said sharply.

'Yes.'

'I am going to be as famous a dancer as there are blue veins over the white marble of Miss Gibbs.'

'Yes, dear,' agreed David noncommittally.

3

I

THE HIGH parabolas of Schumann fell through the narrow
brick court and splashed against the red walls in jangling
crescendo. Alabama traversed the dingy passage behind the
stage of the Olympia Music Hall. In the gray gloom the name
of Raquel Meller faded across a door marked with a scaling
gold star; the paraphernalia of a troupe of tumblers obstructed
the stairway. She mounted seven flights of stairs worn soft and
splintery with the insecure passage of many generations of
dancers and opened the studio door. The hydrangea blue of the
walls and the scrubbed floor hung from the skylight like the
basket of a balloon suspended in the ether. Effort and
aspiration, excitement, discipline, and an overwhelming
seriousness flooded the vast barn of a room. A muscular girl
stood in the centre of this atmosphere winding the ends of space
about the rigidity of her extended thigh. Round and round she
went, and, dropping the thrill of the exciting spiral to the low,
precise organization of a lullaby, brought herself to an orgastic
pause. She walked awkwardly across to Alabama.

'I have a lesson with Madame at three,' Alabama addressed
the girl in French. 'It was arranged by a friend.'

'She is coming soon,' the dancer said with an air of
mockery. 'You will get ready, perhaps?'

Alabama couldn't decide whether the girl was ridiculing the
world in general or Alabama in particular, or, perhaps,
herself.

123

'You have danced a long while?' asked the dancer.

'No. This is my first lesson.'

'Well, we all begin sometime,' said the girl tolerantly.

She twirled blindingly three or four times to end the conversation.

'This way,' she said, indicating her lack of interest in a novice. She showed Alabama into the vestibule.

Along the walls of the dressing room hung the long legs and rigid feet of flesh and black tights moulded in sweat to the visual image of the decisive tempos of Prokofiev and Sauguet, of Poulenc and Falla. The bright, explosive carnation of a ballet-skirt projected under the edges of a face towel. In a corner the white blouse and pleated skirt of Madame hung behind a faded gray curtain. The room reeked of hard work.

A Polish girl with hair like a copper-wire dishcloth and a purple, gnomish face bent over a straw chest sorting torn sheets of music and arranging a pile of discarded tunics. Odd toe shoes swung from the light. Turning the pages of a ragged Beethoven album, the Pole unearthed a faded photograph.

'I think it is her mother,' she said to the dancer.

The dancer inspected the picture proprietorily; she was the ballerina.

'I think, ma chère Stella, that it is Madame herself when she was young. I shall keep it!' She laughed lawlessly and authoritatively – she was the centre of the studio.

'No, Arienne Jeanneret. It is I who will keep it.'

'May I see the picture?' asked Alabama.

'It is certainly Madame herself.'

Arienne handed the picture to Alabama with a shrug of dismissal. Her motions had no continuity; she was utterly immobile between the spasmodic electric vibrations that propelled her body from one cataclysmic position to another.

The eyes of the picture were round and sad and Russian, a dreamy consciousness of its own white dramatic beauty gave the face weight and purpose as if the features were held together by spiritual will. The forehead was bound by a broad metallic strip after the fashion of a Roman charioteer. The hands posed in experimental organization on the shoulders.

'Is she not beautiful?' asked Stella.

124

'She's not un-American,' Alabama answered.

The woman reminded her obscurely of Joan; there was the same transparence about her sister that shone through the face in the picture like the blinding glow of a Russian winter. It was perhaps a kindred intensity of heat that had worn Joan to that thin external radiance.

The girl turned quickly, listening to the tired footsteps of some one hesitantly traversing the studio.

'Where have you found that old picture?' Madame's voice, broken with sensitivity, would have you believe that it was apologetic. Madame smiled. She was not humorless, but no manifestation of her emotions intruded on the white possessed mysticism of her face.

'In the Beethoven.'

'Before,' Madame said succinctly, 'I turned out the lights in my apartment and played Beethoven. My sitting room in Petrograd was yellow and always full of flowers. I said then to myself, "I am too happy. This cannot last."' She waved her hand resignedly and raised her eyes challengingly to Alabama.

'So my friend tells me you want to dance? Why? You have friends and money already.' The black eyes moved in frank childish inspection over Alabama's body, loose and angular as those silver triangles in an orchestra – over her broad shoulder blades and the imperceptible concavity of her long legs, fused together and controlled by the resilient strength of her thick neck. Alabama's body was like a quill.

'I have been to the Russian ballet,' Alabama tried to explain herself, 'and it seemed to me – Oh, I don't know! As if it held all the things I've always tried to find in everything else.'

'What have you seen?'

'*La Chatte*, Madame, I *must* do that some day!' Alabama replied impulsively.

A faint flicker of intrigued interest moved the black eyes recessionally. Then the personality withdrew from the face. Looking into her eyes was like walking through a long stone tunnel with a gray light shining at the other end, sloshing blindly through dank dripping earth over a moist curving bottom.

125

'You are too old. It is a beautiful ballet. Why have you come to me so late?'

'I didn't know before. I was too busy living.'

'And now you have done all your living?'

'Enough to be fed up,' laughed Alabama.

The woman moved quietly about amongst the appurtenances of the dance.

'We will see,' she said, 'make yourself ready.'

Alabama hastily dressed herself. Stella showed her about tying her toe shoes back of her ankle bones so the knot of the ribbon lay hid in a hollow.

'About *La Chatte*—' said the Russian.

'Yes?'

'You cannot do that. You must not build your hopes so high.'

The sign above the woman's head said, 'Do Not Touch the Looking Glass' in French, English, Italian, and Russian. Madame stood with her back to the huge mirror and gazed at the far corners of the room. There was no music as they began.

'You will have the piano when you have learned to control your muscles,' she explained. 'The only way, now that it is so late, is to think constantly of placing your feet. You must always stand with them *so*.' Madame spread her split satin shoes horizontally. 'And you must stretch *so* fifty times in the evenings.'

She pulled and twisted the long legs along the bar. Alabama's face grew red with effort. The woman was literally stripping the muscles of her thighs. She could have cried out with pain. Looking at Madame's smoky eyes and the red gash of her mouth, Alabama thought she saw malice in the face. She thought Madame was a cruel woman. She thought Madame was hateful and malicious.

'You must not rest,' Madame said. 'Continue.'

Alabama tore at her aching limbs. The Russian left her alone to work at the fiendish exercise. Reappearing, she sprayed herself unconcernedly before the glass with an atomizer.

'Fatiguée?' she called over her shoulder nonchalantly.

126

'Yes,' said Alabama.

'But you must not stop.'

After a while the Russian approached the bar.

'When I was a little girl in Russia,' she said impassively, 'I did four hundred of those every night.'

Rage rose in Alabama like the gurgling of gasoline in a visible tank. She hoped the contemptuous woman knew how much she hated her. 'I will do four hundred.'

'Luckily, the Americans are athletic. They have more natural talent than the Russians,' Madame remarked. 'But they are spoiled with ease and money and plenty of husbands. That is enough for today. You have some eau de Cologne?'

Alabama rubbed herself with the cloudy liquid from Madame's atomizer. She dressed amongst the confused startled eyes and naked bodies of a class which drifted in. The girls spoke hilariously in Russian. Madame invited her to wait and see the work.

A man sat sketching on a broken iron chair; two heavy bearded personages of the theatre pointed to first one, then another of the girls; a boy in black tights with his head in a bandana package and the face of a mythical pirate pulverized the air with ankle beats.

Mysteriously the ballet grouped itself. Silently it unfolded its mute clamor in the seductive insolence of black jetés, insouciant pas de chats, the abandon of many pirouettes, launched its fury in the spring and stretch of the Russian stchay, and lulled itself to rest in a sweep of cradling chassés. Nobody spoke. The room was as still as a cyclone centre.

'You like it?' said Madame implacably.

Alabama felt her face flush with a hot gush of embarrassment. She was very tired from her lesson. Her body ached and trembled. This first glimpse of the dance as an art opened up a world. 'Sacrilege!' she felt like crying out to the posturing abandon of the past as she thought ignominiously of *The Ballet of the Hours* that she had danced ten years before. She remembered unexpectedly the exaltation of swinging sideways down the pavements as a child and clapping her heels in the air. This was close to that old forgotten feeling that she couldn't stay on the earth another minute.

'I *love* it. What is it?'

The woman turned away. 'It is a ballet of mine about an amateur who wanted to join a circus,' she said. Alabama wondered how she'd thought those nebulous amber eyes were soft; they seemed to be infernally laughing at her. Madame went on: 'You will work again at three tomorrow.'

Alabama rubbed her legs with Elizabeth Arden muscle oil night after night. There were blue bruises inside above the knee where the muscles were torn. Her throat was so dry that at first she thought she had fever and took her temperature and was disappointed to find that she had none. In her bathing suit she tried to stretch on the high back of a Louis Quatorze sofa. She was always stiff, and she clutched the gilt flowers in pain. She fastened her feet through the bars of the iron bed and slept with her toes glued outwards for weeks. Her lessons were agony.

At the end of a month, Alabama could hold herself erect in ballet position, her weight controlled over the balls of her feet, holding the curve of her spine drawn tight together like the reins of a race horse and mashing down her shoulders till they felt as if they were pressed flat against her hips. The time moved by in spasmodic jumps like a school clock. David was glad of her absorption at the studio. It made them less inclined to use up their leisure on parties. Alabama's leisure was a creaky muscle-sore affair and better spent at home. David could work more freely when she was occupied and making fewer demands on his time.

At night she sat in the window too tired to move, consumed by a longing to succeed as a dancer. It seemed to Alabama that, reaching her goal, she would drive the devils that had driven her – that, in proving herself, she would achieve that peace which she imagined went only in surety of one's self – that she would be able, through the medium of the dance, to command her emotions, to summon love or pity or happiness at will, having provided a channel through which they might flow. She drove herself mercilessly, and the summer dragged on.

The heat of July beat on the studio skylight and Madame sprayed the air with disinfectant. The starch in Alabama's organdy skirts stuck to her hands and sweat rolled into her eyes till she couldn't see. Choking dust rose off the floor, the intense glare threw a black gauze before her eyes. It was humiliating that Madame should have to touch her pupil's ankles when they were so hot. The human body was very insistent. Alabama passionately hated her inability to discipline her own. Learning how to manage it was like playing a desperate game with herself. She said to herself, 'My body and I,' and took herself for an awful beating: that was how it was done. Some of the dancers worked with a bath towel pinned around their necks. It was so hot under the burning roof that they needed something to absorb the sweat. Sometimes the mirror swam in red heat waves if Alabama's lesson came at the hours when the direct sun fell on the glass overhead. Alabama was sick of moving her feet in the endless battements without music. She wondered why she came to her lessons at all: David had asked her to swim at Corne-Biche in the afternoon. She felt obscurely angry with Madame that she had not gone off in the cool with her husband. Though she did not believe that the careless happy passages of their first married life could be repeated – or relished if they were, drained as they had been of the experiences they held – still, the highest points of concrete enjoyment that Alabama visualized when she thought of happiness, lay in the memories they held.

'Will you pay attention?' Madame said. 'This is for you.' Madame moved across the floor mapping the plan of a simple adagio.

'I can't do it,' said Alabama. She began negligently, following the path of the Russian. Suddenly she stopped. 'Oh, but it is beautiful!' she said rapturously.

The ballet mistress did not turn around. 'There are many beautiful things in the dance,' she said laconically, 'but you cannot do them – yet.'

After her lesson, Alabama folded her soaking clothes into her valise. Arienne wrung out her tights in pools of sweat on the floor. Alabama held the ends while she squeezed and twisted. It cost a lot of sweat to learn to dance.

'I am going away for a month,' Madame said one Saturday.

'You can continue here with Mlle. Jeanneret. I hope that when I come back you will be able to have the music.'

'Then I can't have my lesson on Monday?' She had given so much of her time to the studio that it was like being precipitated into a void to think of life without it.

'With Mademoiselle.'

Alabama felt great hot tears rolling inexplicably down her face as she watched the tired figure of their teacher disappear into the dusty fog. She ought to be glad of the respite; she had expected to be glad.

'You must not cry,' the girl said to her kindly. 'Madame must go away for her heart to Royat.' She smiled gently at Alabama. 'We will get Stella to play for your lessons at once,' she said with the air of a conspirator.

Through the heat of August they worked. The leaves dried and decayed in the basin of St-Sulpice; the Champs-Elysées simmered in gasoline fumes. There was nobody in Paris; everybody said so. The fountains in the Tuileries threw off a hot vaporous mist; midinettes shed their sleeves. Alabama went twice a day to the studio. Bonnie was in Brittany visiting friends of Nanny. David drank with the crowds of people in the Ritz Bar celebrating the emptiness of the city together.

'Why will you never come out with me?' he said.

'Because I can't work next day if I do.'

'Are you under the illusion that you'll ever be any good at that stuff?'

'I suppose not; but there's only one way to try.'

'We have no life at home any more.'

'You're never there anyway – I've got to have something to do with myself.'

'Another female whine – I have to do my work.'

'I'll do anything you want.'

'Will you come with me this afternoon?'

They went to Le Bourget and hired an aeroplane. David drank so much brandy before they left that by the time they were over the Porte St-Denis he was trying to get the pilot to take them to Marseilles. When they got back to Paris he urged Alabama to get out with him at the Café Lilas. 'We'll find somebody and have dinner,' he said.

'David, I can't honestly. I get so sick when I drink. I'll have to have morphine if I do, like last time.'

'Where are you going?'

'I'm going to the studio.'

'Yet you can't stay with me! What's the use of having a wife? If a woman's only to sleep with there are plenty available for that—'

'What's the use of having a husband or anything else? You suddenly find you have them all the same, and there you are.'

The taxi whirred through the rue Cambon. Unhappily she climbed the steps. Arienne was waiting.

'What a sad face!' she said.

'Life is a sad business, isn't it, my poor Alabama?' said Stella.

When the preliminary routines at the bar were over, Alabama and Arienne moved to the centre of the floor.

'Bien, Stella.'

The sad coquetries of a Chopin mazurka fell flat on the parched air. Alabama watched Arienne searching for the mental processes of Madame. She seemed very squat and sordid. She was the première danseuse of the Paris Opéra, nearly at the top. Alabama began sobbing inaudibly.

'Lives aren't as hard as professions,' she gasped.

'Well,' Arienne cackled exasperated, 'this is not a pension de jeunes filles! Will you do the step your own way if you do not like the way I do?' She stood with her hands on her hips, powerful and uninspired, implying that Alabama's knowledge of the step's existence imposed on her the obligation to perform it. Somebody had to master the thing; it was there in the air. Arienne had put it there, let Arienne do it.

'It is for you, you know, that we work,' said Arienne harshly.

'My foot hurts,' said Alabama petulantly. 'The nail has come off.'

'Then you must grow a harder one. Will you begin? Dva, Stella!'

Miles and miles of pas de bourrée, her toes picking the floor like the beaks of many feeding hens, and after ten thousand miles you got to advance without shaking your breasts.

Arienne smelled of wet wool. Over and over she tried. Her ankles turned; her comprehension moved faster than her feet and threw her out of balance. She invented a trick: you must pull with your spirit against the forward motions of the body, and that gave you the tenebrous dignity and economy of effort known as style.

'But you are a *bête*, an *impossible*!' screeched Arienne. 'You wish to understand it before you can do it.'

Alabama finally taught herself what it felt like to move the upper part of her body along as if it were a bust on wheels. Her pas de bourrée progressed like a flying bird. She could hardly keep from holding her breath when she did it.

When David asked about her dancing she adopted a superior manner. She felt he couldn't have understood if she had tried to explain about the pas de bourrée. Once she did try. Her exposition had been full of 'You-see-what-I-means' and 'Can't-you-understands,' and David was annoyed and called her a mystic.

'Nothing exists that can't be expressed,' he said angrily.

'You are just dense. For me, it's quite clear.'

David wondered if Alabama had ever really understood any of his pictures. Wasn't any art the expression of the inexpressible? And isn't the inexpressible always the same, though variable – like the X in physics? It may represent anything at all, but at the same time, it's always actually X.

Madame came back during the September drouth.

'You have made much progress,' she said, 'but you must get rid of your American vulgarities. You surely sleep too much. Four hours is enough.'

'Are you better for your treatments?'

'They put me in a cabinet,' she laughed. 'I could only stay with somebody holding my hand. Rest is not *commode* for tired people. It is not good for artists.'

'It has been a cabinet here this summer,' said Alabama savagely.

'And you still want to dance *La Chatte*, poor?'

Alabama laughed. 'You will tell me,' she said, 'when I do well enough to buy myself a tutu?'

Madame shrugged her shoulders, 'Why not now?' she said.

'I'd like to be a fine dancer first.'

'You must work.'

'I work four hours a day.'

'It is too much.'

'Then how can I be a dancer?'

'I do not know how anybody can be anything,' said the Russian.

'I will burn candles to St. Joseph.'

'Perhaps that will help; a Russian saint would be better.'

During the last days of the hot weather David and Alabama moved to the Left Bank. Their apartment, tapestried in splitting yellow brocade, looked out over the dome of St-Sulpice. Old women hatched in the shadows about the corners of the cathedral; the bells tolled incessantly for funerals. The pigeons that fed in the square ruffled themselves on their window ledge. Alabama sat in the night breezes, holding her face to the succulent heavens, brooding. Her exhaustion slowed up her pulses to the tempo of her childhood. She thought of the time when she was little and had been near her father – by his aloof distance he had presented himself as an infallible source of wisdom, a bed of sureness. She could trust her father. She half hated the unrest of David, hating that of herself that she found in him. Their mutual experiences had formed them mutually into an unhappy compromise. That was the trouble: they hadn't thought they would have to make any adjustments as their comprehensions broadened their horizons, so they accepted those necessary reluctantly, as compromise instead of as change. They had thought they were perfect and opened their hearts to inflation but not alteration.

The air grew damp with autumn maze. They dined here and there amongst the jewelled women glittering like bright scaled fish in an aquarium. They went for walks and taxi rides. A growing feeling of alarm in Alabama for their relationship had tightened itself to a set determination to get on with her work. Pulling the skeleton of herself over a loom of attitude and arabesque she tried to weave the strength of her father and the young beauty of her first love with David, the happy oblivion of her teens and her warm protected childhood into a magic cloak. She was much alone.

David was a gregarious person; he went out a great deal. Their life moved along with a hypnotic pound and nothing seemed to matter short of murder. She presumed they wouldn't kill anybody – that would bring the authorities; all the rest was bunk, like Jacques and Gabrielle had been. She didn't care – she honestly didn't care a damn about the loneliness. Years later, she was surprised to remember that a person could have been so tired as she was then.

Bonnie had a French governess who poisoned their meals with 'N'est-ce pas, Monsieur?' and 'Du moins, j'aurais pensée.' She chewed with her mouth open and the crumbs of sardines about the gold fillings of her teeth nauseated Alabama. She ate staring out on the bare autumnal court. She would have got another governess, but something was sure to happen with things at such a tension and she thought she'd wait.

Bonnie was growing fast and full of anecdotes of Josette and Claudine and the girls at her school. She subscribed to a child's publication, outgrew the guignol and began to forget her English. A certain reserve manifested itself in her dealings with her parents. She was very superior with her old English-speaking Nanny, who took her out on the days of Mademoiselle's 'sortie': exciting days when the apartment reeked of Coty's L'Origan and Bonnie incurred eruptions on her face from the scones at Rumpelmayer's. Alabama could never make Nanny admit that Bonnie had eaten them; Nanny insisted the spots were in the blood and that it was better for them to come out, hinting at a sort of exorcising of hereditary evil spirits.

David bought Alabama a dog. They named him 'Adage.' The femme de chambre addressed him as 'Monsieur' and cried when he was spanked so nobody could ever house-train the beast. They kept him in the guest room with the photographic likenesses of the apartment owner's immediate family peering through the fumes of his saleté.

Alabama felt very sorry for David. He and she appeared to her like people in a winter of adversity picking over old garments left from a time of wealth. They repeated themselves to each other; she dragged out old expressions that she knew

134

he must be tired of; he bore her little show with a patent mechanical appreciation. She felt sorry for herself. She had always been so proud of being a good stage manager.

November filtered the morning light to a golden powder that hung over Paris stabilizing time till the days stayed at morning all day long. She worked in the gray gloom of the studio and felt very professional in the discomfort of the unheated place. The girls dressed by an oil stove that Alabama bought for Madame; the dressing room reeked of glue from the toe shoes warming over the thin blaze, of stale eau de Cologne, and of poverty. When Madame was late, the dancers warmed themselves by doing a hundred relevés to the chanted verses of Verlaine. The windows could never be opened because of the Russians, and Nanny and May, who had worked with Pavlova, said the smell made them sick. May lived at the Y.W.C.A. and wanted Alabama to come to tea. One day, as they were going down the steps together, she said to Alabama that she could not dance any more, that she was quite sick.

'Madame's ears are so filthy, my dear,' she said, 'it makes me quite sick.'

Madame had made May dance behind the others. Alabama laughed at the girl's disingenuousness.

There was Marguerite, who came in white, and Fania in her dirty rubber undergarments, and Anise and Anna who lived with millionaires and dressed in velvet tunics, and Céza in gray and scarlet – they said she was a Jew – and somebody else in blue organdie, and thin girls in apricot draperies like folds of skin, and three Tanyas like all the other Russian Tanyas, and girls in the starkness of white who looked like boys in swimming, and girls in black who looked like women, a superstitious girl in mauve, and one dressed by her mother who wore cerise to blind them all in that pulsating gyroscope, and the thin pathetic femininity of Marte who danced at the Opéra Comique and swept off belligerently after classes with her husband.

Arienne Jeanneret dominated the vestibule. She dressed with her face to the wall and had many preparations for rubbing herself and bought fifty pairs of toe-slippers at a time, which she gave to Stella when she'd worn them a week. She kept the girls quiet when Madame was giving a lesson. The vulgarity of her hips repelled Alabama but they were good friends. It was with Arienne that she sat in the café under the Olympia after their lessons and drank the daily Cap Corse with seltzer. Arienne took her backstage at the Opéra where the dancer was well-respected, and Arienne came to lunch with Alabama. David hated her guts because she tried to give him moral lectures about his opinions and his drinking, but she was not bourgeoise: she was gamine, full of strident jokes about firemen and soldiers, and Montmartre songs about priests and peasants and cuckolds. She was almost an elf, but her stockings were always wrinkled and she talked in sermons.

She took Alabama to see Pavlova's last performance. Two men like Beerbohm cartoons asked to see them home. Arienne refused.

'Who are they?' asked Alabama.

'I do not know – subscribers to the Opéra.'

'Then why do you talk to them if you've never met them?'

'One does not meet the patrons of the first three rows of the National Opéra; the seats are reserved for men,' said Arienne. She herself lived with her brother near the Bois. Sometimes she cried in the dressing room.

'Zambelli still dancing *Coppélia*!' she'd say. 'You don't know how difficult life is, Alabama, you with your husband and your baby.' When she cried the black came off her eyelashes and dried in lumps like a wet water-color. There was a spiritual open space between her gray eyes that seemed as pure as an open daisy field.

'Oh, *Arienne*!' said Madame enthusiastically. 'There's a dancer! When she cries it is not for nothing.' Alabama's face grew colorless with fatigue and her eyes sank in her head like the fumes of autumnal fires.

Arienne helped her to master the entrechats.

'You must not rest when you come down after the spring,' she said, 'but you must depart again immediately, so that the impetus of the first leap carries you through the others like the bouncing of a ball.'

'Da,' said Madame, 'da! da! – But it is not enough.' It was never enough to please Madame.

She and David slept late on Sundays, dining at Foyot's or some place near their home.

'We promised your mother to come home for Christmas,' he said over many tables.

'Yes, but I don't see how we can go. It's so expensive, and you haven't finished your Paris pictures.'

'I'm glad you are not too disappointed because I had decided to wait until spring.'

'There's Bonnie's school, too. It would be a shame to switch just now.'

'We'll go for Easter, then.'

'Yes.'

Alabama did not want to leave Paris where they were so unhappy. Her family grew very remote with the distention of her soul in stchay and pirouette.

Stella brought a Christmas cake to the studio, and two chickens for Madame that she had received from her uncle in Normandy. Her uncle wrote her that he could send no more money: the franc was down to forty. Stella made her living copying sheet music, which ruined her eyes and left her starving. She lived in a garret and got sinus trouble from the drafts, but she would not give up wasting her days at the studio.

'What can a Pole do in Paris?' she said to Alabama. What can anybody do in Paris? When it comes to fundamentals, nationalities do not count for much.

Madame got Stella a job turning pages for musicians at concerts, and Alabama paid her ten francs a pair for darning her toe shoes on the ends to keep them from slipping.

Madame kissed them all on both cheeks for Christmas, and they ate Stella's cake. It was as much of a Christmas as she would have at their apartment, thought Alabama without emotion – that was because she hadn't put any interest into their Christmas at home.

Arienne sent Bonnie an expensive kitchen outfit as a present. Alabama was touched when she thought how her friend probably needed the money it cost. Nobody had any money.

'I shall have to give up my lessons,' said Arienne. 'The pigs at the Opéra pay us a thousand francs a month. I cannot live on it.'

Alabama invited Madame to dinner and to see a ballet. Madame was very white and fragile in a pale-green evening dress. Her eyes were fixed on the stage. A pupil of hers was dancing *Le lac des Cygnes*. Alabama wondered what passed behind those yellow Confucian eyes as she watched the white sifting stream of the ballet.

'It is much too small nowadays,' the woman said. 'When I danced things were of a different scale.'

Alabama looked incredulous. 'Twenty-four fouettés, she did,' she said. 'What more can anybody do?' It had physically hurt her to see the ethereal steely body of the dancer snapping and whipping itself in the mad convolutions of those turns.

'I do not know what they can do. I only know that I did something else,' said the artist, 'that was better.'

She did not go backstage after the performance to congratulate the girl. She and Alabama and David went to a Russian cabaret. At the table next to theirs sat Hernandara trying to fill a pyramid of champagne glasses by pouring into the top one only. David joined him; the two men sang and shadow-boxed on the dance floor. Alabama was ashamed and afraid that Madame would be offended.

But Madame had been a princess in Russia with all the other Russians.

'They are like puppies playing,' she said. 'Leave them. It is pretty.'

'Work is the only pretty thing,' said Alabama, '—at least, I have forgotten the rest.'

'It is good to amuse oneself when one can afford it,' Madame spoke reminiscently. 'In Spain, after a ballet, I drank red wine. In Russia it was always champagne.'

Through the blue lights of the place and the red lamps in iron grilles, the white skin of Madame glowed like the arctic sun on an ice palace. She did not drink much but ordered caviar and smoked many cigarettes. Her dress was cheap; that saddened Alabama – she had been such a great dancer in her time. After the war she had wanted to quit, but she had no money and kept her son at the Sorbonne. Her husband fed himself on dreams of the Corps des Pages and quenched his thirst with reminiscences till there was nothing left of him but a bitter aristocratic phantom. The Russians! suckled on a gallant generosity and weaned on the bread of revolution, they haunt Paris! Everything haunts Paris. Paris is haunted.

Nanny came to Bonnie's Christmas tree, and some friends of David's. Alabama thought dispassionately of Christmas in America. They did not sell little frosted houses to hang on Christmas trees in Alabama. In Paris the florists' were filled with Christmas lilacs, and it rained. Alabama took flowers to the studio.

Madame was enraptured.

'When I was a girl, I was a miser for flowers,' she said. 'I loved the flowers of the fields and gathered them in bouquets and boutonnières for the guests who came to my father's house.' These little details from the past of so great a dancer seemed glamorous and poignant to Alabama.

By springtime, she was gladly, savagely proud of the strength of her Negroid hips, convex as boats in a wood carving. The complete control of her body freed her from all fetid consciousness of it.

The girls carried away their dirty clothes to wash them. There was heat incubating again in the rue des Capucines and another set of acrobats at the Olympia. The thin sunshine laid pale commemoration tablets on the studio floor, and Alabama was promoted to Beethoven. She and Arienne kidded along the windy streets and roughhoused in the studio, and Alabama drugged herself with work. Her life outside was like trying to remember in the morning a dream from the night before.

II

'Fifty-one, fifty-two, fifty-three – but I tell you, Monsieur, you must give me the message. I occupy the position of the advisor of Madame – fifty-four, fifty-five—'

Hastings surveyed the panting body coldly. Stella lapsed

into a technically seductive attitude. She had often seen Madame behave just so. She stared into his face as if she were in possession of some vital secret, and awaited his application for an introduction to the mystery. Her petits battements had been well done. She was quite 'réchauffé' for so early in the afternoon.

'It was Mrs. David Knight that I wanted to see,' said Hastings.

'Our Alabama! She will surely be here before long. She is a dear, Alabama,' cooed Stella.

'There was nobody at home at the apartment, so they told me to come here.' Hastings' eyes roved about incredulously as if there must be some mistake.

'Oh, she!' said Stella. 'She is always here. You have only to wait. If Monsieur will excuse me—?'

Fifty-seven, fifty-eight, fifty-nine. At three hundred and eighty Hastings rose to leave. Stella sweated and blew like a porpoise making believe she hated the difficulties of the self-imposed bar work. She made believe she was a beautiful galley-slave whom Hastings might possibly be wanting to purchase.

'Just tell her I came, will you?' he said.

'Of course, and that you went away. I am sorry that what I can do is not more interesting for Monsieur. There is a class at five if Monsieur would care to—'

'Yes, tell her I went away.' He stared about him distastefully. 'I don't suppose she'd be free for a party, anyway.'

Stella had been so much in the studio that she had absorbed an air of complete confidence in her work like all the pupils of Madame. If people who watched were not fascinated, it must be some lack in themselves of æsthetic appreciation.

Madame allowed Stella to work without paying; many dancers did the same who had no money. When there was money they paid – that was the Russian system.

The crash of a suitcase bumping up the stairs announced the arrival of a student.

'A friend has called,' she said importantly. It was inconceivable to the isolated Stella that a visit could be without consequence. Alabama, too, was forgetting the old casual

140

modulations of life. Against the violent twist and thump of tour jeté nothing stood out but the harshest, most dissonant incident.

'What did they want?'

'How should I know?'

A vague unreasoning dread filled Alabama – she must keep the studio apart from her life – otherwise one would soon become as unsatisfactory as the other, lost in an aimless, impenetrable drift.

'Stella,' she said, 'if they should come again – if any one should come here for me, you will always say you don't know anything about me – that I am not here.'

'But why? It is for the appreciation of your friends that you will dance.'

'No, no!' Alabama protested. 'I cannot do two things at once – I wouldn't go down the Avenue de l'Opéra leaping over the traffic cop with pas de chat, and I don't want my friends rehearsing bridge games in the corner while I dance.'

Stella was glad to share in any personal reactions to life, that side of her own being an empty affair boxed by attics and berated by landladies.

'Very well! Why should life interfere with us artists?' she agreed pompously.

'Last time he was here my husband smoked a cigarette in the studio,' continued Alabama in an attempt to justify the clandestine protestations.

'Oh,' Stella was scandalized. 'I see. If I had been here, I would have told him about the awfulness of smells when one is working.'

Stella dressed herself in the worn-out ballet skirts of other dancers and pink gauze shirts from the Galeries Lafayette. She pinned the shirt down over the yoke of the skirt with big safety-pins to form a basque. She lived at the studio during the day, clipping the stems of the flowers the pupils brought Madame to keep them fresh, polishing the great mirror, repairing the music with strips of adhesive, and playing for lessons when the pianist was absent. She thought of herself as councillor to Madame. Madame thought of her as a nuisance.

Stella was very conscientious about earning her lessons. If

any one else tried to do the smallest thing for Madame, it precipitated a scene of sulks and weeping. Her dreamy Polish eyes were faded to the yellowish green of scum on a stagnant pool by the glaze of starvation and intensity. The girls bought her croissants and café au lait at midday and called her 'ma chère.' Alabama and Arienne gave her money on one pretext or another. Madame gave her old clothes and cakes. In return she told them each separately that Madame had said they were making more progress than the others and juggled the working hours in Madame's little book so that her eight-hour day sometimes held nine or ten one-hour periods. Stella lived in an air of general intrigue.

Madame was severe with the girl. 'You know you can never dance, why do you not get work to do?' she scolded. 'You will be old, I will be old – then what will become of you?'

'I have a concert next week. I will have twenty francs for turning pages. Oh, Madame, please let me stay!'

No sooner had Stella the twenty francs than she approached Alabama. 'If you would give me the rest,' she pleaded, persuasively, 'we could buy a medicine cabinet for the studio. Only last week some one turned an ankle – we should have means to disinfect our blisters.' Stella talked incessantly about the cabinet until Alabama went with her one morning to get it. They waited in the golden sunshine crystallizing the gilt front of Au Printemps for the store to open. The thing cost a hundred francs and was to be a surprise for Madame.

'You may give it to her, Stella,' said Alabama, 'but I am going to pay. You cannot afford such an extravagance.'

'No,' mourned Stella, 'I have no husband to pay for me! Hélas!'

'I give up other things,' Alabama replied crossly. She couldn't feel resentment against the misshapen, melancholy Pole.

Madame was displeased.

'It is ridiculous,' she said. 'There is not room for so bulky an affair in the dressing room.' When she saw Stella's frantic eyes, gluey with disappointment, she added, 'But it will be very convenient. Leave it. Only you must not spend your money on me.'

She delegated to Alabama the job of seeing that Stella bought her no more presents.

Madame argued over the dried raisins and licorice bonbons that Stella brought to leave on her table and about the Russian bread she brought in little packages; bread with cheese cooked inside and bread with sugar pellets, caraway bread and glutinous black tragedian breads, breads hot from the oven smelling of innocence, and mouldy epicurean breads from Yiddish bakeries. Anything Stella had money to buy, she bought for Madame.

Instead of curbing Stella, Alabama absorbed the aimless extravagance of the girl. She couldn't wear new shoes; her feet were too sore. It seemed a crime owning new dresses to smell them up with eau de Cologne and leave them hanging all day long against the studio walls. She thought she could work better when she felt poor. She had abandoned so many of the occasions of exercising personal choice that she spent the hundred-franc notes in her purse on flowers, endowing them with all the qualities of the things she might have bought under other circumstances, the thrill of a new hat, the assurance of a new dress.

Yellow roses she bought with her money like Empire satin brocade, and white lilacs and pink tulips like moulded confectioner's frosting, and deep-red roses like a Villon poem, black and velvety as an insect wing, cold blue hydrangeas clean as a newly calcimined wall, the crystalline drops of lily of the valley, a bowl of nasturtiums like beaten brass, anemones pieced out of wash material, and malignant parrot tulips scratching the air with their jagged barbs, and the voluptuous scrambled convolutions of Parma violets. She bought lemon-yellow carnations perfumed with the taste of hard candy, and garden roses purple as raspberry puddings, and every kind of white flower the florist knew how to grow. She gave Madame gardenias like white kid gloves and forget-me-nots from the Madeleine stalls, threatening sprays of gladioli, and the soft, even purr of black tulips. She bought flowers like salads and flowers like fruits, jonquils and narcissus, poppies and ragged robins, and flowers with the brilliant carnivorous qualities of Van Gogh. She chose from windows filled with metal balls and cactus gardens of the florists near the rue de la Paix, and from the florists uptown who sold mostly plants and purple iris, and from florists on the Left Bank whose shops were lumbered up with the wire frames of designs, and from outdoor markets where the peasants dyed their roses to a bright apricot, and stuck wires through the heads of the dyed peonies.

Spending money had played a big part in Alabama's life before she had lost, in her work, the necessity for material possessions.

Nobody was rich at the studio but Nordika. She came to her lessons in a Rolls-Royce, sharing her hours with Alacia, who had the same essence as a Bryn Mawr graduate, she was so practical. It was Alacia who took His Highness away from Nordika, but Nordika hung on to the money and they made a go of it together some way. Nordika was the pretty one like a blonde ejaculation, and Alacia was the one who had moved Milord to pity. Nordika was tremulous with a glassy excitement that she tried to repress – they said in the ballet that Nordika's excitement ruined all of her costumes. Nordika couldn't go around vibrating in a void so her friend managed to anchor her feet enough to the ground to keep the car. Both of them threatened to leave Madame's studio because Stella hid a half-eaten can of shrimp behind their mirror, where it slowly soured. Stella said to the girls that the smell was dirty clothes. When they found what it really was, they were merciless to poor Stella. Stella liked having the chic Nordika and her friend in the class because they were almost the same as an audience.

'Polissonne!' they said to Stella. 'It is bad enough to eat shrimp at home without bringing it here like a stink bomb.'

Stella had so little room at home that she had to keep her trunk jammed out the attic window half in the open. A can of shrimp would have asphyxiated her in the small place.

'Don't mind,' said Alabama. 'I will take you to Prunier's for shrimp.'

Madame said Alabama was a fool to take Stella to Prunier's for shrimp. Madame could remember the days when she and her husband had eaten caviar together in the butchery fumes

144

of the rue Duphot. Forever, to Madame, a presage of disaster lay in the conjured image of the oyster bar – revolutions would almost certainly follow excursions to Prunier's, and poverty and hard times. Madame was superstitious; she never borrowed pins and had never danced in purple, and she somehow thought of trouble in connection with the fish she had loved so well when she could afford it. Madame was very afraid of any luxury.

The saffron in the bouillabaisse made Alabama sweat under the eyes and turned the Barsac tasteless. During the lunch Stella fidgeted across the table and folded something into her napkin. The girl was not as impressed as Alabama would have liked with Prunier's.

'Barsac is a monkish wine,' suggested Alabama absently.

Secretively Stella extracted whatever it was she dredged from the bottomless soup. She was too engrossed to answer. She was as absorbed as a person searching for a dead body.

'What on earth are you doing, ma chère?' It irritated Alabama that Stella was not more enthusiastic. She resolved never to take another poor person to a rich man's place; it was a waste of money.

'Sh – sh – sh! Ma chère Alabama, it is pearls I have found – big ones, as many as three! If the waiters know they will claim them for the establishment, so I make a cache in my napkin.'

'Really,' asked Alabama, 'show me!'

'When we are in the street. I assure you it is so. We will grow rich, and you will have a ballet and I will dance in it.'

The girls finished their lunch breathlessly. Stella was too excited to make her usual senseless protestations about paying the check.

In the pale filtrations of the street they opened the napkin carefully.

'We will buy Stella a present,' she crowed.

Alabama inspected the globular yellow deposits.

'They're only lobster eyes,' she pronounced decisively.

'How should I know? I have never eaten lobsters before,' said Stella phlegmatically.

Imagine living your life with your only hope of finding pearls and fortunes and the unexpected stewed in the heart of

145

a bouillabaisse! It was like being a child and keeping your eyes forever glued to the ground looking for a lost penny – only children do not have to buy bread and raisins and medicine cabinets with the pennies they find on the pavement!

Alabama's lessons began the day at the studio.

In the cold barracks the maid scrubbed and coughed. The woman rubbed her fingers unfeelingly through the flame of the oil stove, pinching the wick.

'The poor woman!' said Stella, 'she has a husband who beats her at night – she has showed me the places – her husband has no jaw-bone since the war. We should give her something, perhaps?'

'Don't *tell* me about it, Stella! We can't be sorry for everybody.'

It was too late – Alabama had already noticed the caked black blood under the woman's fingernails where they were split by the stiff brush in her freezing pail of eau de Javelle. She gave her ten francs and hated the woman for making her sorry. It was bad enough working in the cold asthmatic dust without knowing about the maid.

Stella broke the thorns from the rose stems and gathered the shattered petals off the floor. She and Alabama shivered and worked quickly to get warm.

'Show me again how Madame has shown you in your private lessons,' urged Stella.

Alabama went over and over for her the breathless contraction and muscular abandon necessary to attain elevation. You did the same thing for years, and after three years you might lift yourself an inch higher – of course, there was always the chance that you wouldn't.

'And you must, after the effort of launching your body is accomplished, let it fall in mid-air – this way.' She heaved her body with a stupendous inflation off the floor and came to rest limply, like a deflated balloon.

'Oh, but you will be a dancer!' the girl sighed gratefully, 'but I do not see *why*, since you have already a husband.'

'Can't you understand that I am not trying to get anything – at least, I don't think I am – but to get rid of some of myself?'

'Then why?'

'To sit this way, expectant of my lesson, and feel that if I had not come the hour that I own would have stood vacant and is waiting for me.'

'Is your husband not angry that you are so much away?'

'Yes. He is so angry that I must be away even more to avoid rows about it.'

'He does not like the dance?'

'Nobody does, only dancers and sadists.'

'Incorrigible! Teach me again about the jeté.'

'You cannot do it – you are too fat.'

'Teach me and I shall be able to play it on the piano for your lessons.'

When anything went wrong with the adagio, in silent and controlled rage, Alabama blamed the girl.

'You hear something far away,' said Madame, suggesting.

Alabama could not manage to convey hearing with the lines of her body. She was humiliated to listen with her hips.

'I hear only Stella's discords,' she whispered fiercely. 'She does not keep time.'

Madame withdrew herself when her pupils quarrelled.

'A dancer's supposed to lead the music,' she said succinctly. 'There is no melody in ballet.'

One afternoon David came with some old friends.

Alabama was angry with Stella when she saw him there.

'My lessons are not a circus. Why did you let them come in?'

'It was your *husband*! I cannot stand in front of the door like a dragon.'

'Failli, cabriole, cabriole, failli, soubresaut, failli, coupé, ballonné, ballonné, ballonné, pas de basque, deux tours.'

'Isn't that "Tales from the Vienna Woods"?' asked the tall chic Dickie, smoothing herself over.

'I don't see why Alabama didn't take from Ned Weyburn,' said the elegant Miss Douglas with her hair like a porphyry tomb.

The yellow sun of the afternoon poured a warm vanilla sauce in the window. 'Failli, cabriole,' Alabama bit her tongue.

Running to the window to spit the quick blood, she was

overwhelmingly conscious of the woman beside her. The blood trickled down her chin.

'What is it, chérie?'

'Nothing.'

Miss Douglas said indignantly, 'I think it's ridiculous to work like that. She can't be getting any fun out of it, foaming at the mouth that way!'

Dickie said, 'It's abominable! She'll never be able to get up in a drawing room and do *that*! What's the good of it?'

Alabama had never felt so close to a purpose as she did at that moment. 'Cabriole, failli' – 'Why' was something the Russian understood and Alabama almost understood. She felt she would know when she could listen with her arms and see with her feet. It was incomprehensible that her friends should feel only the necessity to hear with their ears. That was 'Why.' Fierce loyalty to her work swelled in Alabama. Why did she need to explain?

'We'll meet you at the corner in the bistro,' said David's note.

'You will join your friends?' Madame asked disinterestedly as Alabama read.

'No,' answered Alabama abruptly.

The Russian sighed. 'Why not?'

'Life is too sad, and I will be too dirty after my lesson.'

'What will you do at home alone?'

'Sixty fouettés.'

'Do not forget the pas de bourrée.'

'Why can I not have the same steps as Arienne,' stormed Alabama, 'or at least as Nordika? Stella says that I dance nearly as well.'

So Madame led her through the intricacies of the waltz from *Pavillon d'Armide*, and Alabama knew that she did the thing like a child jumping rope.

'You see,' said Madame, 'not yet! It is difficult to dance for Diaghilev.'

Diaghilev called his rehearsals at eight in the morning. His dancers left the theatre around one at night. From the requisite work with their maître de ballet they came direct to the studio. Diaghilev insisted that they live at so much nervous tension that movement, which meant dancing to them, became a necessity, like a drug. They worked incessantly.

One day there was a wedding in his troupe. Alabama was surprised to see the girls in street clothes, in furs and shadow lace as they congregated at the studio. They appeared older; there was a distinction about them that came from the consciousness of their beautiful bodies even in their cheap clothes. If they weighed more than fifty kilos, Diaghilev protested in his high screeching voice, 'You must get thin. I cannot send my dancers to a gymnasium to fit them for adagio.' He never thought of the women as dancers, except the stars. An allegiance to his genius as strong as a cult determined all their opinions. The quality that set them off from other dancers was his insistence on their obliteration of self to the integral purpose of his ballet. There was no *petite marmite* in his productions, nor in the people that he produced out of ragged Russian waifs, some of them. They lived for the dance and their master.

'What are you doing with your face?' Madame would say scathingly. 'It is not a cinema we are making. You will please to keep it as expressionless as you can.'

'Race, dva, tree, race, dva, tree—'

'Show me, Alabama,' Stella cried in despair.

'How can I show you? I can't do it myself,' she answered irritably. She was angry when Stella placed her in the same class with herself. She said to herself that she would give Stella no more money to teach her her place. But the girl came to her tearfully smelling of butter and the mechanics of life, offering an apple she had bought for Alabama or a sack of mint tips, and Alabama gave her ten francs anyway, to pay for the apple.

'If you were not here,' Stella said, 'how could I live? My uncle can send me no more money.'

'How can you live when I have gone to America?'

'Other people will come – perhaps from America.' Stella smiled improvidently. Though she talked a great deal about the difficulties of the future, it was impossible for her to think further ahead than a day.

Maleena came to give Stella money. She wanted to open a studio of her own, and she offered Stella the job as her pianist if she could get enough pupils away from the classes of Madame. It was Maleena's mother who wanted to do the dishonest thing – she had herself been a dancer but not a big one.

The mother was as bloated as the delicatessen sausages that kept her alive, and half-blinded by the vicissitudes of life. In her pudgy, greasy hands she held a lorgnette and peered at her daughter. 'See,' she said to Stella. 'Pavlova cannot do "sauts sur les pointes" like that! There is no dancer like my Maleena. You will get your friends to come to our studio?'

Maleena was chicken-breasted; she performed the dance like a person administering lashes with a scourge.

'Maleena is like a flower,' the old lady said. When Maleena perspired she smelled of onions. Maleena pretended that she loved Madame. She was an old pupil – her mother thought Madame should have got her a job with the Russian ballet.

In watering the floor before class the watering-can slipped in Stella's hands and drenched the parquet over Maleena's place in line. She did not dare complain imagining that Madame would suspect her hostility.

'Failli, cabriole, cabriole, failli—'

Maleena slipped in the puddle and split her kneecap.

'I knew our chest would be useful,' said Stella. 'You will help me with the bandage, Alabama.'

'—Race, Dva, Tree!'

'The roses are dead,' Stella reminded Alabama reproachfully. She begged for the old organdy skirts which would not meet across her back and gapped scandalously over her dingy tights. Alabama had them made with four ruffles on a broad band that bound her hips – five francs it cost to get them ironed in a French laundry. There was a red-and-white check for weather like Normandy, a chartreuse for decadent days, pink for her lessons at midday, and sky blue for late afternoon. In the mornings she liked white skirts best to match the colorless reflection on the skylight.

For the waist she bought cotton bicycle shirts and faded them in the sun to pastel shades, burnt orange to wear over the pink, green for the pale chartreuse. It was a game to Alabama discovering new combinations. The habitual flamboyance expressed in her street dress flowered in this less restricted medium. She wore a chosen color for every mood.

David complained that her room smelled of eau de Cologne. There was always a pile of dirty clothes from the studio dumped in the corner. The voluminous ruffles of the skirts wouldn't fit in the closets or drawers. She wore herself to a frazzle, and didn't notice about the room.

Bonnie came in one day to say good morning. Alabama was late; it was half-past seven; the damp of the night air had taken the stiffening out of her skirt. She turned crossly to Bonnie. 'You haven't brushed your teeth this morning,' she said irritably.

'Oh, but I have!' said the little girl defiantly, angry at her mother's suspicion. 'You told me to always before I did anything in the mornings.'

'I told you to, so you just thought you wouldn't today. I can see the brioche still on the front ones,' Alabama pursued.

'I did so brush them.'

'Don't lie to me, Bonnie,' said her mother angrily.

'It's you who's a lie!' flared Bonnie recklessly.

'Don't you dare say that to me!' Alabama grabbed the small arms and slapped the child soundly over the thighs. The short explosive sound warned her that she had used more force than she had intended. She and her daughter stared at each other's red reproachful faces.

'I'm sorry,' said Alabama pathetically. 'I didn't mean to hurt you.'

'Then why did you slap me?' protested the child, full of resentment.

'I meant to make it just hard enough to show you that you have to pay for being wrong.' She did not believe what she said, but she had to offer some explanation.

Alabama hastily left the apartment. On her way past Bonnie's door down the corridor she paused.

'Mademoiselle?'

'Oui, Madame?'

'Did Bonnie brush her teeth this morning?'

'Naturally! Madame has left orders that that is to be tended to first thing on rising, though I personally think it spoils the enamel—'

'Damn it,' said Alabama viciously to herself, 'there were nevertheless crumbs. What can I say to make up to Bonnie for the sense of injustice she must have?'

Nanny brought Bonnie to the studio one afternoon when Mademoiselle was out. The dancers spoiled her dreadfully; Stella gave her candy and sweets, and Bonnie choked and sputtered, rubbing her hands through the melted chocolate that plastered her mouth, Alabama had been so severe about her not making a noise that the child tried not to cough. Stella led the little red-faced, gasping girl into the vestibule, patting her over the back.

'You will dance also,' she said, 'when you are bigger?'

'No,' said Bonnie emphatically, 'it is too "sérieuse" to be the way Mummy is. She was nicer before.'

'Madam,' said Nanny, 'I was really astonished at how well you do, really. You do nearly as well as the others. I wonder if I should like it – it must be very good for you.'

'Lord,' Alabama said infuriated.

'We must all have something to do, and Madam never plays bridge,' persisted Nanny.

'We get something to do and as soon as we've got it, it gets us.' Alabama wanted to say 'Shut up!'

'Isn't that always the way?'

When David suggested coming again to the studio Alabama protested.

'Why not?' he said, 'I should think you would want me to see you practice.'

'You wouldn't understand,' she answered egotistically. 'You will just see that I am given only the things I can't do and discourage me.'

The dancers worked always beyond their strength.

'Why "déboulé"?' Madame expostulated. 'You do that already – passably.'

'You're so thin,' said David patronizingly. 'There's no use killing yourself. I hope that you realize that the biggest

152

difference in the world is between the amateur and the professional in the arts.'

'You might mean yourself and me—' she said thoughtfully.

He exhibited her to his friends as if she were one of his pictures.

'Feel her muscle,' he said. Her body was almost their only point of contact.

The saillants of her sparse frame glowed with the gathering despair of fatigue that lit her interiorly.

David's success was his own – he had earned his right to be critical – Alabama felt that she had nothing to give to the world and no way to dispose of what she took away.

The hope of entering Diaghilev's ballet loomed before her like a protecting cathedral.

'You're not the first person who's ever tried to dance,' David said. 'You don't need to be so sanctimonious about it.'

Alabama was despondent, nourishing her vanity on the questionable fare of Stella's liberal flattery.

Stella was the butt of the studio. The girls, angry and jealous of each other, took out their spite and ill-temper on the clumsy, massive Pole. She made such an effort to please that she was always in the way of everybody – she flattered them all.

'I can't find my new tights – four hundred francs they cost,' flared Arienne. 'I have not got four hundred francs to throw from the window! There have never been thieves before in the studio.' She glared at the dancers and fixed on Stella.

Madame was called to quell the rising insults. Stella had put the tights in Nordika's chest. Nordika said angrily that she would have to have her tunics dry-cleaned; it was unnecessary, her saying that; Arienne was immaculate.

It was Stella who placed Kira behind Arienne that she might better learn by imitating the fine technician. Kira was a beautiful girl with long brown hair, and high voluptuous curves. She was a protégée – nobody knew of whom, but she was unable to move without supervision.

'Kira!' shrieked Arienne, 'will spoil my dancing! She sleeps at the bar and sleeps on the floor. You would think this is a rest-cure!'

Kira's voice was cracked. 'Arienne,' she wheedled, 'you will help me with my batterie?'

'You have no batterie,' stormed Arienne, 'outside of a batterie de cuisine, perhaps, and I would have Stella know that I form my own protégées.'

When Stella had to tell Kira to move farther down the bar, Kira cried and went to Madame.

'What has Stella to do with where I stand?'

'Nothing,' answered Madame, 'but since she lives here, you must not notice her more than the walls.'

Madame never said much. She seemed to expect the girls to quarrel. Sometimes she discussed the qualities of yellow or cerise or Mendelssohn. Inevitably the sense of her words was lost for Alabama, drifting off into that dark mournful harvest of the tides of the sea of Marmara, the Russian language.

Madame's brown eyes were like the purple bronze footpaths through an autumn beech wood where the mold is drenched with mist, and clear fresh lakes spurt up about your feet from the loam. The classes swayed to the movements of her arms like an anchored buoy to the tides. Saying almost nothing in that ghoulish Eastern tongue, the girls were all musicians and understood that Madame was exhausted with their self-assertion when the pianist began the pathetic lullaby from the entre'acte of *Cleopatra*; that the lesson was going to be interesting and hard when she played Brahms. Madame seemed to have no life outside her work, to exist only when she was composing.

'Where does Madame live, Stella?' asked Alabama curiously.

'But, ma chère, the studio is her home,' said Stella, 'for us anyway.'

Alabama's lesson was interrupted one day by men with measuring rods. They came and paced the floor and made laborious estimates and calculations. They came again at the end of the week.

'What is it?' said the girls.

'We will have to move, chéries,' Madame answered sadly. 'They are making a moving-picture studio of my place here.'

At her last lesson, Alabama searched behind the dismantled

154

segments of the mirror for lost pirouettes, for the ends of a thousand arabesques.

There was nothing but thick dust, and the traces of hairpins rusted to the walls where the huge frame had hung.

'I thought I might find something,' she explained shyly, when she saw Madame looking at her curiously.

'And you see there is nothing!' said the Russian, opening her hands. 'But in my new studio you may have a tutu,' she added. 'You asked me to tell you. Perhaps in its folds, who knows what you may find.'

The fine woman was sad to leave those faded walls so impregnated with her work.

Alabama had sweated to soften the worn floor, worked with the fever of bronchitis to appease the drafts in winter, candles were burning at St-Sulpice. She hated to leave, too.

She and Stella and Arienne helped Madame to move her piles of old abandoned skirts, worn toe shoes, and discarded trunks. As she and Arienne and Stella sorted and arranged these things redolent of the struggle for plastic beauty, Alabama watched the Russian.

'Well?' said Madame. 'Yes, it is very sad,' she said implacably.

III

The high corners of the new studio in the Russian Conservatory carved the light to a diamond's facets.

Alabama stood alone with her body in impersonal regions, alone with herself and her tangible thoughts, like a widow surrounded by many objects belonging to the past. Her long legs broke the white tutu like a statuette riding the moon.

'Khorosho,' the ballet mistress said, a guttural word carrying the sound of hail and thunder over the Steppes. The Russian face was white and prismatic as a dim sun on a block of crystal. There were blue veins in her forehead like a person with heart trouble, but she was not sick except from much abstraction. She lived a hard life. She brought her lunch to the studio in a little valise: cheese and an apple, and a Thermos

155

full of cold tea. She sat on the steps of the dais and stared into space through the sombre measures of the adagio.

Alabama approached the visionary figure, advancing behind her shoulder blades, bearing her body tightly possessed, like a lance in steady hands. A smile strained over her features painfully – pleasure in the dance is a hard-earned lesson. Her neck and chest were hot and red; the back of her shoulders strong and thick, lying over her thin arms like a massive yoke. She peered gently at the white lady.

'What do you find in the air that way?'

There was an aura of vast tenderness and of abnegation about the Russian.

'Forms, child, shapes of things.'

'It is beautiful.'

'Yes.'

'I will dance it.'

'Well, pay attention to the design. You do well the steps, but you never follow the configuration: without that, you cannot speak.'

'You will see if I can do it.'

'Go, then! Chérie, it is my first rôle.'

Alabama yielded herself to the slow dignity of the selfless ritual, to the voluptuous flagellation of the Russian minors. Slowly she moved to the protestations of the adagio from *Le Lac des Cygnes*.

'Wait a minute.'

Her eyes caught the white transparent face in the glass. The two smiles met and splintered.

'But I will do it if I break my leg,' she said, beginning again.

The Russian gathered her shawl about her shoulders. From a deep mysticism she said tentatively and without conviction, 'It is not worth that trouble – then you could not dance.'

'No,' said Alabama, 'it's not worth the trouble.'

'Then, little one,' sighed the aging ballerina, 'you will do it – just right.'

'We will try.'

The new studio was different. Madame had less space to spare; she gave fewer lessons for nothing. There was no room in the dressing room to practice changement de pieds. The tunics were cleaner since there was no place to leave them to dry. There were many English girls in the classes who still believed in the possibility of both living and dancing, filling the vestibule with gossip of boat rides on the Seine and soirées in the Montparnasse.

It was awful in the afternoon classes. A black fog from the station hung over the studio skylight, and there were too many men. A Negro classicist from the Folies-Bergère appeared at the bar. He had a gorgeous body but the girls laughed. They laughed at Alexandre with his intellectual face and glasses – he used to own a box at the ballet in Moscow when he had been in the army. They laughed at Boris, who stopped in the café next door for ten drops of valerian before his lessons; they laughed at Schiller because he was old and his face was puffy from years of make-up like a bartender's or a clown's. They laughed at Danton because he could toe dance, though he tried to restrain how superb he was to look at. They laughed at everybody except Lorenz – nobody could have laughed at Lorenz. He had the face of an eighteenth-century faun; his muscles billowed with proud perfection. To watch his brown body ladling out the measures of a Chopin mazurka was to feel yourself anointed with whatever meaning you may have found in life. He was shy and gentle, though the finest dancer in the world, and sometimes sat with the girls after classes, drinking coffee from a glass and munching Russian rolls soggy with poppy seeds. He understood the elegant cerebral abandon of Mozart, and had perceived the madnesses against which the consciousness of the race sets up an early vaccine for those intended to deal in reality. The voluptés of Beethoven were easy for Lorenz, and he did not have to count the churning revolutions of modern musicians. He said he could not dance to Schumann, and he couldn't, being always ahead or behind the beat whipping the romantic cadences beyond recognition. He was perfection to Alabama.

Arienne bought her way free from laughter with gnomish venom and an impeccable technique.

'What a wind!' somebody would cry.

'It is Arienne turning,' was the answer. Her favorite

157

musician was Liszt. She played on her body as if it were a xylophone, and had made herself indispensable to Madame. When Madame called out ten or so consecutive steps only Arienne could put them together. Her rigid insteps and the points of her toe shoes sliced the air like a sculptor's scalpel, but her arms were stubby and could not reach the infinite, frustrated by the weight of great strength and the broken lines of too much muscle. She loved telling how when she had been operated on the doctors came to look anatomically at the muscles in her back.

'But you have made much progress,' the girls said to Alabama, crowding before her to the front of the class.

'You will leave a place for Alabama,' corrected Madame.

She did four hundred battements every night.

Arienne and Alabama split the cost of the taxi each day as far as the Place de la Concorde. Arienne insisted that Alabama come to lunch at her apartment.

'I go so much with you,' she said. 'I do not like to be indebted.'

It was a desire to discover what they were mutually jealous of in each other that drew them together. In both of them there was an undercurrent of disrespect for discipline which allied them in a hoydenish comradeship.

'You must see my dogs,' said Arienne. 'There is one who is a poet and the other who is very well trained.'

There were ferns, silvery in the sun, on little tables and many autographed photographs.

'I have no photographs of Madame.'

'Perhaps she will give us one.'

'We can buy one from the photographer who made the proofs the last year she danced in the ballet,' suggested Arienne illicitly.

Madame was both pleased and angry when they carried the photographs to the studio.

'I will give you better ones,' she said.

She gave Alabama a picture of herself in *Carnaval* in a wide polka-dotted dress which her fingers held like a butterfly wing. Madame's hands constantly surprised Alabama: they were not long and thin; they were stubby. Arienne never got her picture, and she begrudged Alabama the photograph and grew more jealous than ever.

Madame gave a house-warming at the studio. They drank many bottles of sweet champagne that the Russians provided, and ate the sticky Russian cakes. Alabama contributed two magnums of Pol Roger Brut, but the Prince, Madame's husband, had been educated in Paris, and he took them home to drink for himself.

Alabama was nauseated from the gummy pastry – the Prince was delegated to ride with her in the taxi.

'I smell lily of the valley everywhere,' she said. Her head swam with the heat and the wine. She held on to the straps of the car to keep herself from throwing-up.

'You are working too hard,' said the Prince.

His face was gaunt in the passing flares from the street lamps. People said he kept a mistress on the money he had from Madame. The pianist kept her husband; he was sick – almost everybody kept somebody else. Alabama could barely remember when that would have offended her – it was just the exigencies of life.

David said he would help her to be a fine dancer, but he did not believe that she could become one. He had made many friends in Paris. When he came from his studio he nearly always brought somebody home. They dined out amongst the prints of Montagné's, the leather and stained glass of Foyot's, the plush and bouquets of the restaurants around the Place de l'Opéra. If she tried to induce David to go home early, he grew angry.

'What right have you to complain? You have cut yourself off from all your friends with this damn ballet.'

With his friends they drank Chartreuse along the boulevards under the rose-quartz lamps, and the trees, wielded by the night over the streets like the feathery fans of acquiescent courtesans.

Alabama's work grew more and more difficult. In the mazes of the masterful fouetté her legs felt like dangling hams; in the swift elevation of the entrechat cinq she thought her breasts hung like old English dugs. It did not show in the mirror. She was nothing but sinew. To succeed had become an obsession. She worked till she felt like a gored horse in the bull ring, dragging its entrails.

At home, the household fell into a mass of dissatisfaction without an authority to harmonize its elements. Before she left the apartment in the morning Alabama left a list of things for lunch which the cook never bothered to prepare – the woman kept the butter in the coal-bin and stewed a rabbit every day for Adage and gave the family what she pleased to eat. There wasn't any use getting another; the apartment was no good anyway. The life at home was simply an existence of individuals in proximity; it had no basis of common interest.

Bonnie thought of her parents as something pleasant and incalculable as Santa Claus that had no real bearing on her life outside the imprecations of Mademoiselle.

Mademoiselle took Bonnie for promenades in the Luxembourg Gardens, where the child seemed very French in her short white gloves bowling her hoop between the beds of metallic zinnias and geraniums. She was growing fast; Alabama wanted her to start training for the ballet – Madame had promised to give her a début when she found time. Bonnie said she didn't want to dance, an incomprehensible aversion to Alabama. Bonnie reported that Mademoiselle walked with a chauffeur in the Tuileries. Mademoiselle said it was beneath her dignity to contest the supposition. The cook said the hairs in the soup were from the black moustachios of Marguerite, the maid. Adage ate up in a silk canapé. David said the apartment was a pest house: the people upstairs played 'Punchinello' at nine in the morning on their gramophone and cut short his sleep. Alabama spent more and more time at the studio.

Madame at last took Bonnie as a pupil. It was thrilling to her mother to see her little legs and arms seriously follow the sweeping movements of the dancer. The new Mademoiselle had worked for an English Duke; she complained that the atmosphere of the studio was not fit for the little girl. That was because she couldn't speak Russian. She thought the girls were Fiends Infernal jabbering in the cacophony of a strange tongue and posturing immodestly before the mirror. The new Mademoiselle was a lady neurasthenic. Madame

160

said Bonnie did not seem to have talent, but it was too soon to tell.

One morning Alabama came early to her lesson. Paris is a pen-and-ink drawing before nine o'clock. To avoid the thick traffic of the Boulevard des Batignolles, Alabama tried the Metro. It smelled of fried potatoes, and she slipped in the spit on the dank stairs. She was afraid of getting her feet crushed in the crowd. Stella waited for her in tears in the vestibule.

'You must take my part,' she said, 'Arienne does nothing but abuse me; I mend her shoes and piece her music and Madame has offered me to gain money by playing for her lessons and she refuses.'

Arienne was bent over her straw chest in the dark, packing.

'I shall never dance again,' she said. 'Madame has time for children, time for amateurs, time for everybody, but Arienne Jeanneret must work at hours when she cannot get a decent pianist to play.'

'I do my best. You have only to tell me,' Stella sobbed.

'I am telling you. You are a nice girl, but you play the piano like a cochon!'

'If you would only explain what you want,' pled Stella. It was horrible to see the dwarfish face red and swollen with fright and tears.

'I explain at this instant. I am an artist, not a teacher of piano. So Arienne goes that Madame may continue her kindergarten.' She, too, was crying angrily.

'If anybody goes, Arienne,' said Alabama, 'it will be me. Then you may have your hour again.'

Arienne turned to her, sobbing.

'I have explained to Madame that I cannot work at night after my rehearsals. My lessons cost money; I cannot afford them. I must make progress when I am here. I pay the same as you,' sobbed Arienne.

She turned defiantly to Alabama.

'I live by my work,' she said contemptuously.

'Children have to begin,' said Alabama. 'It was you who said one must begin sometime – the first time I ever saw you.'

'Certainly. Then let them begin like the others, with the less great.'

'I will share my time with Bonnie,' Alabama said at last. 'You must stay.'

'You are very good.' Arienne laughed suddenly. 'Madame is a weak woman – always for something new,' she said. 'I will stay, however, for the present.'

She kissed Alabama impulsively on her nose.

Bonnie protested her lessons. She had three hours a week of Madame's time. Madame was fascinated by the child. The woman's personal emotions had to be wedged in between the spacings of her work since it was incessant. She brought Bonnie fruit and chocolate langue-de-chat, and took great pains with the placing of her feet. Bonnie became her outlet for affection; the emotions of the dance were of a sterner stuff than sentimental attachments. The little girl ran continually through the apartment in leaps and pas de bourrée.

'My God,' said David. 'One in the family is enough. I can't stand this.'

David and Alabama passed each other in the musty corridors hastily and ate distantly facing each other with the air of enemies awaiting some gesture of hostility.

'If you don't stop that humming, Alabama, I'll lose my mind,' he complained.

She supposed it *was* annoying the way the music of the day kept running through her head. There was nothing else there. Madame told her that she was not a musician. Alabama thought visually, architecturally, of music – sometimes it transformed her to a faun in twilit spaces unpenetrated by any living soul save herself; sometimes to a lone statue to forgotten gods washed by the waves on a desolate coast – a statue of Prometheus.

The studio was redolent of rising fortunes. Arienne passed the Opéra examinations first of her group. She permeated the place with her success. She brought a small group of French into the class, very Degas and coquettish in their long ballet skirts and waistless backs. They covered themselves with perfume, and said the smell of the Russians made them sick. The Russians complained to Madame that they could not breathe with the smell of French musk in their noses. Madame sprinkled the floor with lemon-oil and water to placate them all.

'I am to dance before the President of France,' cried Arienne jubilantly one day. 'At last, Alabama, they have begun to appreciate La Jeanneret!'

Alabama could not suppress a surge of jealousy. She was glad for Arienne; Arienne worked hard and had nothing in her life but the dance. Nevertheless, she wished it could have been herself.

'So I must give up my little cakes and Cap Corse and live like a saint for three weeks. Before I begin my schedule I want to give a party, but Madame will not come. She goes out to dine with you – she will not go out with Arienne. I ask her why – she says, "But it is different – you have no money." I will have money some day.'

She looked at Alabama as if she expected her to protest the statement. Alabama had no convictions whatsoever on the subject.

A week before Arienne danced, the Opéra called a rehearsal that fell at the time of her lesson with Madame.

'So I will work in the hour of Alabama,' she suggested.

'If she can change with you,' said Madame, 'for a week.'

Alabama couldn't work at six in the afternoon. It meant that David dined alone and that she couldn't get home until eight. She was all day at the studio as it was.

'Then we cannot do that,' said Madame.

Arienne was tempestuous. She lived at a terrible nervous pitch dividing her resistance between the opera and the studio.

'And this time I go for good! I will find someone who will make me a great dancer,' she threatened.

Madame only smiled.

Alabama would not oblige Arienne; the two girls worked in a state of amicable hatred.

Professional friendship would not bear close inspection – best everybody for herself, and interpret things to conform to personal desires – Alabama thought like that.

Arienne was intractable. Outside the province of her own genre, she refused to execute the work of the class. With the tears streaming down her face, she sat on the steps of the dais and stared into the mirror. Dancers are sensitive, almost primitive people: she demoralized the studio.

The classes filled with dancers other than Madame's usual pupils. The Rubenstein ballets were rehearsing and dancers were being paid enough to afford lessons with Madame again. Girls who had been to South America drifted back to town from the disbanded Pavlova troupe – the steps could not always be the tests of strength and technique to suit Arienne. It was the steps that moulded the body and offered it bit by bit to the reclaiming tenors of Schumann and Glinka that Arienne hated most – she could only lose herself in the embroiling rumbles of Liszt and the melodrama of Leoncavallo.

'I will go from this place,' she said to Alabama, 'next week.' Arienne's mouth was hard and set. 'Madame is a fool. She will sacrifice my career for nothing. But there are others!'

'Arienne, it is not like that that one becomes one of the great,' said Madame, 'you must rest.'

'There is nothing I can do here any more; I had better go away,' Arienne said.

The girls ate nothing but pretzels before the morning class – the studio was so far away from their homes they couldn't get breakfast in time; they were all irritable. The winter sun came in bilious squares through the fog and the gray buildings about the Place de la République took on the air of a cold caserne.

Madame called upon Alabama to execute the most difficult steps alone before the others with Arienne. Arienne was a finished ballerina. Alabama was conscious of how much she must fall short of the fine concision that marked the French girl's work. When they danced together the combinations were mostly steps for Arienne rather than the lyrical things that Alabama did best, yet always Arienne cried out that the steps were not for her. She protested to the others that Alabama was an interloper.

Alabama bought Madame flowers which wilted and shrivelled in the steam of the overheated studio. The place being more comfortable, more spectators came to the classes. A critic of the Imperial Ballet came to witness one of

Alabama's lessons. Impressive, reeking of past formalities, he left at the end on a flood of Russian.

'What did he say?' asked Alabama when they were alone. 'I have done badly – he will think you are a bad teacher.' She felt miserable at Madame's lack of enthusiasm: the man was the first critic of Europe.

Madame gazed at her dreamily. 'Monsieur knows what kind of a teacher I am,' was all she said.

In a few days the note came:

On the advice of Monsieur – I am writing to offer you a solo début in the opera *Faust* with the San Carlos Opera of Naples. It is a small rôle, but there will be others later. In Naples there are pensions where one can live very comfortably for thirty lire a week.

Alabama knew that David and Bonnie and Mademoiselle couldn't live in a pension that cost thirty lire a week. David couldn't live in Naples at all – he had called it a postcard city. There wouldn't be a French school for Bonnie in Naples. There wouldn't be anything but coral necklaces and fevers and dirty apartments and the ballet.

'I must not get excited,' she said to herself. 'I must work.'

'You will go?' said Madame expectantly.

'No. I will stay, and you will help me to dance *La Chatte*.'

Madame was noncommittal. Looking into the woman's fathomless eyes was like walking over a stretch of blistering pebbles through a treeless, shadeless August as Alabama searched them for some indication.

'It is hard to arrange a début,' she said. 'One should not refuse.'

David seemed to feel that there was something accidental about the note.

'You can't do that,' he said. 'We've got to go home this spring. Our parents are old, and we promised last year.'

'I am old, too.'

'We have some obligations,' he insisted.

Alabama no longer cared. David was a better person at heart than she to care about hurting people, she thought.

'I don't want to go to America,' she said.

Arienne and Alabama teased each other mercilessly. They worked harder and more consistently than the others. When they were too tired to put on their clothes after classes, they sat on the floor of the vestibule laughing hysterically and slapping each other with towels drenched in eau de Cologne or Madame's lemon-water.

'And I think—' Alabama would say.

'Tiens!' shrieked Arienne. 'Mon enfant begins to think. Ah! Ma fille, it is a mistake – all the thinking you do. Why do you not go home and mend your husband's socks?'

'Méchante,' Alabama answered. 'I will teach you to criticize your elders!' The wet towel fell with a smack across Arienne's rigid buttocks.

'Give me more room. I cannot dress so near to this polissonne,' retorted Arienne. She turned to Alabama seriously and looked at her questioningly. 'But it is true – I have no more place here since you have filled the dressing room with your fancy tutus. There is nowhere to hang my poor woollens.'

'Here is a new tutu for you! I make you a present!'

'I do not wear green. It brings bad luck in France.' Arienne was offended.

'If I had a husband to pay I, too, could buy them for myself,' she pursued disagreeably.

'What business of yours is it who pays? Or is that all the patrons of your first three rows can talk to you about?'

Arienne shoved Alabama into the group of naked girls. Somebody pushed her hurriedly back into Arienne's gyrating body. The eau de Cologne spilled over the floor and gagged them. A swat of the towel-end landed over Alabama's eyes. Groping about she collided with Arienne's hot, slippery body.

'Now!' shrieked Arienne. 'See what you have done! I shall go at once to a magistrate and have it constaté!' She wept and hurled Apache invective at the top of her lungs. 'It is not today that it shows but tomorrow. I will have a cancer! You have hit me in the breast from a bad spirit! I will have it constaté, so when the cancer develops you will pay me much money, even if you are at the ends of the earth! You will pay!' The whole studio listened. The lesson Madame was giving outside could not continue, the noise was so loud. The Russians took sides with the French or the Americans.

'Sale race!' they shrieked indiscriminately.

'One can never have confidence in the Americans!'

'One must never trust the French!'

'They are too nervous, the Americans and the French.'

They smiled long, superior Russian smiles as if they had long ago forgotten why they were smiling: as if the smile were a hallmark of their superiority to circumstance. The noise was deafening yet somehow surreptitious. Madame protested – she was angry with the two girls.

Alabama dressed as fast as she could. Out in the fresh air her knees trembled as she waited for a taxi. She wondered if she was going to take cold from her soaking hair under her hat.

Her upper lip felt cold and peppery with drying sweat. She had put on a stocking that wasn't her own. What was it all about, she said to herself – fighting like two kitchen maids and just barely getting along on the ends of their physical resources, all of them?

'My God!' she thought. 'How sordid! How utterly, unmitigatedly sordid!'

She wanted to be in some cool and lyrical place asleep on a cool bed of ferns.

She did not go to the afternoon class. The apartment was deserted. She could hear Adage clawing at his door to get out. The rooms hummed with emptiness. In Bonnie's room she found a red carnation such as they give away in restaurants fading in a marmalade pot.

'Why don't I get *her* some flowers?' she asked herself.

A botched attempt at a doll's tutu lay on the child's bed; the shoes by the door were scuffed at the toes. Alabama picked up an open drawing-book from the table. Inside Bonnie had designed a clumsy militant figure with mops of yellow hair. Underneath ran the legend, 'My mother is the most beautiful lady in the world.' On the page opposite, two figures held hands gingerly; behind them trailed Bonnie's conception of a dog. 'This is when my Mother and Father go

167

out walking,' the writing said. 'C'est trés chic, mes parents ensemble!'

'Oh, God!' thought Alabama. She had almost forgotten about Bonnie's mind going on and on, growing. Bonnie was proud of her parents the same way Alabama had been of her own as a child, imagining into them whatever perfections she wanted to believe in. Bonnie must be awfully hungry for something pretty and stylized in her life, for some sense of a scheme to fit into. Other children's parents were something to them besides the distant 'chic,' Alabama reproached herself bitterly.

All afternoon she slept. Out of her subconscious came the feeling of a beaten child, and her bones ached in her sleep and her throat parched like blistering flesh. When she woke up she felt as if she had been crying for hours.

She could see the stars shining very personally into her bedroom. She could have lain in bed for hours listening to the sounds from the streets.

Alabama went only to her private lessons to avoid Arienne. As she worked she could hear the girl's cackling laugh in the vestibule raking over the arriving class for support. The girls looked at her curiously. Madame said she must not mind Arienne.

Dressing herself hurriedly, Alabama peeped between the dusty curtains at the dancers. The imperfections of Stella, the manoeuvres of Arienne, the currying of favor, the wrangling over the front line appeared to her in the moated sun falling through the glass roof like the grovelling, churning movement of insects watched through the sides of a glass jar.

'Larvae!' said the unhappy Alabama contemptuously.

She wished she had been born in the ballet, or that she could bring herself to quit altogether.

When she thought of giving up her work she grew sick and middle-aged. The mile and miles of pas de bourrée must have dug a path inevitably to somewhere.

Diaghilev died. The stuff of the great movement of the Ballet Russe lay rotting in a French law court – he had never been able to make money.

Some of his dancers performed around the swimming pool

at the Lido to please the drunk Americans in summer; some of them worked in music-hall ballets; the English went back to England. The transparent celluloid décor of *La Chatte* that had stabbed its audience with silver swords from the spotlights of Paris and Monte Carlo, London and Berlin lay marked 'No Smoking' in a damp, ratty warehouse by the Seine, locked in a stone tunnel where a gray light from the river sloshed over the dark, dripping earth and over the moist, curving bottom.

'What's the use?' said Alabama.

'You can't give up all that time and work and money for nothing,' said David. 'We'll try to arrange something in America.'

That was nice of David. But she knew she'd never dance in America.

The intermittent sun disappeared from the skylight over her last lesson.

'You will not forget your adagio?' said Madame. 'You will send me pupils when you go to America?'

'Madame,' Alabama answered suddenly, 'do you think I could still go to Naples? Will you see the man immediately and tell him that I will leave at once?'

Looking into the woman's eyes was like watching those blocks of black-and-white pyramids where there are sometimes six and sometimes seven squares. Looking into her eyes was to experience an optical illusion.

'So!' she said. 'I am sure the place is still open. You will leave tomorrow? There is no time to waste.'

'Yes,' said Alabama, 'I will go.'

4

I

DAHLIAS stuck out of green tins at the station flower stalls like the paper fans that come with pop-corn packages; the oranges were piled like Minie balls along the newsstands; the windows of the buffet de la gare sported three American grapefruit like the balls of a gastronomic pawnshop. Saturated air hung between the train windows and Paris like a heavy blanket.

David and Alabama filled the second class wagon-lit with brassy cigarette smoke. He rang for an extra pillow.

'If you need anything I'll always be there,' he said.

Alabama cried and swallowed a spoonful of yellow sedative.

'You'll get awfully sick of telling people how I'm getting along—'

'I'm going to Switzerland as soon as we can close the apartment – I'll send Bonnie to you when you're ready to have her.'

A demi-Perrier sizzled in the car window. David choked on the dank must.

'It's silly to travel second class. Won't you let me have them change you to first?' he said.

'I'd rather feel I could afford it from the beginning.'

The weight of their individual reactions separated them like a barrage. Unconscious relief buckled their parting with sad constraint – innumerable involuntary associations smothered their good-byes in platonic despair.

'I'll send you some money. I'd better be getting off.'

'Good-bye – Oh, David!' she called as the train shoved away. 'Be sure to have Mademoiselle get Bonnie's underwear from Old England—'

'I'll tell her – good-bye, dear!'

Alabama stuck her head inside the dim incandescence of the train lit like a spiritualist's seance. Her face flattened to a stone carving in the mirror. Her suit wasn't right for second class; Yvonne Davidson had made it out of the reflections of an Armistice parade – the lines of the horizon-blue helmet and the sweep of the cape were too generous for the constraint of the scratchy lace-covered benches. Alabama went over her plans sympathetically to herself as a mother might soothe an unhappy child. She couldn't see the maîtresse de ballet till the day after she got there. It was nice of Mademoiselle to give her a bunch of maguey; she was sorry she had forgotten it on the mantelpiece at home. She had some dirty clothes in the laundry, too – Mademoiselle could pack them with the linen when they moved. She supposed David would leave the linen at the American Express. It wouldn't be hard packing, they had so little junk: a broken tea-set, relic of a pilgrimage to Valence from St-Raphaël, a few photographs – she was sorry she hadn't brought the one of David taken on the porch in Connecticut – some books, and David's crated paintings.

The glow from the electric signs blared over Paris in the distance like the glare of a pottery kiln. Her hands sweated under the coarse red blanket. The carriage smelled like the inside of a small boy's pocket. Her thoughts insistently composed jibberish in French to the click of the car wheels.

> La belle main gauche l'éther compact,
> S'étendre dans l'air qui fait le beau
> Trouve la haut le rhythm intact
> Battre des ailes d'un triste oiseau.

Alabama got up to look for a pencil.

'Le bruit constant de mille moineaux,' she added. She wondered if she'd lost the letter – no, it was in her Cutex-box.

She must have gone to sleep – it was hard to tell in a train. Tramping in the corridors awoke her. This must be the border. She rang the bell. Nobody came for ages. A man in the green uniform of a circus animal-trainer appeared at last.

'Water?' said Alabama ingratiatingly.

The man stared blankly about the wagon. There was no response in the smooth enigma of his fascinated countenance.

'Acqua, de l'eau wat*aire*,' Alabama persisted.

'Fräulein rings,' commented the man.

'Listen,' said Alabama. She raised her arms in the motions of the Australian crawl and finished with a tentative compromise between exaggerated swallows and a gargle. She faced the guard anticipatorily.

'No, no, No!' he cried out in alarm and vanished from the compartment.

Alabama got out her Italian phrase book and rang again.

'Do' – veh pos' – so com – prar' – eh ben – ze' – no,' the book said. The man laughed hilariously. She must have lost the place.

'Nothing,' Alabama told him reluctantly and went back to her composing. The man had driven the rhythm out of her head. She was probably in Switzerland by now. She couldn't remember whether or not it was Byron who had crossed the Alps with the curtains of his carriage down. She tried to see out of the window – some milk cans glistened in the dark. What she should have done about Bonnie's underwear was to have had it made by a seamstress. Mademoiselle would see to it. She got up and stretched, holding on to the sliding door.

The man informed her disparagingly that she couldn't open the doors in the second class and she couldn't have breakfast served in a couchette.

The country from the windows of the diner next day was flat like the land from which the sea has receded with sparse feather-duster trees tickling the bright sky. Little clouds foamed over the placidity aimlessly as froth from a beer pail; castles tumbled over the round hills like crowns awry; nobody sang 'O Sole Mio.'

There was honey for breakfast and bread like a stone mallet. She was afraid to change in Rome without David. The

172

Rome station was full of palms; the fountains scrubbed the baths of Caracalla with sprays of sunshine opposite the terminus. In the open friendliness of the Italian air, her spirits rose.

'Ballonné, deux tours,' she said to herself. The new train was filthy. There were no carpets on the floor and it smelled of the Fascisti, of guns. The signs pronounced a litany; Asti Spumanti, Lagrima Christi, Spumoni, Tortoni. She didn't know what it was she had lost – the letter was still in the Cutex. Alabama took possession of herself as a small boy walking in a garden might close his hand over a firefly.

'Cinque minuti mangiare,' said the attendant.

'All right,' she said, counting on her fingers, 'una, due, tre – It's all right,' she assured him.

The train swerved this way and that, trying to avoid the disorder of Naples. The cabbies had forgotten to move their cabs off the car rails, sleepy men forgot which way they were going in the middle of the streets, children spread their mouths and soft hurt eyes and forgot the emotion of crying. White dust blew about the city; delicatessens sold sharp smells, cubes and triangles and wicker globes of odor. Naples shrunk in the lamplight from its public squares, suppressed by a great pretense of discipline, quelled by its blackened stone façades.

'Venti lire!' expostulated the cabby.

'The letter,' said Alabama haughtily, 'said I could *live* on thirty lire a week in Naples.'

'Venti, venti, venti,' carolled the Italian without turning around.

'It's going to be difficult not being able to communicate,' thought Alabama.

She gave the man the address the maîtresse had sent her. Flourishing his whip grandiloquently, the cabby urged the horse's hoofs pendulously through the munificence of the night. As she gave the man his money his brown eyes swung on hers like cups set on a tree to catch a precious sap. She thought he would never quit looking.

'Signorina will like Naples,' he said surprisingly. '"The city's voice is soft like solitude's."'

The cab clumped away through the red and green lights set about the brim of the bay like stones in the filigree of a Renaissance poison-cup. The syrupy drippings of the fly-specked south seeped up on the breeze that blew the vast aquamarine translucence into emotional extinction.

The light from the pension entry shone in globular drops in Alabama's fingernails. Her movements gathered up inconsequential stirrings of the air as she passed inside leaving no traces on the stillness behind her.

'Well, I've got to live here,' said Alabama, 'so that's all there is to that.'

The landlady said the room had a balcony – it did, but there wasn't any floor to the balcony; the iron rails joined the peeling pink wash of the outside walls. However, there was a lavabo with gigantic spouts sticking out over the bowl and splashing the square of oilcloth underneath. The breakwater curved its arm about the ball of blue night from her window; the smell of pitch rose from the harbor.

Alabama's thirty lire bought a white iron bed that had obviously once been green, a maple wardrobe with a bevelled mirror opalling the Italian sun, and a rocker made of a strip of Brussels carpet. Cabbage three times a day, a glass of Amalfi wine, gnocchi on Sundays, and the chorus of 'Donna' by the loafers beneath the balcony at night were all included in the price. It was a huge room with no shape, being all bays and corners till it gave her a sense of inhabiting a whole apartment. There is a suggestion of gilt about everything in Naples, and though Alabama could not find a trace of it in her room, she felt somehow as if the ceilings were encrusted with goldleaf. Footfalls rose from the pavements below in sumptuous warm reminiscence. Nights fell out of the classics; the merest suggestion of people floated off into view, fantastic excrescences of happy existence; cacti speared the summer; the backs of fish glinted in the open boats below like mica splinters.

Madame Sirgeva conducted her classes on the stage of the opera house. She complained incessantly about the price of the lights; the piano sounded very ineffectual in the Victorian chasms. The darkness from the wings and the dimness between the three globes she kept burning overhead divided the stage into small intimate compartments. Madame paraded her ghost through the sway of tarlatan, the creak of toe shoes, the subdued panting of the girls.

'No noise, less noise,' she reiterated. She was as pale and dyed and shrivelled and warped by poverty as a skin that has been soaked under acid. The black dye in her hair, coarse as the stuffing of a pillow, was yellow along the part; she taught her girls in puffed-sleeved blouses and pleated skirts which she wore on the street afterward beneath her coat.

Swirling round and round like an exercise in penmanship, Alabama threaded the line through the spots of light.

'But you are like Madame!' said Madame Sirgeva. 'We were at the Imperial School together in Russia. It was I who taught her her entrechats, though she never did them properly. Mes enfants! There are four counts to a quatre-temps, please, p – l – e – a – s – e!'

Alabama clamorously dropped her person bit by bit into the ballet like pieces dropped through a mechanical piano.

The girls were unlike the Russians. Their necks were dirty and they came to the theatre with paper bags filled with thick sandwiches. They ate garlic; they were fatter than the Russians and their legs were shorter; they danced with bent knees and their Italian-silk tights crinkled over their dimples.

'God and the Devil!' shrieked Sirgeva. 'It is Moira who is never in step, and the ballet goes on in three weeks.'

'Oh, Maestra!' remonstrated Moira. 'Molto bella!'

'Oh,' gasped Madame, turning to Alabama. 'You see? I provide them with steel shoes to hold up their lazy feet and the moment I turn my back they dance flatfoot – and I am paid only sixteen hundred lire for all that! Thank heavens, I have *one* from a Russian school!' The mistress went on like a churning piston-rod. She sat in the humid closed opera house with a seal cape about her shoulders, faded and dyed like her hair, coughing into her handkerchief.

'Mother Maria,' sighed the girls. 'Sanctified Mary!' They drew together in frightened groups in the gloom. They were suspicious of Alabama because of her clothes. Over the backs of the canvas chairs in the dingy dressing room she flung her things: two hundred dollars' worth of black tulle 'Adieu Sagesse,' moss roses floating through a nebula like seeds in a strawberry ice, costly nebula – one hundred, two hundred dollars; some yellow clownish fringe, a chartreuse hooded cloak, white shoes, blue shoes, buckles for Bobby Shafto, silver buckles, steel buckles, hats and red sandals, shoes with the signs of the Zodiac, a velvet cape soft as the roof of an old château, a cap of pheasant's feathers – she hadn't realized in Paris that she had had so many clothes. She would have to wear them out now that she was living on six hundred lire a month. She was glad of all those clothes that David had bought her. After the class, she dressed amidst the fine things with the purposeful air of a father inspecting a child's toy.

'Holy Mother,' whispered the girls shyly, fingering her lingerie. Alabama was cross when they did that; she didn't want them smearing sausage over her chiffon step-ins.

She wrote to David twice a week – their apartment appeared to her far away, and dull. Rehearsals were coming – any life compared with that seemed dreary. Bonnie answered on little paper with French nursery rhymes on the heading.

Dearest Mummy—

I was the hostess while Daddy put on his cuff-buttons for a lady and gentleman. My life is working quite well. Mademoiselle and the chambermaid said they never saw a box of paints so pretty as the one you sent. I jumped of joy with the paintbox and made some pictures of des gens à la mer, nous qui jouons au croquet et une vase avec des fleurs dedans d'après nature. When we are Sunday in Paris, I go to Catechism to learn of the horrible sufferings of Jesus Christ.

Your loving daughter,
Bonnie Knight.

Alabama took the yellow sedative at night to forget Bonnie's letters. She made friends with a dark Russian girl blowing through the ballet like a sirocco. Together they went to the Galleria. In the blank stone enclosure where footsteps spattered like steady rain, they sat over their beers. The girl refused to believe that Alabama was married; she lived in constant hopes of meeting the man who provided her friend with so much money, and of stealing him away. Crowds of men passing arm in arm eyed them callously and disdainfully – they wouldn't pick up women who went to the Galleria at night alone, they seemed to say. Alabama showed her friend Bonnie's picture.

'You are happy,' said the girl. 'One is happier when one doesn't marry.' Her eyes were a deep brown that glowed red and clear like violin rosin when she was exhilarated by a little alcohol. On especial occasions she wore a pair of black net teddies with lavender bows that she had bought when she worked in the chorus of the Ballet Russe before Diaghilev died.

Rehearsing in the big empty theatre, the troupe went over and over the *Faust* ballet. The orchestra leader conducted Alabama's three-minute solo like lightning. Madame Sirgeva did not dare to speak to the Maestro. At last with tears in her eyes, she stopped the performance.

'You are killing my girls,' she wept. 'It is inhuman!'

The man threw his stick across the piano; the hair stood up on his head like grass sprouting on a clay scalp.

'Sapristi!' he screamed. 'The music is written so!'

He dashed distractedly out of the Opera House and they finished without music. The following afternoon the Maestro was more determined, the music went faster than ever. He had looked up a copy of the original score; he had never made an error. The arms of the violins rose above the stage bent and black as grasshopper legs; the Maestro snapped his backbone like a rubber slingshot, flinging the fast chords up over the footlights with an impossible rapidity.

Alabama was unused to a slanting stage. To habituate herself she worked alone at lunch time after the morning class, turning, turning. The slant threw her turns out of balance. She worked so hard that she felt like an old woman by a fireside in a far Nordic country as she sat on the floor dressing afterwards. The telescoping vacation blue and brighter blue of the Bay of Naples was blinding to stumble through on her way home. Alabama's feet were bleeding as she fell into bed.

When at last her first performance was over she sat on the base of a statue of the 'Venus de Milo,' outside the studded doors of the Opera greenrooms; Pallas Athene stared at her across the musty hall. Her eyes throbbed with the beat of her pulse, her hair clung like Plasticine about her head; 'Bravo' and 'Benissimo' for the ballet rang about her ears like persistent gnats. 'Well, it's done,' she said.

She didn't dare look at the girls in the dressing room; she tried to hold on to the magic for a long time. She knew her eyes would see the sagging breasts like dried August gourds, and wound themselves on the pneumatic buttocks like lurid fruits in the pictures of Georgia O'Keefe.

David had telegraphed a basket of calla lilies. 'From your two sweethearts' the card should have read, but it had come through the Neapolitan florist 'sweat-hearts.' She didn't laugh. She hadn't written to David in three weeks. She plastered her face with coldcream and sucked on the half-lemon she had brought in her valise. Her Russian friend embraced her. The ballet girls seemed to be waiting about for something more to happen; no men waited in the shadows of the opera door. The girls were mostly ugly, and some of them were old. Their faces were vacuous and so stretched with fatigue that they would have fallen apart save for the cordlike muscles developed by years of hard breathing. Their necks were pinched and twisted like dirty knots of mending thread when they were thin, and when they were fat the flesh hung over their bones like bulging pastry over the sides of paper containers. Their hair was black with no nuances to please the tired senses.

'Jesu!' they cried in admiration, 'the lilies! How much can they have cost? They are fit for a cathedral!'

Madame Sirgeva kissed Alabama gratefully.

'You have done well! When we give the ballet programme for the year, you will have the stellar rôle – these girls are too ugly. I can do nothing with them. There was no interest in ballet before – now we shall see! Do not worry. I will write to Madame! Your flowers are beautiful, piccola ballerina,' she finished softly.

Alabama sat in her window listening to the night chorus of 'Donna.'

'Well,' she sighed distractedly, 'there should be something to do after a success.'

She put her wardrobe in order and thought of her friends in Paris. Sunday friends with satin-coated wives toasting impeccable accents in the sun of foreign plages; tumultuous friends drowning the Chopin in modern jazz in vintage wines; cultured friends hanging over David like a group of relations over a first-born. They would have taken her out somewhere. Calla lilies, in Paris, would not have been tied with a white tulle bow.

She sent David the clippings from the paper. They were agreed that the ballet was a success, and that the new addition to Madame Sirgeva's corps was a competent dancer. She had promise and should be given a bigger rôle, the papers said. Italians like blondes; they said Alabama was as ethereal as a Fra Angelico angel because she was thinner than the others.

Madame Sirgeva was proud of those notices. It seemed more important to Alabama that she should have discovered a new make of toe shoe from Milan; the shoes were soft as air. Alabama ordered a hundred pairs – David sent her the money. He was living in Switzerland with Bonnie. She hoped he had bought Bonnie woollen bloomers – up to the age of ten girls need to have their stomachs protected. At Christmas he wrote her that he had bought Bonnie a blue ski-suit, and sent her Kodak snaps of the snow and of the two of them falling down the hills together.

Asthmatic Christmas bells tolled over Naples; flat metallic sheets of sound like rustled sheafs of roofing. The steps about the public places were filled with jonquils and roses dyed orange, dripping red water. Alabama went to see the wax Nativities at Benediction. There were calla lilies everywhere and tapers and worn, bland faces smiling convulsively over the season. From the reflection of the candle flicker on the gilt, from the chants that rose and fell like the beating of the tides on amorphous shores before the birth of man, from the spattering tread of the women with heads bound in lace veils, Alabama absorbed a sense of elation as if she marched to the righteous tune of spiritual organization. The surplices of the priests in Naples were of white satin, lush with passion

179

flowers and pomegranates. During the services Alabama thought of Bourbon princes and hemophilia, papal counts, and maraschino cherries. The gleam of gold damask on the altar was as warm and rich as what it represented. Her thoughts prowled about her introspection like leopards in a cage at the zoo. Her body was so full of static from the constant whip of her work that she could get no clear communication with herself. She said to herself that human beings have no right to fail. She did not feel what failure was. She thought of Bonnie's tree. Mademoiselle could get it together as well as she.

Unexpectedly she laughed, tapping her spirit experimentally like a piano being tuned.

'There's a lot in religion,' she said to her Russian friend, 'but it has too much meaning.'

The Russian told Alabama about a priest she had known who became so aroused by the tales he had heard in the Confessional that he got drunk on the Holy Sacrament. He drank so much during the week that there wasn't any communion to give to the penitents on Sunday, who had also been drinking during the week and needed a pick-me-up. His church became known as a lousy dump that borrowed its blood of Christ from the synagogue, the girl said, and lost many customers, amongst them herself.

'I,' the girl rambled on, 'used to be very religious. Once in Russia when I found my carriage was being drawn by a white horse I got out and walked three miles through the snow to the theatre and I got pneumonia. Since, I have cared less for God – between the priests and white horses.'

The Opera gave *Faust* three times during the winter, and Alabama's tea-rose tarlatan that had risen at first like a frozen fountain wore streaked and crushed. She loved the lessons the morning after a performance – the let-down and still floral calm like the quiet of an orchard in bloom that followed the excitement, and her face's being pale, and the traces of make-up washed out of the corner of her eyes with perspiration.

'Stations of the Cross!' moaned the girls, 'but my legs ache, and I am sleepy! My mother beat me last night because I was late; my father refuses me Bel Paese – I cannot work on goat cheese!'

'Ah,' the fat mothers deflated themselves, 'bellissima, my daughter – she should be ballerina, but the Americans grab everything. But Mussolini will show them, Holy Sacrament!'

For the end of Lent the Opera demanded a whole programme of ballet; Alabama at last was to dance ballerina of *Le Lac des Cygnes*.

As the ballet went into rehearsal, David wrote asking if she would like Bonnie for two weeks. Alabama got permission to miss a morning class to meet her child at the station. A swishing army officer helped Bonnie and Mademoiselle out of the train into the Neapolitan jargon of sound and color.

'Mummy,' the child cried excitedly. 'Mummy!' She clung about Alabama's knees adoringly; a soft wind swept her bangs back in little gusts. Her round face was as flushed and translucent as the polish on the day of her arrival. The bones had begun to come up in her nose; her hands were forming. She was going to have those wide-ended fingers of a Spanish primitive like David. She was very like her father.

'She has given an excellent example to the travellers,' said Mademoiselle straightening her hair.

Bonnie clung to her mother bristling with resentment of Mademoiselle's proprietary air. She was seven, had just begun to sense her position in the world, and was full of the critical childish reserves that accompany the first formations of social judgment.

'Is your car outside?' she bubbled.

'I haven't any car, dear. There's a flea-bitten horse-cab that's much nicer to take us to my pension.'

A determination not to manifest her disappointment showed in Bonnie's face.

'Daddy has a car,' she said critically.

'Well, here we travel in chariots.' Alabama deposited her on the crinkled linen covers of the voiture.

'You and Daddy are very "chic,"' Bonnie went on speculatively. 'You should have a car—'

'Mademoiselle, did you tell her that?'

'Certainly, Madame. I should like to be in Mademoiselle Bonnie's place,' said Mademoiselle emphatically.

'I suppose I shall be very rich,' said Bonnie.

'My God, no! You must get things like that out of your head. You will have to work to get what you want – that's why I wanted you to dance. I was sorry to hear you had given it up.'

'I did not like dancing, except the presents. At the end Madame gave me a little silver evening bag. Inside there was a glass and a comb and real powder – that part I liked. Would you like to see it?'

From a small valise she produced an incomplete pack of cards, several frayed paper dolls, an empty match-box, a small bottle, two souvenir fans, and a notebook.

'I used to make you keep your things in better order,' commented Alabama, staring at the untidy mess.

Bonnie laughed. 'I do more as I please now,' she said. 'Here is the bag.'

Handling the little silver envelope, an unexpected lump rose to Alabama's throat. A faint scent of eau de Cologne brought back the glitter on the crystal beads of Madame; the music hammering the afternoon to a beaten-silver platter, David and Bonnie waiting at dinner, swirled in her head like snowflakes settling in a glass paperweight.

'It's very pretty,' she said.

'Why do you cry? I will let you carry it sometime.'

'It's the smell makes my eyes water. What have you got in your suitcase that smells so?'

'But, Madame,' expostulated Mademoiselle, 'it is the very same mixture they make for the Prince of Wales. One takes one part lemon, one part eau de Cologne, one part Coty's jasmine, and—'

Alabama laughed. '—And you shake it up, and pour off two parts ether and half a dead cat!'

Bonnie's eyes widened disdainfully.

'You can take it in trains for when your hands are soiled,' she protested, 'or for if you have the "vertige."'

'I see – or in case the engine runs out of oil. Here's where we get out.'

The cab shook itself to an indeterminate stop before the pink boarding house. Bonnie's eyes wandered incredulously over the flaking wash and the hollow entry. The doorway smelled of damp and urine; stone steps cradled the centuries in their worn centres.

'Madame has not made a mistake?' protested Mademoiselle querulously.

'No,' Alabama said cheerfully. 'You and Bonnie have a room to yourselves. Don't you *love* Naples?'

'I hate Italy,' pronounced Bonnie. 'I like it better in France.'

'How do you know? You've just got here.'

'The Italians are very dirty, isn't it?' Mademoiselle reluctantly parted with an unclassifiable facial expression.

'Ah,' said the landlady, smothering Bonnie in a vast convex embrace. 'Mother of God, it is a beautiful child!' Her breasts hung over the stunned little girl like sandbags.

'Dieu!' Mademoiselle sighed. 'These Italians are a religious people!'

The Easter table was decorated with lugubrious crosses made of dried palmetto leaves. There was gnocchi and vino da Capri for dinner, and a purple card with cupids pasted in the centre of gold radiations resembling medals of state. In the afternoon they walked along the pulverized white roads and up the steep alleys gashed with bright rags hung out to dry in the glare. Bonnie waited in her mother's room while Alabama prepared for rehearsal. The child amused herself by sketching in the rocker.

'I cannot make a good likeness,' she announced, 'so I have changed to caricature. It is Daddy when he was a young man.'

'Your father's only thirty-two,' said Alabama.

'Well, that's quite old, wouldn't you say?'

'Not so old as seven, my dear.'

'Oh, of course – if you count backwards,' agreed Bonnie.

'And if you begin in the middle, we are a very young family all round.'

'I should like to begin when I am twenty, and have six children.'

'How many husbands?'

'Oh, no husbands. They shall, perhaps, be away at the

time,' said Bonnie vaguely. 'I have seen them so in the movies.'

'What was that remarkable film?'

'It was about dancing, so Daddy took me. There was a lady in the Russian Ballet. She had no children but a man and they both cried a lot.'

'It must have been interesting.'

'Yes. It was Gabrielle Gibbs. Do you like her, Mummy?'

'I've never seen her except in life, so I couldn't say.'

'She is my favorite actress. She is a very pretty lady.'

'I must see the picture.'

'We could go if we were in Paris. I could carry my silver sac de soirée.'

Every day during rehearsals, Bonnie sat in the cold theatre with Mademoiselle lost under the dim trimmings like rose and gold cigar-bands, terrified by the seriousness and the emptiness and Madame Sirgeva. Alabama went over and over the adagio.

'Blue devils,' gasped the maîtresse. 'Nobody has done that with two turns! Ma chère Alabama – you will see with the orchestra that it cannot be!'

On their way home they passed a man ponderously swallowing frogs. The frogs' legs were tied to a string, and he pulled them up again out of his stomach, as many as four at a time. Bonnie gloated with disgusted delight. It made her quite sick to see; she was fascinated.

The pasty food at the boarding house gave Bonnie a rash.

'It is ringworm from the filth,' said Mademoiselle. 'If we stay, Madame, it may turn to erysipelas,' she threatened. 'Besides, Madame, our bath is dirty.'

'It is quite like broth, mutton broth,' corroborated Bonnie distastefully, 'only without the peas!'

'I had wanted to give Bonnie a party,' said Alabama.

'Could Madame suggest where I might get a thermometer?' Mademoiselle interjected hastily.

Nadjya, the Russian, unearthed a little boy for Bonnie's party. Madame Sirgeva incalculably furnished a nephew. Though all of Naples was covered with buckets of anemones and night-blooming stock, pale violets like enamelled breast-pins, straw-flowers and bachelor's-buttons, and the covetous enveloping bloom of azaleas, the landlady insisted upon decorating the children's table with poisonous pink-and-yellow paper flowers. She produced two children for the party, one with a sore under its nose, and one who had had to have its head recently shaved. The children arrived in corduroy pants worn over the seat like a convict's head. The table was loaded with rock cakes and honey and warm pink lemonade.

The Russian boy brought a monkey which hopped about the table tasting from all the jams and throwing the spoons about recklessly. Alabama watched them under the scraggly palms from the low sill of her room; the French governess tore ineffectually about on the outskirts of their activities.

'Tiens, Bonnie! Et toi, ah, mon pauvre chou-chou!' she shrieked without pause.

It was a witch's incantation. What magic philter was the woman brewing to be drunk by the passing years? Alabama's senses floated off on dreams. A sharp scream from Bonnie startled her back to reality.

'Ah, quelle sale bête!'

'Well, come here, dear, we'll put iodine on it,' Alabama called from the casement.

'So Serge takes the monkey,' Bonnie stammered, 'and he th – r – o – ws him at me, and he is horrible, and I hate the children of Naples!'

Alabama held the child on her knee. Her body felt very little and helpless to her mother.

'Monkeys have to have *something* to eat,' Alabama teased.

'You are lucky he has not bitten your nose,' Serge commented unsolicitously. The two Italians were only concerned about the animal, rubbing him affectionately and soothing him with dreamy Italian prayer like a love song.

'Che – che – che,' chittered the parakeet.

'Come,' said Alabama. 'I will tell you a story.'

The young eyes hung suspended on her words like drops of rain under a fence rail; their little faces followed hers like pale pads of clouds beneath the moon.

'I would never have come,' declaimed Serge, 'if I had known there wasn't going to be Chianti!'

'Nor I, Hail Mary!' echoed the Italians.

'Don't you want to hear about the Greek temples, all bright reds and blues?' Alabama insisted.

'Si, Signora.'

'Well – they are white now because the ages have worn away their original, dazzling—'

'Mummy, may I have the compote?'

'Do you want to hear about the temples or not?' said Alabama crossly. The table came to a dead expectant silence. 'That's all I know about them,' she concluded, feebly.

'Then may I please now have the compote?' Bonnie dripped the purple stain down the knife-pleats of her best dress.

'Doesn't Madame feel that we have had enough for one afternoon?' said Mademoiselle in dismay.

'I feel sick, a little,' confessed Bonnie. She was ghastly pale.

The doctor said he thought it was the climate. Alabama forgot to get the emetic he prescribed at the drug store and Bonnie lay in bed for a week, living on lime-water and mutton broth while her mother rehearsed the waltz. Alabama was distracted; Madame Sirgeva had been right – she couldn't do two turns with the orchestra unless it slowed up. The Maestro was adamant.

'Mother of women,' the girls breathed from the dark corners. 'She will break her back so!'

Somehow she got Bonnie well enough to board the train. She bought them a spirit lamp for the voyage.

'But what will we do with it, Madame?' asked Mademoiselle suspiciously.

'The British always have a spirit lamp,' explained Alabama, 'so when the baby gets croup they can take care of it. We never have anything, so we get to know the inside of many hospitals. The babies all come out the same, only later in life some prefer spirit lamps and some prefer hospitals.'

'Bonnie has not got croup, Madame,' Mademoiselle reproved huffily. 'Her illness is the result solely of our visit.' She wanted the train to start to extricate herself and Bonnie from Neapolitan confusions. Alabama wanted also to be extricated.

'We should have taken the train-de-luxe,' said Bonnie. 'I am in rather a hurry to get to Paris.'

'This is the train-de-luxe, snob!'

Bonnie gazed at her mother in impassive skepticism.

'There are many things in the world you don't know, Mummy.'

'It's just barely possible.'

'Ah,' fluttered Mademoiselle approvingly, 'Au 'voir, Madame, au 'voir! And good luck!'

'Good-bye, Mummy. Do not dance too hard!' called Bonnie perfunctorily as the train moved off.

The poplar trees before the station jingled their tops like pockets full of silver money; the train whistled mournfully as it rounded a bend.

'For five lire,' said Alabama to the dog-eared cab driver, 'you must take me to the Opera House.'

She sat alone that night without Bonnie. She hadn't realized how much fuller life was with Bonnie there. She was sorry she hadn't sat more with her child when she was sick in bed. Maybe she could have missed rehearsals. She had wanted her child to see her dance the ballet. In one more week of rehearsal she would have her début as a ballerina!

Alabama threw the broken fan and the pack of picture postcards that Bonnie had left behind in the wastebasket. They seemed hardly worth sending after her to Paris. She sat down to mend her Milanese tights. The Italian toe shoes were good but Italian tights were too heavy – they cut your thighs on the arabesque croisé.

II

'D'you have a good time?'

David met Bonnie under the pink explosive apple trees where Lake Geneva spread a net below the undulating acrobacies of the mountains. Opposite the Vevey Station a bridge of pencil strokes clipped pleasantly over the river; the mountains braced themselves out of the water on the Dorothy Perkins stems and thongs of purple clematis. Nature had padded every crack and crevice with floral stuffing; narcissus banded the mountains in a milky way, the houses tethered themselves to the earth with browsing cows and pots of geraniums. Ladies in lace with parasols, ladies in linen with white shoes, ladies in tangerine smiles patronized the elements in the station square. Lake Geneva, pounded for so many summers by the cruel brightness, lay shaking its fist at the high heavens swearing up at God from the security of the Swiss Republic.

'Lovely,' replied Bonnie succinctly.

'How was Mummy?' pursued David.

Dressed in a catalogue of summer, even Bonnie noticed that his clothes were a little amazing, suggesting a studied sartorial selection. He was dressed in pearly gray and he looked as if he had stepped down inside his angora sweater and flannel pants with such precision that he had hardly deranged their independent decorative purpose. If he hadn't been so handsome he could never have achieved so speculative and tentative an effect. Bonnie was proud of her father.

'Mummy was dancing,' said Bonnie.

Deep shadows sprawled about the streets of Vevey like lazy summer drunkards; clouds full of moisture floated like lily pads in the luminous puddle of the sky.

They mounted the hotel bus.

'The rooms, Prince,' said the sad, suave hotel man, 'will be eight dollars a day because of the fête.'

The valet carried their luggage to a white-and-gold encrusted suite.

'Oh, what a beautiful sitting room!' ejaculated Bonnie. 'There is even a telephone. Such "élégance"!'

She spun about switching on the lurid floor lamps.

'And I have a room to myself, and a bath of my own,' she hummed. 'It was nice of you, Daddy, to give Mademoiselle "vacances"!'

'How would the royal visitor like her bath?' said David.

'Well – cleaner, please, than in Naples.'

'Was your bath dirty in Naples?'

'Mummy said "no"—' said Bonnie hesitantly, 'but Mademoiselle said "yes." Everybody gives me much contrary advice,' she confided.

'Alabama should have seen to your bath,' said David.

He heard the thin treble voice singing to itself in the tub, 'Savez-vous planter les choux—' There was no sound of splashing.

'Are you washing your knees?'

'I haven't got to them yet – "à la manière de chez-nous, à la manière de chez-nous"—'

'Bonnie, you *must* hurry up.'

'Can I stay up till ten o'clock tonight? – "on les plante avec le nez"—'

Bonnie tore giggling through the rooms.

The sun winked in the gold braid, the curtains blew softly in the ghostly breeze, the lamps glowed like abandoned campfires under their pink shades in the daylight. The flowers in the room were pretty. There must be a clock. Round and round the child's brain raced contentedly. The tops of the trees outside were shiny blue.

'Didn't Mummy *say* anything?' said David.

'Oh, yes,' said Bonnie, 'she gave me a party.'

'That was nice; tell me about it.'

'Well,' said Bonnie, 'there was a monkey, and I was sick, and Mademoiselle cried about the preserves on my dress.'

'I see – well, what did Mummy say?'

'Mummy said if it weren't for the orchestra she could do two turns.'

'It must have been very interesting,' said David.

'Oh, yes,' Bonnie compromised, 'it was very interesting. Daddy—'

'Yes, dear?'

'I love you, Daddy.'

David laughed in little sharp jerks like a person making tatting.

'Well, you'd better.'

'I think so too. Do you think I could sleep in your bed tonight?'

'Of course not!'

'It would be very comfortable.'

'Your own is just the same.'

The child's tone changed to sudden practicality. 'It's safer near you. No wonder Mummy liked sleeping in your bed.'

'How silly!'

'When I am married all my family will sleep together in a large bed. Then I shall be quite easy about them, and they will not be afraid of the dark,' went on the child. 'You liked being near your parents until you had Mummy, didn't you?'

'We had our parents – then we had you. The present generation is always the one without the comfort of people to lean on.'

'Why?'

'Because solace, Bonnie, is an affair of retrospect and expectation. If you don't hurry up, our friends will be here before you are dressed.'

'Are there children coming?'

'Yes, I am taking the family of one of my friends for you to meet. We are going to Montreux to see the dancing. But,' said David, 'the sky is clouding over. It looks like rain.'

'Daddy, I hope not!'

'So do I. Something always spoils a party, monkeys or rain. There are our friends now.'

Behind their governess three blond children traversed the hotel court through the thin sun pinking suggestively the trunks of the firs.

'Bonjour,' said Bonnie, extending her hand limply in a juvenile interpretation of a grande dame. Inconsistently she pounced on the little girl. 'Oh, but you are dressed as Alice in Wonderland!' she shrieked.

The child was several years older than Bonnie.

'Grüss Gott,' she answered demurely, 'you too have on a pretty dress.'

'Et bonjour, Mademoiselle!' The two little boys were younger. They clambered over Bonnie with the stiff military formality of the Swiss school boy.

The children were very decorative under the vista of cropped plane trees. The green hills stretched away like a canvas sea to faint recesses of legend. Pleasantly loitering mountain vegetation dangled over the hotel front in swaying clots of blue and mauve. The childish voices droned through the mountain clarity conversing intimately in the sense of seclusion conveyed by the overhanging Alps.

190

'What is this "it" I saw in the papers?' said the eight-year-old voice.

'Don't be silly, it's only sex-appeal,' answered the voice of ten.

'Only beautiful ladies can have it in the movies,' said Bonnie.

'But sometimes, don't men have it too?' said the little boy disappointed.

'Father says everybody does,' called the older girl.

'Well, Mother said only a few. What did your parents say, Bonnie?'

'They didn't say anything, since I had not read it in the papers.'

'When you are older,' said Genevra, 'you will – if it is still there.'

'I saw my father in a shower bath,' offered the smallest boy expectantly.

'That's nothing,' sniffed Bonnie.

'Why is it nothing?' the voice insisted.

'Why is it something?' said Bonnie.

'I have swimmed with him naked.'

'Children – children!' reproved David.

Black shadows fell on the water, echoes of nothing poured down the hills and steamed over the lake. It began to rain; a Swiss downpour soaked the earth. The flat bulbous vines about the hotel windows bled torrents over the ledges; the heads of the dahlias bent with the storm.

'How can they have the fête in the rain?' the children cried in dismay.

'Perhaps the ballet will wear their "caoutchouc" as we have done,' said Bonnie.

'I'd rather they had trained seals anyway,' said the little boy optimistically.

The rain was a slow sparkling leak from a lachrymose sun. The wooden platforms about the estrade were damp and soaked with dye from the wet serpentine and sticky masses of confetti. Fresh wet light through the red and orange mushrooms of shiny umbrellas glowed like a lamp store display; a fashionable audience glistened in bright cellophane slickers.

'What if it rains down his horn?' said Bonnie, as the orchestra appeared beneath the rain-washed set of chinchilla-like mountains.

'But it might be pretty,' protested the boy. 'Sometimes in my bath when I sink beneath the water I make the most beautiful noises by blowing.'

'It is ravishing,' pronounced Genevra, 'when my brother blows.'

The damp air flattened the music like a sponge; girls brushed the rain from their hats; the rolling back of the tarred canvas exposed the slick and dangerous boards.

'It is *Prometheus* they're going to give,' said David, reading the programme. 'I will tell you the story afterwards.'

From a whirr of revolving leaps Lorenz collected his brown magnificence, clenching his fists in the air and chinning the mystery of the mountain sky. His bare rain-polished body tortured itself to inextricable postures, straightened, and dropped to the floor with the suspended float of falling paper.

'Look, Bonnie,' David called, 'there's an old friend of yours!'

Arienne, subduing a technical maze of insolent turns and arrogant twists, represented a pink cupid. Damp and unconvincing, she tenaciously gripped the superhuman exigencies of her rôle. The workman underneath the artist ground out her difficult interpretation.

David felt an overwhelming unexpected surge of pity for the girl going through all that while the spectators thought of how wet they were getting and how uncomfortable they were. The dancers, too, were thinking of the rain, and shivered a little through the bursting crescendo of the finale.

'I liked best the ones in black who fought themselves,' said Bonnie.

'Yes,' said the boy, 'when they were bumping each other it was far best.'

'We'd better stay in Montreux for dinner – it's too wet to drive back,' suggested David.

About the hotel lobby sat many groups with an air of professional waiting; the smell of coffee and French pastry permeated the half-gloom; raincoats trickled in the vestibule.

192

'Bonjour!' yelled Bonnie suddenly, 'you have danced very well, better than in Paris even!'

Sleek and well-dressed Arienne traversed the room. She turned like a mannequin, exhibiting herself. A slight embarrassment covered the gray honest meadow between her eyes.

'I am sorry I am so dégouttante,' she said pretentiously shaking her coat, 'in this old thing from Patou! But you have grown so big!' she fondled Bonnie affectedly. 'And how is your mother?'

'She too is dancing,' said Bonnie.

'I know.'

Arienne freed herself as quickly as she could. She had given her drama of success – Patou was the chosen couturière of the stars of the ballet; only the finest sack-cloth was sewed by Patou. Arienne had said Patou. 'Patou,' she said, emphatically.

'I must go to my room, our étoile is waiting for me there. Au 'voir, cher David! Au 'voir, ma petite Bonnie!'

The children were very dainty about the table, and somehow not an anachronism in this night place that had had music before the war. The wine barred the table with topaz shafts, the beer protested the cold restraint of silver mugs, the children giggled ebulliently beneath parental discipline like boiling water shaking the lid of a sauce-pan.

'I want the hors d'oeuvre,' said Bonnie.

'Why, daughter! It's too indigestible for night.'

'But I want it too!' wailed the boy.

'The old will order for the young,' announced David, 'and I will tell you about "Prometheus" so you will not notice that you are not getting what you want. Prometheus was tied to an immense rock and—'

'May I have the apricot jam?' interrupted Genevra.

'Do you want to hear about Prometheus, or not?' said Bonnie's father impatiently.

'Yes, sir. Oh, yes, of course.'

'Then,' resumed David, 'he writhed there for years and years and—'

'That is in my "Mythologie,"' said Bonnie proudly.

'And then what?' said the little boy, 'after he was writhing.'

'Then what? Well—' David glowed with the exhilaration of

being attractive, laying out the facets of his personality for the children like stacks of expensive shirts for admiring valets. 'Do you remember exactly what *did* happen?' he said lamely to Bonnie.

'No. I've forgot since a long time.'

'If that is all, may I please have the compote?' Genevra politely insisted.

Riding home through the flickering night, the country passed in visions of twinkling villages and cottage gardens obstructing their passage with high sunflower stalks. The children, wrapped in the bright armor of Bonnie's father's car, dozed against the felt cushions. Safe in the glittering car they rode: the car-at-your-disposal, the mystery-car, the Rajah's-car, the death-car, the first-prize, puffing the power of money out on the summer air like a seigneur distributing largesse. Where the night sky reflected the lake they rode like a rising bubble through the bowl of the mercurial, welded globe. They drove through the black impenetrable shadows clouding the road like fumes from an alchemist's laboratory and sped across the gleam of the open mountain top.

'I would not like to be an artist,' said the little boy sleepily, 'unless I could be a trained seal, I wouldn't,' he qualified.

'I would,' said Bonnie. 'They will be having supper when we are already asleep.'

'But,' protested Genevra reasonably, 'we have had our supper.'

'Yes,' Bonnie agreed, 'but supper is always nice to be having.'

'It's not when you're full,' said Genevra.

'Well, when you're full you wouldn't care whether it was nice or not,' said Bonnie.

'Why do you always argue so?' Genevra settled in cold withdrawal against the window.

'Because you interrupted when I was thinking what would be nice.'

'We'll go straight to your hotel,' suggested David. 'You children seem to be tired.'

'Father says conflict develops the character,' said the older boy.

'I think it spoils the evening,' said David.

'Mummy said it ruins the disposition,' contributed Genevra.

Moving about the hotel rooms alone with David, Bonnie approached her father.

'I suppose I should have been much nicer?'

'Yes. Sometimes you will realize that people are more important than digestion, even.'

'They should have made me *feel* nice then, don't you think? They were the company.'

'Children are always company,' said David. 'People are like almanacs, Bonnie – you never can find the information you're looking for, but the casual reading is well worth the trouble.'

'These rooms are very nice,' reflected Bonnie. 'What is that thing in the bathroom where the water squirts out like a hose?'

'I have told you a thousand times not to touch those things! It's a sort of a fire extinguisher.'

'Do they always think there's going to be a fire in the bathroom?'

'Very seldom.'

'Of course,' said Bonnie, 'it would be too bad for the people, but it would be fun to see the excitement.'

'Are you ready for bed? I want you to write to your mother.'

'Yes, Daddy.'

Bonnie sat in the still parlor with its deep majestic windows facing the sepia square, composing.

'Dearest Mummy:

As you will see, we are back in Switzerland—' The room was very big and quiet.

'—It is very interesting to see the Swiss! The hotel-man called Daddy a Prince!'

The curtains waved just softly in the breeze, then lay still.

'—Figurez-vous, Mamman, that would make me a Princess. Imagine them thinking anything so silly—'

There were enough lamps for a room to have, even a big 'chic' room such as this.

'—Mademoiselle Arienne had a Patou dress. She was glad about your success—'

They had even thought of putting flowers to make the room so much prettier at her father's hotel.

'—If I were a Princess, I should always have my own way. I would bring you to Switzerland—'

The cushions were hard but very pretty with their gold tassels hanging down the chair legs.

'—I was glad when you were home—'

The shadows seemed to move. Only babies were frightened of shadows or of moving things at night.

'—I have not many experiences to relate. I am making myself as spoiled as I can—'

There couldn't be anything hiding in the shadows. They just appeared to move that way. Was that the door opening?

'O – o – oh,' shrieked Bonnie in terror.

'Sh – sh – sh,' David reassured the child, holding out the promise of warmth and comfort to his daughter.

'Did I frighten you?'

'No – It was the shadows. I am sometimes silly when I am all by myself.'

'I understand,' he soothed. 'Grown people are too, very often.'

The lights of the hotel fell somnolently over the park opposite; an air of waiting hung over the streets like a flag lying about its staff without a breeze.

'Daddy, I want to sleep with my lights on.'

'What an idea! There's nothing to be afraid of – you've got me and Mummy.'

'Mummy is in Naples,' said Bonnie, 'and if I fall asleep you will surely be going out!'

'All right then, but it's absurd!'

Some hours later when David tiptoed in, he found Bonnie's room dark. Her eyes were much too tightly closed to be unconscious; she had arranged a small crack in the door to the living room to compromise.

'What's keeping you awake?' he said.

'I was thinking,' murmured Bonnie. 'It is better here than with Mummy's success in Italy.'

'But I have success,' said David, 'only I got it before you were born so it just appears the natural order to you!'

Insects reverberated in the trees beside the silent room.

'Was it so awful in Naples?' he pursued.

'Well,' hesitated Bonnie, 'I don't know how it was for Mummy, of course—'

'Didn't she say anything at all about me?'

'She said – let me see – I don't know what Mummy said, Daddy, only she said her piece of advice that she had to give me was not to be a back-seat driver about life.'

'Did you understand?'

'Oh, no,' sighed Bonnie gratefully and complacently.

The summer quavered down from Lausanne to Geneva, trimming the lake like the delicate border of a porcelain plate; the fields yellowed in the heat; the mountains across from their windows yielded up no more details even on the brightest of days.

Bonnie played in sibylline detachment watching the Juras wedge their inky shadows between the rushes at the water's edge. White birds flying in inverted circumflex accented the colorless suggestion of a bounded infinite.

'Has the little one slept well?' asked the people recovering from long illnesses who painted the view in the garden.

'Yes,' answered Bonnie politely, 'but you must not disturb me – I am the watcher who tells when the enemy is coming.'

'Then can I be King of the Castle?' called David from the window, 'and cut off your head if you make a mistake?'

'You,' said Bonnie, 'are a prisoner, and I have pulled out your tongue so you cannot complain – but I am good to you anyway,' she relented, 'so you needn't feel unhappy, Daddy – unless you want to! Of course, it would be *better* to be unhappy, perhaps!'

'All right,' said David, 'I'm one of the unhappiest of people! The laundry has faded my pink shirt, and I've just been invited to a wedding.'

'I don't allow you to go out visiting,' said Bonnie severely.

'Well, then, I'm only half as unhappy as I was.'

'I won't let you play any more if you act that way. You're supposed to be sad and homesick for your wife.'

'Look! I dissolve in tears!' David draped himself like a puppet over the wet bathing suits drying on the window ledge.

The bellboy bringing up the telegram seemed rather surprised to find Monsieur le Prince Américain in such an unusual position. David tore open the envelope.

'Father stricken,' he read. 'Recovery doubtful. Come at once. Try to save Alabama from shock. Devotedly. Millie Beggs.'

David stared trance-like at the white butterflies fluttering under a tree with crooked branches elbowing the ground impassively. He watched his emotions sliding past the present like a letter dropped down a glass chute; the telegram cut into their lives as decisively as the falling blade of a guillotine. Grabbing a pencil he started to write out a telegram to Alabama, decided to telephone, and remembered that the Opera was closed in the afternoon. He sent the wire to the pension.

'What's the matter, Daddy, aren't you playing any more?'

'No, dear; you'd better come in, Bonnie. I've had some bad news.'

'What's happened?'

'Your grandpa's dying, so we'll have to go to America. I'll send for Mademoiselle to stay with you. Mummy will probably come straight to Paris to meet me – unless I sail from Italy.'

'I wouldn't,' advised Bonnie. 'I'd surely go from France.'

They waited distractedly for word from Naples.

The answer from Alabama fell like a shooting star, a cold mass of lead from the heavens. From voluble hysterical Italian, David finally deciphered the message.

'Madame is ill in the hospital since two days. You must come here to save her. There is none to look after her though she refuses us your address, still hoping to be well alone. It is serious. We have no one to count on but you and Jesus.'

'Bonnie,' groaned David, 'where in the hell have I put Mademoiselle's address?'

'I don't know, Daddy.'

198

'Then you'll have to pack for yourself – and be quick.'

'Oh, Daddy,' wept Bonnie, 'I just came from Naples. I don't want to go!'

'Your mother needs us,' was all David said. They caught the midnight express.

It was a little like the Inquisition at the Italian hospital – they had to wait outside with Alabama's landlady and Madame Sirgeva till it opened its doors at two o'clock.

'So much promise,' moaned Madame, 'she would perhaps have been a big dancer in time—'

'And Holy Angels, so young!' murmured the Italian.

'Only of course there wasn't any time,' added Sirgeva sorrowfully. 'She was too old.'

'And always alone, so help me God, Signor,' sighed the Italian reverentially.

The streets ran about the tiny grass plots like geometrical calculations – some learned doctor's half-effaced explanatory diagrams on a slate. A charwoman opened the doors.

David did not mind the smell of the ether. Two doctors talked together in an anteroom about golf-scores. It was the uniforms that made it like the Inquisition, and the smell of green soap.

David felt very sorry for Bonnie.

David didn't believe the English interne had made a hole-in-one.

The doctors told him about the infection from the glue in the box of the toe shoe – it had seeped into a blister. They used the word 'incision' many times over as if they were saying a 'Hail Mary.'

'A question of time,' they repeated, one after the other.

'If she had only disinfected,' said Sirgeva. 'I will keep Bonnie while you go in.'

In the desperate finality of the room, David stared at the ceiling.

'There's nothing the matter with my foot,' screamed Alabama. 'It's my stomach. It's killing me!'

Why did the doctor inhabit another world from hers? Why couldn't he hear what she was saying, and not stand talking about ice-packs?

'We will see,' the doctor said, staring out of the window impassively.

'I've got to have some water! *Please* give me some water!'

The nurse went on methodically straightening the dressings on the wheel-table.

'Non c'è acqua,' she whispered.

She didn't need to be so confidential about it.

The walls of the hospital opened and shut. Alabama's room smelled like hell. Her foot lay off the bed in a yellow fluid that turned white after a while. She had a terrible backache. It was as if she had been beaten with heavy beams.

'I've got to have some orange juice,' she thought she said. No, it was Bonnie who had said that. David will bring me some chocolate ice cream and I will throw it up; it smells like a soda fountain, thrown-up, she thought. There were glass tubes in her ankle like stems, like the headdress of a Chinese Empress – it was a permanent wave they were giving her foot, she thought.

The walls of the room slid quietly past, dropping one over the other like the leaves of a heavy album. They were all shades of gray and rose and mauve. There was no sound when they fell.

Two doctors came and talked together. What did Salonica have to do with her back?

'I've got to have a pillow,' she said feebly. 'Something broke my neck!'

The doctors stood impersonally at the end of the bed. The windows opened like blinding white caverns, entrances to white funnels that fitted over the bed like tents. It was too easy to breathe inside that tented radiance – she couldn't feel her body, the air was so light.

'This afternoon, then, at three,' said one of the men, and left. The other went on talking to himself.

'I can't operate,' she thought he said, 'because I've got to stand here and count the white butterflies to-day.'

'And so the girl was raped by a calla lily,' he said, '—or, no, I believe it was the spray of a shower bath that did the trick!' he said triumphantly.

He laughed fiendishly. How could he laugh so much of

Pulcinella? And he as thin as a matchstick and tall as the Eiffel Tower! The nurse laughed with another nurse.

'It isn't *Pulcinella*,' Alabama thought she said to the nurse. 'It's *Apollon-Musagète*.'

'You wouldn't know. How could I possibly expect you to understand that?' she screamed contemptuously.

Meaningfully the nurses laughed together and left her room. The walls began again. She decided to lie there and frustrate the walls if they thought they could press her between their pages like a bud from a wedding bouquet. For weeks Alabama lay there. The smell of the stuff in the bowl took the skin off her throat, and she spit red mucus.

Those agonizing weeks David cried as he walked along the streets, and he cried at night, and life seemed senseless and over. Then he grew desperate, and murder and violence played in his heart till he wore himself out.

Twice a day he came to the hospital and listened to the doctors telling about blood poison.

Finally they let him see her. He buried his head in the bedclothes and ran his arms underneath her broken body and cried like a baby. Her legs were up in sliding pulleys like a dentist's paraphernalia. The weights ached and strained her neck and back like a mediaeval rack.

Sobbing and sobbing, David held her close. He felt of a different world to Alabama; his tempo was different from the sterile, attenuated rhythms of the hospital. He felt lush and callous, somehow, like a hot laborer. She felt she hardly knew him.

He kept his eyes glued persistently to her face. He hardly dared look at the bottom of the bed.

'Dear, it's nothing,' he said with affected blandness. 'You will be well in no time.' Somehow she was not reassured. He seemed to be avoiding some issue. Her mother's letters did not mention her foot and Bonnie was not brought to the hospital.

'I must be very thin,' she thought. The bedpan cut her spine, and her hands looked like bird claws. They clung to the air like claws to a perch, hooking the firmament as her right to a foot rest. Her hands were long and frail and blue over the knuckles like an unfeathered bird.

Sometimes her foot hurt her so terribly that she closed her eyes and floated off on the waves of the afternoon. Invariably she went to the same delirious place. There was a lake there so clear that she could not tell the bottom from the top; a pointed island lay heavy on the waters like an abandoned thunderbolt. Phallic poplars and bursts of pink geranium and a forest of white-trunked trees whose foliage flowed out of the sky covered the land. Nebulous weeds swung on the current: purple stems with fat animal leaves, long tentacular stems with no leaves at all, swishing balls of iodine and the curious chemical growths of stagnant waters. Crows cawed from one deep mist to another. The word 'sick' effaced itself against the poisonous air and jittered lamely about between the tips of the island and halted on the white road that ran straight through the middle. 'Sick' turned and twisted about the narrow ribbon of the highway like a roasting pig on a spit, and woke Alabama gouging at her eyeballs with the prongs of its letters.

Sometimes she shut her eyes and her mother brought her a cool lemonade, but this happened only when she was not in pain.

David came when anything new occurred like a parent supervising a child who is learning to walk.

'And so – you must know sometime, Alabama,' he said at last. The bottom fell out of her stomach. She could feel the things dropping through.

'I've known for ages,' she said in sickly calm.

'Poor darling – you've still got your foot. It's not *that*,' he said compassionately. 'But you will never be able to dance again. Are you going to mind terribly?'

'Will I have crutches?' she asked.

'No – nothing at all. The tendons are cut and they had to scrape through an artery, but you will be able to walk with a slight limp. Try not to mind.'

'Oh, my body,' she said. 'And all that work for nothing!'

'Poor, my dear one – but it has brought us together again. We have each other, dear.'

'Yes – what's left,' she sobbed.

She lay there, thinking that she had always meant to take

202

what she wanted from life. Well – she hadn't wanted this. This was a stone that would need a good deal of salt and pepper.

Her mother hadn't wanted her boy to die, either, she supposed, and there must have been times when her father hadn't wanted any of them dragging about his thighs and drawing his soul off in lager.

Her father! She hoped they would get home while he was still alive. Without her father the world would be without its last resource.

'But,' she remembered with a sudden sobering shock, 'it will be me who is the last resource when my father is dead.'

III

The David Knights stepped out of the old brick station. The Southern town slept soundless on the wide palette of the cotton-fields. Alabama's ears were muffled by the intense stillness as if she had entered a vacuum. Negroes, lethargic and immobile, draped themselves on the depot steps like effigies to some exhausted god of creation. The wide square, masked in velvet shadows, drowned in the lull of the South, spread like soft blotting paper under man and his heritage.

'So we will find us a beautiful house and live here?' asked Bonnie.

'Que c'est drôle!' ejaculated Mademoiselle. 'So many Negroes! Do they have missionaries to teach them?'

'Teach them what?' asked Alabama.

'Why – religion.'

'Their religion is very satisfactory, they sing a lot.'

'It is well. They are very sympathetic.'

'Will they bother me?' asked Bonnie.

'Of course not. You're safer here than you've ever been in your life. This is where your mother was little.'

'I went to a Negro baptism in that river at five o'clock on a Fourth of July morning. They were dressed in white robes and the red sun slanted down over the muddy water's edge, and I felt very rapturous and wanted to join their church.'

'I would like to see that.'

'Maybe.'

Joan was waiting in the little brown Ford.

Alabama felt like a little girl again to see her sister after so many years. The old town where her father had worked away so much of his life spread before her protectively. It was good to be a stranger in a land when you felt aggressive and acquisitive, but when you began to weave your horizons into some kind of shelter it was good to know that hands you loved had helped in their spinning – made you feel as if the threads would hold together better.

'I'm awfully glad you got here,' Joan said sadly.

'Is grandpa very sick?' said Bonnie.

'Yes, dear. I've always thought Bonnie was such a sweet child.'

'How are your children, Joan?' Joan wasn't much changed. She was conventional, more like their mother.

'Just fine. I couldn't bring them. All this is very depressing for children.'

'Yes. We'd better leave Bonnie at the hotel. She can come out in the morning.'

'Let her just come to say "Hello." Mamma adores her so.' She turned to David. 'She's always liked Alabama better than the rest of us.'

'Junk! Because I'm the youngest.'

The car sped up the familiar streets. The soft inconsequential night, the smell of the gently perspiring land, the crickets in the grass, the heavy trees conspiring together over the hot pavements, lulled the blank fear in Alabama's heart to a sense of impotence.

'Can't we do *anything*?' she said.

'We've done everything. There's no cure for old age.'

'How is Mamma?'

'As brave as she always is – but I'm glad you could come.'

The car stopped before the quiet house. How many nights had she coasted up to that walk just that way to keep from waking her father with the grind of the brakes after dances? The sweet smell of sleeping gardens lay in the air. A breeze from the gulf tolled the pecan trees mournfully back and forth. Nothing had changed. The friendly windows shone in the just benediction of her father's spirit, the door spread open to the just decency of his will. Thirty years he had lived in his house, and watched the scattered jonquils bloom and seen the morning-glories wrinkle in the morning sun and snipped the blight from his roses and admired Miss Millie's ferns.

'Ain't they pretty?' he'd say. Measured, marked only by the absence of an accent, his balanced diction swayed to the aristocracy of his spirit.

He had caught a crimson moth once in the moon vines and pinned it over his mantel on a calendar. 'It's a very good place for it,' he had said, stretching the fragile wings over a railroad map of the South. The Judge had a sense of humor.

Infallible man! How his children had gloated when something went wrong – the unsuccessful operation on a chicken's craw with the Judge's pocketknife and a needle from Millie's sewing basket, an overturned glass of iced tea on the Sunday dinner table, a spot of turkey-dressing on the clean Thanksgiving cloth – these things had rendered the cerebral machinery of the honest man more tangible.

The quick fear of unclassified emotion seized Alabama, an overwhelming sense of loss. She and David climbed the steps. How high those cement slabs that held the ferns had seemed when she was a child jumping from one to the other – and there was the place where she had sat while somebody told her about Santa Claus, and hated the informer and hated her own parents that the myth should be untrue and yet exist, crying out, 'I will believe—'; and there the dry Bermuda grass between the hot bricks had tickled her bare thighs, and there was the limb of the tree her father had forbade her to swing on. It seemed incredible that the thin branch could ever have supported her body. 'You must not abuse things,' her father had corrected.

'It won't hurt the tree.'

'In my judgment it will. If you want to have things, you have got to take care of them.'

He who had had so few things! An engraving of his father and a miniature of Millie, three buckeyes from a Tennessee vacation, a pair of gold cuff buttons, an insurance policy, and some summer socks was what Alabama remembered of his top bureau drawer.

'Hello, darling,' her mother kissed her tremulously, 'and my darling! Let me kiss you on the top of your head.' Bonnie clung to her grandmother.

'Can we see Grandpa, Grandma?'

'It will make you sad, dear.'

The old lady's face was white and reticent. She moved slowly back and forth in the old swing, rocking with gentle condolence their spiritual losses.

'Oh – o – o – o—, Millie,' the Judge's voice called feebly.

The tired doctor came to the porch.

'Cousin Millie, I thought if the children want to see their father, he is conscious now.' He turned kindly to Alabama. 'I'm glad you got here,' he said.

Trembling, she followed his lean, protective back into the room. Her father! Her father! How weak and pale he was. She could have cried out at her inability to frustrate this useless, inevitable waste.

She sat quietly on the bed. Her beautiful father!

'Hello, baby.' His gaze wandered over her face. 'Are you going to stay here awhile?'

'Yes, it's a good place.'

'I've always thought so.'

The tired eyes travelled to the door. Bonnie waited, frightened, in the hall.

'I want to see the baby.' A sweet tolerant smile lit the Judge's face. Bonnie approached the bed timidly.

'Hello, there, baby. You're a little bird,' the man smiled. 'And you're as pretty as two little birds.'

'When will you be well again, Grandpa?'

'Pretty soon. I'm very tired. I'll see you tomorrow.' He waved her aside.

Alone with her father, Alabama's heart sank. He was so thin and little now that he was sick, to have got through so much of life. He had had a hard time providing for them all. The noble completeness of the life withering on the bed before her moved her to promise herself many promises.

'Oh, my father, there are so many things I want to ask you.'

'Baby,' the old man patted her hand. His wrists were no bigger than a bird's. How had he fed them all?

'I never thought you'd known till now.'

She smoothed the gray hair, even Confederate gray.

'I've got to go to sleep, baby.'

'Sleep,' she said, 'sleep.'

She sat there a long time. She hated the way the nurse moved about the room as if her father were a child. Her father knew everything. Her heart was sobbing, and sobbing.

The old man opened his eyes proudly, as was his wont.

'Did you say you wanted to ask me something?'

'I thought you could tell me if our bodies are given to us as counterirritants to the soul. I thought you'd know why when our bodies ought to bring surcease from our tortured minds, they fail and collapse; and why, when we are tormented in our bodies, does our soul desert us as a refuge?'

The old man lay silent.

'Why do we spend years using up our bodies to nurture our minds with experience and find our minds turning then to our exhausted bodies for solace? Why, Daddy?'

'Ask me something easy,' the old man answered very weak and far away.

'The Judge must sleep,' said the nurse.

'I'll go.'

Alabama stood in the hall. There was the light her father turned out when he went up to bed; there was the peg with his hat hanging there.

When man is no longer custodian of his vanities and convictions, he's nothing at all, she thought. Nothing! There's nothing lying on that bed – but it is my father and I loved him. Without his desire, I should never have lived, she thought. Perhaps we are all just agents in a very experimental stage of organic free will. It cannot be that myself is the purpose of my father's life – but it can be that what I can appreciate of his fine spirit is the purpose of my own.

She went to her mother.

'Judge Beggs said yesterday,' said Millie to the shadows, 'that he would like to go for a ride in the little car to see the

207

people on their front porches. He tried all summer to learn to drive, but he was too old. "Millie," he said, "tell that hoary-headed angel to dress me. I want to go out." He called the nurse his hoary-headed angel. He always had a dry sense of humor. He loved his little car.'

Like the good mother she was, she went on and on – as if she could teach Austin to live again by rehearsing all those things. Like a mother speaking of a very young child, she told Alabama about the sick Judge, her father.

'He said he wanted to order some new shirts from Philadelphia. He said he would like some breakfast bacon.'

'He gave Mamma a check for the undertaker for a thousand dollars,' added Joan.

'Yes,' Miss Millie laughed as if at a child's capricious prank. 'Then he said "But I want it back if I don't die."'

'Oh, my poor mother,' thought Alabama, 'and all the time he's going to die. Mamma knows, but she can't say to herself "He's going to die." Neither can I.'

Millie had nursed him so long, sick and well. When he was a young man in the law office and the other clerks no older than himself addressed him already as 'Mr. Beggs,' when he was middle-aged and consumed with poverty and care, when he was old and had more time to be kindly.

'My poor mother,' said Alabama. 'You have given your life for my father.'

'My father said we could be married,' answered her mother, 'when he found that your father's uncle was thirty-two years in the United States Senate and his father's brother was a Confederate General. He came to my father's law office to ask him for my hand. *My* father was eighteen years in the Senate and the Confederate Congress.'

She saw her mother as she was, part of a masculine tradition. Millie did not seem to notice about her own life, that there would be nothing left when her husband died. He was the father of her children, who were girls, and who had left her for the families of other men.

'My father was a proud man,' Millie said, proudly. 'When I was a little girl I loved him dearly. There were twenty of us and only two girls.'

'Where are your brothers?' said David curiously.

'Dead and gone long ago.'

'They were half-brothers,' said Joan.

'It was my own brother who came here in the spring. He went away and said he'd write, but he never did.'

'Mamma's brother was a darling,' Joan said. 'He owned a drug store in Chicago.'

'Your father was very kind to him and took him driving in the car.'

'Why didn't you write to him, Mamma?'

'I did not think to get his address. When I came to live with your father's family I had so much to do I couldn't keep track of my own.'

Bonnie was asleep on the hard porch bench. When Alabama had slept that way as a little girl, her father had carried her upstairs to bed in his arms. David lifted the sleeping child.

'We ought to go,' he said.

'Daddy,' Bonnie whispered, snuggling under his coat lapels. 'My Daddy.'

'You will come again tomorrow?'

'Early in the morning,' Alabama answered. Her mother's white hair was done in a crown around her head like a Florentine saint. She held her mother in her arms. Oh, she remembered how it felt to be close to her mother!

Every day Alabama went to the old house, so clean inside and bright. She brought her father little special things to eat, and flowers. He loved yellow flowers.

'We used to gather yellow violets in the woods when we were young,' her mother said.

The doctors came and shook their heads, and so many friends came that nobody ever had more friends to bring them cakes and flowers, and old servants came to ask about the Judge, and the milkman left an extra pint of milk out of his own pocket to show that he was sorry, and the Judge's fellow-judges came with sad and noble faces like the heads on postage stamps and cameos. The Judge lay in his bed, fretting about money.

'We can't afford this sickness,' he said over and over. 'I've got to get up. It's costing money.'

His children talked it over. They would share the expenses. The Judge would not have allowed them to accept his salary from the State if he had known he was not going to get well. All of them were able to help.

Alabama and David rented a house to be near her parents. It was bigger than her father's house, in a garden with roses and a privet hedge, and iris planted to devour the spring, and many bushes and shrubs under the windows.

Alabama tried to persuade her mother to take a ride. It was months since she had left the house.

'I can't go,' Millie said. 'Your father might want me while I'm away.' She waited constantly for some last illuminating words from the Judge, feeling that he must have something to tell her before he left her alone at the last.

'We'll just stay half an hour,' Millie finally agreed.

Alabama drove her mother past the Capitol, where her father had spent so many years of his life. The clerks sent them roses from the rose bed under his office window. Alabama wondered if his books were covered with dust. Perhaps he would have prepared some last communication there, in one of his drawers.

'How did you happen to marry Daddy?'

'He wanted to marry me. I had many beaux.'

The old lady looked at her daughter as if she expected a protest. She was more beautiful than her children. There was much integrity in her face. Surely she had had many beaux.

'There was one who wanted to give me a monkey. He told my mother monkeys all had tuberculosis. My grandmother looked at him and said, "But you look very healthy to me." She was French, and a very beautiful woman. A young man sent me a baby pig from his plantation, and another sent me a coyote from New Mexico, and one of them drank, and another married Cousin Lil.'

'Where are they all?'

'Dead and gone years ago. I wouldn't know them if I saw them. Ain't the trees pretty?'

They passed the house where her mother and father had met – 'at a New Year's ball,' her mother told her. 'He was the handsomest man there, and I was visiting your Cousin Mary.'

Cousin Mary was old and her red eyes cried continually under her spectacles. There wasn't much left of her, yet she had given a ball on New Year's.

Alabama had never pictured her father dancing.

When she saw him in the casket at the end, his face was so young and fine and humorous, the first thing Alabama thought of was that New Year's ball so many years ago.

'Death is the only real elegance,' she said to herself. She had been afraid to look, afraid of what discoveries she might make in the spent and lifeless face. There was nothing to be afraid of, only plastic beauty and immobility.

There was nothing amongst the papers in his bare skeleton office, and nothing in the box with his insurance premiums except a tiny mouldy purse containing three nickels wrapped in an ancient newspaper.

'It must be the first money he ever earned.'

'His mother gave it to him for laying out the front yard,' they said.

There was nothing amongst his clothes or hid behind his books. 'He must have forgot,' Alabama said, 'to leave the message.'

The State sent a wreath to the funeral and the Court sent a wreath. Alabama was very proud of her father.

Poor Miss Millie! She had a mourning veil pinned over her black straw hat from last year. She had bought that hat to go to the mountains with the Judge.

Joan cried about the black. 'I can't afford it,' she said.

So they didn't wear black.

They didn't have music. The Judge had never liked songs save the tuneless 'Old Grimes' that he sang to his children. They read 'Lead Kindly Light' at the funeral.

The Judge lay sleeping on the hillside under the hickory-nut trees and the oak. From his grave the dome of the Capitol blotted out the setting sun. The flowers wilted, and the children planted jasmine vines and hyacinths. It was peaceful in the old cemetery. Wild flowers grew there, and rose bushes so old that the flowers had lost their color with the years. Crape myrtle and Lebanon cedars shed their barbs over the slabs; rusty Confederate crosses sank into the clematis vines and the burned grass. Tangles of narcissus and white flowers strayed the washed banks and ivy climbing in the crumbling walls. The Judge's grave said:

AUSTIN BEGGS
APRIL, EIGHTEEN FIFTY-SEVEN
NOVEMBER, NINETEEN THIRTY-ONE

But what had her father said? Alabama, alone on the hillside, fixed her eyes on the horizon in an effort to hear again that abstract measured voice. She couldn't remember that he had ever said anything. The last thing he said was:

'This thing is costing money,' and when his mind was wandering, 'Well, son, I could never make money either.' And he had said Bonnie was as pretty as two little birds, but what had he said to her when she was a little girl? She couldn't remember. There was nothing in the mackerel sky but cold spring rain.

Once he had said, 'If you want to choose, you must be a goddess.' That was when she had wanted her own way about things. It wasn't easy to be a goddess away from Olympus.

Alabama ran from the first drops of the bitter drizzle.

'We are certainly accountable,' she said, 'for all the things manifest in others that we secretly share. My father has bequeathed me many doubts.'

Panting, she threw the car into gear and slid off down the already slippery red clay road. She was lonely at night for her father.

'Everybody gives you belief for the asking,' she said to David, 'and so few people give you anything more to believe in than your own belief – just not letting you down, that's all. It's so hard to find a person who accepts responsibilities beyond what you ask.'

'So easy to be loved – so hard to love,' David answered.

Dixie came after a month had passed.

'I've plenty of room now for whoever wants to stay with me,' said Millie sadly.

The girls were much with their mother, trying to distract her.

212

'Alabama, please take the red geranium for your house,' insisted her mother. 'It doesn't matter here any more.'

Joan took the old writing desk and crated it and shipped it away.

'But you must be careful not to let them fix the corner where the Yankee shell fell through my father's roof – that would spoil it.'

Dixie asked for the silver punch bowl, and expressed it to her home in New York.

'Be careful not to dent it,' said Millie. 'It is made by hand from silver dollars that the slaves saved to give to your grandfather after they were freed – you children may choose what you like.'

Alabama wanted the portraits, Dixie took the old bed where she and her mother and Dixie's son had been born.

Miss Millie sought her consolation in the past.

'My father's house was square with crossing halls,' she'd say. 'There were lilacs about the double parlor windows, and an apple orchard far down by the river. When my father died, I carried you children down to the orchard to keep you away from the sadness. My mother was always very gentle, but she was never the same, after.'

'I'd like that old daguerreotype, Mamma,' said Alabama. 'Who is it?'

'My mother and my little sister. She died in a Federal prison during the war. My father was considered a traitor. Kentucky did not secede. They wanted to hang him for not upholding the Union.'

Millie at last agreed to move to a smaller house. Austin would never have stood for the little house. The girls persuaded her. They ranged their memories on the old mantel like a collection of bric-a-brac, and closed the shutters of Austin's house on the light and all of himself left there. It was better so for Millie – that memories should be sharp when one has nothing else to live for.

They all had bigger houses than Austin's and much bigger than the one he left to Millie, yet they came there to Millie feeding on what she remembered of their father and on her spirit, like converts imbibing a cult.

The Judge had said, 'When you're old and sick, you will wish you had saved your money.'

They had, some day, to accept the tightening up of the world – to begin some place to draw in their horizons.

Alabama lay awake thinking at night: the inevitable happened to people, and they found themselves prepared. The child forgives its parents when it perceives the accident of birth.

'We will have to begin all over again,' she said to David, 'with a new chain of associations, with new expectations to be paid from the sum of our experience like coupons clipped from a bond.'

'Middle-aged moralizing!'

'Yes, but we *are* middle-aged, aren't we?'

'My God! I hadn't thought of it! Do you suppose my pictures are?'

'They're just as good.'

'I've got to get to work, Alabama. Why have we practically wasted the best years of our lives?'

'So that there will be no time left on our hands at the end.'

'You are an incurable sophist.'

'Everybody is – only some people are in their private lives, and some people are in their philosophy.'

'Well?'

'Well, the object of the game is to fit things together so that when Bonnie is as old as we are and investigates our lives, she will find a beautiful harmonious mosaic of two gods of the hearthstone. Looking on this vision, she will feel herself less cheated that at some period of her life she has been forced to sacrifice her lust for plunder to protect what she imagines to be the treasure that we have handed on to her. It will lead her to believe that her restlessness will pass.'

Bonnie's voice drifted up from the drive on the evangelistic afternoon.

'And so good-bye, Mrs. Johnson. My mother and father will be very pleased and glad that you have been so kind and delightful about the nice time.'

She mounted the stairs contentedly. Alabama heard her purring in the hall.

214

'You must have had a wonderful time—'

'I hated her stupid old party!'

'Then what was the oration about?'

'You said,' Bonnie stared at her parent contemptuously, 'that I was not polite the last time when I didn't like the lady. So I hope you are glad now with how I was this time.'

'Oh, quite!'

People can't learn about their relations! As soon as they're understood they're over. 'Consciousness,' Alabama murmured to herself, 'is an ultimate betrayal, I suppose.' She had asked Bonnie simply to spare the lady's feelings.

The child played often at her grandmother's house. They played at keeping house. Bonnie was the head of the family; her grandma made an agreeable little girl to have.

'Children were not brought up so strictly when mine were young,' she said. She felt very sorry for Bonnie, that the child should have to learn so much of life before it began for her. Alabama and David insisted on that.

'When your mother was young, she charged so much candy at the corner store that I had an awful time hiding it from her father.'

'Then I will be as Mummy was,' said Bonnie.

'As much as you can get by with,' chuckled her grandmother. 'Things have changed. When I was a child it was the maid and the coachman who argued about whether or not I could carry a demijohn into the church with me on Sundays. Discipline used to be a matter of form and not a personal responsibility.'

Bonnie stared intently at her grandmother.

'Grandma, tell me some more about when you were little.'

'Well, I was very happy in Kentucky.'

'But go on.'

'I can't remember. I was much the same as you.'

'I shall be different. Mummy says I shall be an actress if I want, and go to school in Europe.'

'I went to school in Philadelphia. That was considered a long way then.'

'And I shall be a great lady and wear fine clothes.'

'My mother's silks were imported from New Orleans.'

215

'You don't remember anything else?'

'I remember my father. He brought me toys from Louisville, and thought that girls should marry young.'

'Yes, Grandma.'

'I didn't want to. I was having too good a time.'

'Didn't you have a good time when you were married?'

'Oh, yes, dear, but different.'

'I suppose it can't be always the same.'

'No.'

The old lady laughed. She was very proud of her grandchildren. They were smart, good children. It was very pretty to see her with Bonnie, both of them pretending great wisdom about things, both of them eternally pretending.

'We shall be gone soon,' the little girl sighed.

'Yes,' sighed her grandmother.

'Day after tomorrow we shall be gone,' said David.

Out of the Knights' dining-room windows the trees put out down like new-feathered chicks. The bright, benevolent sky floated across the panes and lifted the curtains in billowing sails.

'You people never stay anywhere,' said the girl with the shanghaied hair, 'but I don't blame you.'

'We once believed,' said Alabama, 'that there were things one place which did not exist in another.'

'Sister went to Paris last summer. She said there were – well, toilets all along the streets – I'd like to see it!'

The cacophony of the table volleyed together and frustrated itself like a scherzo of Prokofiev. Alabama whipped its broken staccato into the only form she knew: schstay, schstay, brisé, schstay, the phrase danced along the convolutions of her brain. She supposed she'd spend the rest of her life composing like that: fitting one thing into another and everything into the rules.

'What are you thinking about, Alabama?'

'Forms, shapes of things,' she answered. The talk pelted her consciousness like the sound of hoofs on a pavement.

'—They say that he kicked her in the bust.'

'The neighbors had to close their doors to keep out the bullets.'

'And four in the same bed. Imagine it!'

'And Jay kept jumping through the transoms, so now they can't rent the house at all.'

'But I don't blame his wife, even if he did promise to sleep on the balcony.'

'She said the best abortionist was in Birmingham, but anyway they went to New York.'

'So Mrs. James was in Texas when it happened, and somehow James got it taken off the records.'

'And the chief of police took her off in a patrol wagon.'

'They met at her husband's grave. There was some suggestion that he had his wife buried next door on purpose, and that's the way it began.'

'So Greek!'

'But, my dear, there are limits to human conduct!'

'But not to human impulses.'

'Pompeii!'

'And nobody wants any homemade wine? I strained it through an old pair of underwear, but it seems to still have a little sediment.' In St-Raphaël, she was thinking, the wine was sweet and warm. It clung like syrup to the roof of my mouth and glued the world together against the pressure of the heat and the dissolution of the sea.

'How is your exhibition?' they said. 'We've seen the reproductions.'

'We love those last pictures,' they said. 'Nobody has ever handled the ballet with any vitality since—'

'I thought,' said David, 'that rhythm, being a purely physical exercise of the eyeball, that the waltz picture would actually give you, by leading the eye in pictorial choreography, the same sensation as following the measure with your feet.'

'Oh, Mr. Knight,' said the women, 'what a wonderful idea!'

The men had been saying 'Attaboy,' and 'Twenty-three skidoo,' since the depression.

Along the paths of their faces the light slept in their eyes like the sails of children's boats reflected in a pond. The rings where stones kicked from the walk sank, widened and disappeared, and the eyes were deep and quiet.

'Oh,' wailed the guests; 'the world is terrible and tragic, and we can't escape what we want.'

'Neither can we – that's why there's a chip off the globe teetering on our shoulders.'

'May I ask what it is?' they said.

'Oh, the secret life of man and woman – dreaming how much better we would be than we are if we were somebody else or even ourselves, and feeling that our estate has been unexploited to its fullest. I have reached the point where I can only express the inarticulate, taste food without taste, smell whiffs of the past, read statistical books, and sleep in uncomfortable positions.'

'When I revert to the allegorical school,' David went on, 'my Christ will sneer at the silly people who do not give a rap about his sad predicament, and you will see in his face that he would like a bite of their sandwiches if somebody would just loosen up his nails for a minute—'

'We shall all come to New York to see it,' they said.

'And the Roman soldiers in the foreground will also be wanting a bite of sandwich, but they will be too jacked up by the dignity of their position to ask for it.'

'When will it be shown?'

'Oh, years and years from now – when I have finished painting everything else in the world.'

On the cocktail tray, mountains of things represented something else; canapés like goldfish, and caviar in balls, butter bearing faces and frosted glasses sweating with the burden of reflecting such a lot of things to stimulate the appetite to satiety before eating.

'You two are lucky,' they said.

'You mean that we've parted with segments of ourselves more easily than other people – granted that we were ever intact,' said Alabama.

'You have an easy time,' they said.

'We trained ourselves to deduce logic from experience,' Alabama said. 'By the time a person has achieved years adequate for choosing a direction, the die is cast and the moment has long since passed which determined the future. We grew up founding our dreams on the infinite promise of American advertising. I *still* believe that one can learn to play the piano by mail and that mud will give you a perfect complexion.'

'Compared to the rest, you are happy.'

'I sit quietly eyeing the world, saying to myself, "Oh, the lucky people who can still use the word 'irresistible.'"'

'We couldn't go on indefinitely being swept off our feet,' supplemented David.

'Balance,' they said, 'we must all have balance. Did you find balance in Europe?'

'You'd do better to have another drink – that's what you came for, isn't it?'

Mrs. McGinty had short white hair and the face of a satyr, and Jane had hair like a rock whirlpool, and Fannie's hair was like a thick coating of dust over mahogany furniture, Veronica's hair was dyed with a dark aisle down the centre part, Mary's hair was country hair, like Maude's, and Mildred's hair was like the draperies of the 'Winged Victory,' flying.

'And they said he had a platinum stomach, my dear, so that his food just dropped into a little sack when he ate. But he lived for years like that.'

'That hole in the top of his head was to blow him up by, though he pretended that he got it in the war.'

'So she cut her hair after first one painter then another, till finally she came to the cubists and camouflaged her scalp.'

'And I told Mary she wouldn't like the hashish, but she said that she must get something out of her hard-earned disillusion, so there she is, in a permanent trance.'

'But it wasn't the Rajah, I tell you! It was the wife of the man who owns the Galeries Lafayette,' Alabama insisted to the girl who wanted to talk about living abroad.

They rose to leave the pleasant place.

'We've talked you to death.'

'You must be dead with packing.'

'It's death to a party to stay till digestion sets in.'

'I'm dead, my dear. It's been wonderful!'

219

'So good-bye, and please come back to see us on your wanderings.'

'We'll always be back to see the family.'

Always, Alabama thought, we will have to seek some perspective on ourselves, some link between ourselves and all the values more permanent than us of which we have felt the existence by placing ourselves in our father's setting.

'We will come back.'

The cars drove away from the cement drive.

'Good-bye!'

'Good-bye!'

'I'm going to air the room a little,' said Alabama. 'I wish people wouldn't set wet glasses down on rented furniture.'

'Alabama,' said David, 'if you would stop dumping ash trays before the company has got well out of the house we would be happier.'

'It's very expressive of myself. I just lump everything in a great heap which I have labelled "the past," and, having thus emptied this deep reservoir that was once myself, I am ready to continued.'

They sat in the pleasant gloom of late afternoon, staring at each other through the remains of the party; the silver glasses, the silver tray, the traces of many perfumes; they sat together watching the twilight flow through the calm living room that they were leaving like the clear cold current of a trout stream.

A NOTE ON THE TEXT

By Matthew J. Bruccoli

SAVE ME THE WALTZ was written during January and February 1932 in Montgomery and at Phipps Clinic of Johns Hopkins Hospital; and it was sent to Maxwell Perkins at Scribner's in March 1932.[1] The version that Perkins first saw had not been read by F. Scott Fitzgerald, for Zelda Fitzgerald was anxious to succeed without her husband's help. The original manuscript and typescripts have disappeared; but the first draft appears to have been a much more personal document – that is, more transparently about the Fitzgeralds' marriage – and, indeed, David Knight was originally named Amory Blaine after the hero of *This Side of Paradise*, who was an autobiographical character. When Fitzgerald did read the novel, he was disturbed on two counts: he felt it exposed too much of his private life; and he thought it drew upon material he had written for *Tender is the Night*, which was then in progress.

The story of the publication of *Save Me the Waltz* can be traced through Fitzgerald's correspondence. On 16 March – some four days after Zelda Fitzgerald sent the novel to Perkins – Fitzgerald instructed him not to decide anything until it was revised.[2] Although he clearly wanted his wife to have a success and praised the novel to Perkins, Fitzgerald was concerned that the original version would injure both of them – but especially him:

[1] Zelda Fitzgerald to Maxwell Perkins, c. 12 March 1932. Scribner's files.
[2] F. Scott Fitzgerald to Maxwell Perkins, 16 March 1932. Scribner's files.

221

Turning up in a novel signed by my wife as a somewhat anemic portrait painter with a few ideas lifted from Clive Bell, Leger, etc. puts me in an absurd & Zelda in a ridiculous position. The mixture of fact & fiction is calculated to ruin us both, or what is left of us, and I can't let it stand. Using the name of a character I invented to put intimate facts in the hands of the friends and enemies we have accumulated *en route* – my God, my books made her a legend and her single intention in this somewhat thin portrait is to make me a non-entity.[3]

He urged his wife to revise and no doubt helped her, but the extent of his labor is by no means clear in the absence of the working papers. It seems likely, though, that the assumption that he actually rewrote *Save Me the Waltz* is false. The available documents indicate that his work was advisory. On 25 March he wired Perkins that the novel would require only minor revisions and that it was a fine novel; but three days later he informed Perkins that the whole middle section needed to be rewritten.[4] By 2 May he was able to report: 'Zelda's novel is now good, improved in every way. It is new. She has largely eliminated the speakeasy-nights-and-our-trip-to-Paris atmosphere.'[5] The letter warns Perkins against exciting her with too-generous praise.

On or about 14 May Fitzgerald sent the revised novel, stating:

It is a good novel now, perhaps a very good novel – I am too close to tell. . . . (At first she refused to revise – then she revised completely, added on her own suggestion and has

[3] Quoted in Andrew Turnbull, *Scott Fitzgerald* (New York: Scribner's, 1962), p. 207. This letter was presumably written to Zelda Fitzgerald's psychiatrist.

[4] F. Scott Fitzgerald to Maxwell Perkins, 25 and 28 March, 1932. Scribner's files.

[5] F. Scott Fitzgerald to Maxwell Perkins, before 2 May 1932. Quoted in *The Letters of F. Scott Fitzgerald*, ed. Andrew Turnbull (New York: Scribner's, 1963), pp. 226–27.

changed what was a rather flashy and self-justifying 'true confessions' that wasn't worthy of her into an honest piece of work. She can do more with galleys but I can't ask her to do more now.) – But now praise will do her good, within reason.[6]

In the Fitzgerald Papers at the Princeton University Library are the typescript printer's copy for *Save Me the Waltz* and five sets of galley proofs. The typescript is clean copy, almost certainly prepared by a typist, with only a few authorial corrections and printer's or editor's queries. The proof consists of two sets of very heavily revised – not just corrected – galleys, two duplicate sets, and one set of paged final galleys:

A. First galleys, author's revised set. 2 gal 1 – 2 gal 82.
B. Duplicate of A, revised at beginning only.
C. Second galleys, author's revised set. 2 gal 1 – 2 gal 77.
D. Duplicate of C, unmarked.
E. Page final galleys, unmarked, Pp. 1–287.

In revising the first galleys, Zelda Fitzgerald completely rewrote the opening of Chapter 2, the account of the visit by Alabama's parents to the Knights. Twenty-five pages of typed copy were substituted for the original thirty-three. At the same time ten pages of typescript revisions for part three of Chapter 2 were prepared.

The two sets of revised galleys are drastically worked over, but almost all the marks are in Zelda Fitzgerald's hand. Fitzgerald did not systematically work on the surviving proofs: only eight of the words written on them are clearly in his hand.

---

[6] F. Scott Fitzgerald to Maxwell Perkins, c. 14 May 1932. Quoted in *Letters*, pp. 228–29. Curiously, this letter warns Perkins not to discuss the novel with Ernest Hemingway, who had *Death in the Afternoon* coming out that season and who would therefore regard *Save Me the Waltz* as competition.

Fitzgerald's estimate of *Save Me the Waltz* was later revised downward. On 8 February 1936, he wrote Harold Ober: 'Please don't have anybody read Zelda's book because it is a bad book!' (*Letters*, p. 402).

Perhaps the wholesale revisions discouraged the proofreaders, or perhaps the author resisted editorial help – but whatever the reasons, apart from troublesome authorial idiosyncracies of style and usage, there are hundreds of appalling errors that almost certainly affected reader response.[7]

The size of the initial printing has not been determined, but it was probably a depression run of no more than 3,000 copies. Judging from the scarcity of copies, the run may have been considerably smaller. There is, by the way, no evidence to suggest that Fitzgerald provided a subvention for publication. *Save Me the Waltz* was never reprinted in America; but in 1953 Grey Walls Press published a new edition in England.

Copy-text for the present edition is the October 1932 Scribner's first printing. The Grey Walls text has not been consulted. Some 550 emendations have been made in the copy-text; they are all listed in the hardbound edition of *Save Me the Waltz* published by the Southern Illinois University Press.[8] An attempt has been made to verify problematical readings against the galleys – but the galleys are so densely revised that it is not always possible to determine what the author intended. In emending copy-text no attempt has been made to improve the author's style or even to make more than the really necessary corrections. Baffling sentences have not been solved, and puzzling words have been left wherever they make sense. Much of the unusual quality of *Save Me the Waltz* comes from its odd prose; no good purpose would be served by tampering with it. One might well be tempted to reproduce a completely uncorrected text in the hope of retaining the bouquet of the 1932 publication, were it not for

[7] At least two reviews specifically complained about the proofreading – *New York Times Book Review* (16 October) and *Bookman* (November). These and three other reviews all commented on the unusual word usage – *Boston Transcript* (30 November), *Saturday Review of Literature* (22 October), and *Forum* (December).

[8] I am indebted to Mr. Alexander Clark, Curator of Manuscripts, Princeton University Library; Prof. Henry Dan Piper; and Beatrice R. Moore, editor extraordinary.

the fact that both author and publisher intended to print a mechanically correct text.

The eyes of Madame – Alabama's ballet teacher – are variously described as *black*, *smoky*, *amber*, *yellow*, *brown*, and *black-and-white*. These readings have not been emended.

Arienne's last name is given as *Jeannert*, *Jeanneret* (twice), and *Jeannerette* (twice). The spelling has been regularized to *Jeanneret*.

The word *stchay* or *schtay* or *schstay* – presumably a Russian ballet term – has not been verified; it has not been regularized.

Of the two shows mentioned at 47., only *Sally* was at the New Amsterdam Theatre; *Two Little Girls in Blue* was at the George M. Cohan.

The word *house* – not *houses*, or *blouses* – at 105.34 appears in the TS. It was queried in proof and marked *stet* by the author. The reading remained *house* through final paged galleys; but it was changed to *houses* in the book when *humming* in the preceding sentence was emended to *which hummed*. Neither change appears to have been authorial, although the change to *which hummed* is a necessary correction. The editor has restored the authorial reading *house* – but he does not understand it.

VINTAGE CLASSICS

Vintage launched in the United Kingdom in 1990, and was originally the paperback home for the Random House Group's literary authors. Now, Vintage is comprised of some of London's oldest and most prestigious literary houses, including Chatto & Windus (1855), Hogarth (1917), Jonathan Cape (1921) and Secker & Warburg (1935), alongside the newer or relaunched hardback and paperback imprints: The Bodley Head, Harvill Secker, Yellow Jersey, Square Peg, Vintage Paperbacks and Vintage Classics.

From Angela Carter, Graham Greene and Aldous Huxley to Toni Morrison, Haruki Murakami and Virginia Woolf, Vintage Classics is renowned for publishing some of the greatest writers and thinkers from around the world and across the ages – all complemented by our beautiful, stylish approach to design. Vintage Classics' authors have won many of the world's most revered literary prizes, including the Nobel, the Man Booker, the Prix Goncourt and the Pulitzer, and through their writing they continue to capture imaginations, inspire new perspectives and incite curiosity.

In 2007 Vintage Classics introduced its distinctive red spine design, and in 2012 Vintage Children's Classics was launched to include the much-loved authors of our childhood. Random House joined forces with the Penguin Group in 2013 to become Penguin Random House, making it the largest trade publisher in the United Kingdom.

@vintagebooks